Andrea, Thank ... hp
in

A ROOMFUL OF BIRDS

A ROOMFUL OF BIRDS

Scottish Short Stories
1990

Introduction by Deirdre Chapman

COLLINS
8 Grafton Street, London W1
1990

William Collins Sons & Co. Ltd
London·Glasgow·Sydney·Auckland
Toronto·Johannesburg

First published 1990

A Roomful of Birds © Elizabeth Burns 1990; *Club Les Anges* © William Boyd 1990; *The Trader* © Michael Cannon 1990; *No New Heroes* © Felicity Carver 1990; *Toddle-Bonny and the Bogeyman* © Douglas Dunn 1990; *The Pilgrim* © Margaret Elphinstone 1990; *The Siege* © Ronald Frame 1990; *Incubus* © Dorothy Johnston 1990; *The Hill Street Public Conveyance* © Frank Kuppner 1990; *Strawberries* © Candia McWilliam 1990; *Some Notes On His Departure* © James Meek 1990; *William* © Willie Orr 1990; *Ildico's Story* © Peter Regent 1990; *The Farmer's Wife* © Frank Shon 1990; *Experience* © Alexander McCall Smith 1990; *Letters From Another Place* © Esther Woolfson 1990.

The Publisher acknowledges the financial assistance of the Scottish Arts Council in the publication of this volume.

BRITISH LIBRARY CATALOGUING IN PUBLICATION DATA

A Roomful of Birds
1. Short stories in English.
Scottish writers, 1990. Anthologies
823'.01'089411 [FS]

ISBN 0-00223705-9 (h/b)
ISBN 0-00223706-7 (pbk)

Photoset in Linotron Imprint by
Rowland Phototypesetting Ltd
Bury St Edmunds, Suffolk
Printed and Bound in Great Britain by
William Collins Sons and Co. Ltd, Glasgow

CONTENTS

Preface by Deirdre Chapman   vii

Elizabeth Burns   3
A ROOMFUL OF BIRDS

William Boyd   18
CLUB LES ANGES

Michael Cannon   29
THE TRADER

Felicity Carver   41
NO NEW HEROES

Douglas Dunn   55
TODDLE-BONNY AND THE BOGEYMAN

Margaret Elphinstone   76
THE PILGRIM

Ronald Frame   99
THE SIEGE

Dorothy Johnston   114
INCUBUS

Frank Kuppner   125
THE HILL STREET PUBLIC CONVEYANCE

Candia McWilliam   130
STRAWBERRIES

James Meek   140
SOME NOTES ON HIS DEPARTURE

Willie Orr   148
WILLIAM

Peter Regent ILDICO'S STORY	163
Frank Shon THE FARMER'S WIFE	171
Alexander McCall Smith EXPERIENCE	184
Esther Woolfson LETTERS FROM ANOTHER PLACE	196
Biographical Notes	215

PREFACE

Grave, equanimous, unhurried, in good spirits, some people sit down in a small room to choose stories. A pleasant practice, one would think, and on the increase. Echoes of all the stories they have read are in their heads and comments on them are on bits of paper. The comments are on things which can be articulated but which in the first instance are simply felt. Feelings are what this is about.

The writers' feelings: the writer of a short story has initially perhaps ten minutes of a stranger's disposable attention in which to fix him with an image – disturbing, ironical, visual, wayward or universal – as close as possible to the one in the writer's mind. It won't be a replica – readers aren't fax machines – but some of the writer's craft lies in knowing the failings of readers. For this reason writers' feelings must be disciplined.

The readers' feelings: whether the object is to give prizes or to fill a book, the selectors (representative readers) go through a similar process. Tea is served and biscuits are eaten. Choices are put forward. Surprise is felt. Cups are refilled. Moral and intellectual superiority is experienced (did he read that or what?) as they begin to discern in one another the disfiguring stamp of personality. Fairness is set aside as each asks of the others that he be no more than a tuning fork vibrating to the writer's creative impulse with no added twangs of his own, while at the same time each retains the right to his own subjectivity. Readers' feelings are essentially undisciplined.

Echoes in the head: arguments are advanced for being moved, or, always more fluently, failing to be moved by certain stories. Fictional situations are related anecdotally to life experiences. The selectors marvel at one another's depravity.

Bits of paper: technique – rational, civilized, almost quantifiable technique – is what brings accord. The echoes in the head can be unreliable extensions of the writer's image; they

PREFACE

can embroider or tidy up what was unfinished or overdone. A selection by one person would rely heavily on these echoes but for agreement amongst several the intention of the writer must be matched by his success in carrying it through. The near misses from this volume are those writers who spoke to one of us – John Linklater, Jonathan Warner or myself – but failed to persuade the other two.

There were few persuasive near misses this year, and having no bank of subsidiary mutually agreeable stories to draw on, fighting was fierce and protracted. There will always be some stories that, however polished, reflect assumptions about life that one or other of the selectors cannot condone. Exclusion can become more urgent than inclusion.

One reading of this dearth of moderately good stories is that there is not a limitless supply of potential writers out there. *Communication* is a growth area, creative writing perhaps is not. Many of the contributions were raw slices of life, barely disguised as fiction. Many of the writers were careless or, more likely, unaware of the effect they were creating. It is good to find that people are increasingly articulating experience, but this is not the place for that.

The best of writing overcomes the failings and the reservations of the individual reader, makes him feel clever, perceptive, extended. We are lucky to have here work from some of the best of Scottish writers.

Often they achieve their efforts obliquely, Candia McWilliam using detail, William Boyd humour to project learning experiences. Elizabeth Burns's 'A Roomful of Birds', which gives this collection its title, is similarly about personal survival through observation and quick wits, while in the stories of Ronald Frame and Douglas Dunn growth and action are the threats, continuity the lifeline.

An annual collection like this has no fixed focus; it is as variable as the impulses of the small number of writers represented. As our afternoon became evening we felt happy that our final choice reflected the diverse, often subjective, increasingly worldly themes of contemporary Scottish writers.

DEIRDRE CHAPMAN

SCOTTISH
SHORT STORIES

A ROOMFUL OF BIRDS
Elizabeth Burns

Today the colour of the sky in the spaces of the windowpanes is white. I hear rain faltering down through the laurel leaves to the ground. I lie awake a long time listening to it before she stirs. I can hear her breath, *souffle* is their word for it, exactly the way it sounds. I lie there perfectly still, counting the thirty-six windowpanes, lapping up these last moments before day begins, of rain tapping on laurel before the snuffly moaning sound of a baby waking up begins. OK, Isabelle, I'm coming.

   Not that they were not kind to me when I arrived: a hot bath with white towels as big as sheets, clover soap that really smelt of fields and white ginger shampoo for my hair, the liquid not white nor ginger scented but colourless and scentless. We have our own bathroom, Isabelle and I. It is very spacious and white with big windows looking out over the lawn. After the bath I felt fresh as clover and ginger and very French, practising the words in my head ready for intelligent conversation with my new employers. Shiny clean and ready to hold this tiny girl in my arms and start taking care of her. Fabienne disdains her daughter and cannot be bothered with motherhood which is why she requires me. An alliance forms between us, the little milk-plump child and I.

   After the meadowy bath, Fabienne gave me tea from a glass teapot: you could see the liquid, gold as peat water, and the tea leaves shifting like plant life. When she gave the child into my arms I was fearful for the teapot that Isabelle had her eyes fixed on, but her little bunch of fingers was not strong enough to budge it. One hand around the baby, the other holding the thin white china cup. I sipped my tea, gone cold, and talked in halting French.

'Treat this place as your home,' they told me. All those pleasing formalities that fall from the lips of new employers. But if I were to treat it as a home, were I ever to have it as I'd really like, they would have me out and beheaded if it were the revolution times again: the travelling guillotine would be here for me. Or rather I suppose it would be the other way around: I the revolutionary and they the chateau owners for the chop.

I have thought a lot about the revolution times and take some gory comfort in imagining how it happened here, how the lords were murdered and the serfs set free. How the gates were stormed and the roof burnt. It is all wood, the roof: they restored it and one day Fabienne took me up to see the great carved rafters. 'Such a pity, what they did in the revolution,' she said, as though its only effect was the destruction of her roof. 'And later, of course, the owners had to sell off so much of the land, so what's left here is very little indeed of what there once was.' She told me this sadly and apologetically, as though I might have required an even larger garden for my strolls.

She has the guiltlessness of the rich, although she has only recently married into Philippe's money. Guilt slides off her like rain off laurel leaves. How else could she saunter downstairs in a negligée at eleven to make herself a *café au lait*, knowing that someone else was up at dawn to change her baby's nappy?

It is a gentle lovely place for spring here, up in the hills looking out across a grey-green valley. There is an abundance of wildflowers which I gathered in bunches for my room. This information was passed on by the cleaning lady, and Philippe said to me one day: 'It would be better if you did not have these hedgerow flowers in your room. They use a spray for the weeds in the vineyards and traces of it may get onto the flowers. I do not think it is wise to have them in the house.'

I tell him that a trace of weedkiller doesn't bother me, but that does not allay his worries. 'It is better to err on the side of caution,' he says, in English. That is a phrase he relishes on his tongue.

A ROOMFUL OF BIRDS

I have resigned myself to a flowerless room, though sometimes I manage to get flowers at the market in town, but Fabienne doesn't like to linger there, she prefers the 'specialist shops' as she calls them. But sometimes I have purchased jonquils or freesias or lily-of-the-valley, their stems bound together with fine pink wool.

Fabienne. I love her name, I say it over and over to myself. It is part of her glamour. Fabienne. Fabulous. Fabergé. And Philippe. I like their names together like that. Fabienne, Philippe and Isabelle. A family. I imagine her signing the expensive tasteful Christmas cards for all of them.

Philippe keeps canaries. They told me that when I arrived. Later Fabienne confided to me: 'They're his new obsession. It used to be the sheep – he wanted to play at being a farmer – but they took up too much time. We've just got the two old ones now. He took the rest to be slaughtered.'

I have never seen such fat spoilt sheep. They do not sleep outside, though he lets them stay out munching the lush grass until the sun goes down, like children allowed to stay up late. Then he calls them in by name and beds them down in straw and feeds them special granules that he keeps in a lidded bucket so that rats are not attracted. They don't know how lucky they are, these plump French sheep. If they saw a moor and the skimpy thin grass between the heather, they would prefer an abattoir. But the sheep are the last of an old obsession. Now we have the canaries.

Such colours when he first opened the door of the room. I had thought until then that canaries were yellow, all the same colour as the paint named after them, or a tee-shirt in a mail order catalogue. But no, canary yellow, it seems, is the most boring colour you can have. It is far better – far more interesting and far more profitable, Philippe tells me – to breed them in different colours. They are all shades from a pale, pale yellow that is almost white, through to deep oranges and browns and reds, and some are a patchy mixture. There is a set of pale peachy birds that I admire, and those white ones with the few yellow feathers. Some are a deep flamey orange, one almost fluorescent. There is a rusty colour, and some are a soft donkey brown flecked with gold. There are ones as red as robins, and ones so brown as to be taken for starlings, though Philippe would never confess to such a thought. The orange ones, he tells me, are the rarest, and have to be fed a special pâté, as he calls it, so that they keep their colour. He opens a tin of dry beige powdery stuff. I had expected it to be orange, like flamingoes eating shrimps to keep them pink.

'A pinch of this' – he takes the powder between his fingers – 'and they will always retain their colour. It must never be neglected.'

He sees to the canaries the moment he arrives back from the bank and has changed out of his manager's suit. They are as serious as his life.

I walk up and down this lane from the chateau to the main road. I know its wildflowers and its scents, in the morning, in the evening, on a hot day or after rain. I know where the wild sorrel grows: I pick leaves of it and chew it as I walk until the lemony flavour comes. It makes good soup, but of course Philippe would never allow a hedgerow soup. There is a corner where buttercups and wild orchids are rampant together. Their colours daze me, and I lift up Isabelle so she can see them too. She likes it when I touch the stems and make the spots of gold and purple move. And when she sees the cows gobbling the grass and mooing she laughs. She gets excited when a tractor passes or a dog barks. She is curious over everything.

'Look at the scarecrow, Isabelle,' I say as we pass the stick with the blue jacket amongst the vines, or, 'Look at the tulips, Isabelle,' as we see them in a garden, splash splash splash of colour.

I show her how the blossom drapes like a shawl across the lane, or tell her how the black charred trunk of a tree was hit by lightning.

Fabienne says the thunderstorms are terrible in summer, though there is a lightning conductor on the chateau, of course. Philippe would not be without it.

I talk to Isabelle in English always so she will imbibe its

sounds. I want her to grow up with the knowledge of it in her head, so that suddenly, when I am long gone from this place, she will spurt it out and people will wonder at her eloquence. And she will say, 'Oh, I had an English nanny once . . .'

Just now she gurgles in no language at all. She is a happy dribbly child. Big brown eyes like the cows we admire every morning. Little gold tufts of hair. A snub nose. And of course exquisite clothes. Anyone could tell I'm not her mother because I dress so badly. No style at all. Just throw on some jeans while she's crying to get up, and a tee-shirt that smells usually of baby sick and has a milky stain somewhere. I wish I were like Fabienne who looks glamorous even when she's bleary-eyed and in her night clothes. Isabelle will be the same one day. She has glamour in her blood, I think.

Twice a week we go shopping in the market town. I am only there to carry the parcels and to push Isabelle's pram, but it is a glimpse of life outside the chateau.

I take the chance to post my letters. Fabienne would take them and do it for me, but I do not want her eyes on the envelopes, the names of my friends. I like to place the letters myself in the part of the letterbox that says 'other destinations'. We do not go to the post office for stamps, it would be too tiresome to wait in the queue, Fabienne says. So instead I go to a tobacconist that sells stamps across the road from where she buys her vegetables. I tell her – assertively, because I am determined on it – that I'm just going across the road for stamps. I run out of the vegetable shop, leaving Isabelle and the parcels, and am back before Fabienne has decided between asparagus tips or artichoke hearts.

The postman. My ears are sharp listening every morning for his van. He drives up to the gate, and if we are in the garden he hands the letters to me. Otherwise they go in the box which is set right inside the wall so that when you take the letters out they have a little of the dust of crumbled stone on them. Or sometimes we meet the postman on the road, Isabelle and I out for our stroll, and then I can carry the letters home in my pocket, anticipating.

Letters are gold dust. They help to keep me sane. I have friendships in the outside world, I do exist beyond this place. I sleep with the letters under my pillow so that I will dream of home. By day I dream of Paris, imagining myself there. I live on these dreams of past and future, save them up and eat them as I lie in bed awake or as I walk along the country roads pushing and pushing the pram.

My eating here is furtive. 'Have what you like,' says Fabienne casually. But I sneak to the fridge, guilty, gape at its open arms of food, not used to these vast amounts: the cheeses, the pâtés, the creamy desserts and yoghurts, the thick sweet fruit juices. And there are the bowlfuls of exotic fruits, the baskets of crusty bread and a cupboard that is entirely filled with varieties of biscuits and chocolates. At the pâtisserie Fabienne buys cakes and brings them home in a white cardboard box tied with thin gold ribbon. When you open it up, there are the cakes nestling in their paper cases, spilling cream. I am offhand about these pâtisserie extravagances, but actually they are a solace to me: I crave and devour them, their delicious excessiveness. I save them, like letters, for times when I am alone. Then sneak up to my room to eat them with a mug of fresh brewed coffee, tiptoeing up the spiral stairs, hoping I will not meet one of them on the way, and that Isabelle will not wake, and that my coffee will stay hot. Then curled up on my bed among the cushions, and almond paste, coffee cream, chocolate icing, fresh strawberries, choux pastry: you are my pleasures and delights.

I despise myself for this: for the smallness of my pleasures in a shrunken world.

Last Sunday, when Philippe got back from Mass – he always goes, so he can be seen by his clients, while Fabienne stays in bed all morning, waiting for him to return with the cream cakes and the Sunday papers he brings back from town – he asked me if I would do an extra job that afternoon, if they went out with Isabelle. He said he would put a bit extra on my pay that week. 'It's the canaries,' he said. 'Soon it will be warm enough for them to be outside, so I need to have the aviary prepared.'

The aviary was an enormous wire cage beside the gate of the chateau. He said it needed to be scrubbed with a wire brush to get the rust off and then repainted for the summer. He said he couldn't bear to let the birds into it in its present state of repair.

I thought of the money, though he wouldn't say how much, and agreed. They went off to see some friends in town, Isabelle crying as they bundled her into the car along with a box of cakes and a bottle of wine.

When they came back at dusk I was halfway through the painting. My skin was rust coloured and my hair full of the flakes of it. Fabienne said she'd put 'baby' to bed, but only, I think, because she thought I might get dirt on her clothes.

Philippe hovered around outside, pacing about outside the aviary, running his finger along the unpainted bars to see how well I'd scrubbed the rust off. I carried on painting, standing inside the cage of the aviary, dipping my paintbrush, saying nothing. Suddenly there was a scrunching metal sound, and he was at the door of the cage with a key in his hand and then was turning it in the lock. I was so startled I cried out, no words, just some kind of noise. He said nothing, just gave me his bank manager's glimmer of a smile, then unlocked the door again and said, 'Pretty little canary.'

I dropped the paintbrush and ran, all rusty, up the spiral stairs to my room, to my dear silk-skinned baby. Out of the window, I saw him pottering off to see to his canaries.

I have begun to stay up in my room in the evenings when he gets home from work. Fabienne tries to get me to stay downstairs with them – she likes someone to chatter to, and Philippe never says much – but I pretend I can hear Isabelle crying and run off upstairs to my room.

Every week I count my money that I keep at the back of a drawer in the bureau. I suppose I should have a bank account but it's always so rushed in town with the shopping and posting of letters, and Fabienne would find it tiresome to wait in a queue. So I just keep it in an envelope in a drawer and every time I count it I think of Paris. For the aviary he only gave me fifty francs.

Walking endless country roads pushing Isabelle's pram, I remember my mother telling me how she used to walk for miles with me when I was a baby, just to get out of the house of her mother-in-law, whose house they lived in, and who used to lecture my mother on the right way to bring up a baby. At least there are no lectures from Fabienne. She has no ideas at all on the right way to bring up a baby, and doesn't care either.

Some days with Isabelle I walk for miles. At least I sleep well, at least I accomplish something in the day. I hate it when it rains and we are confined indoors. On fine days, I fill the pram with supplies and we visit the little villages round about. Some of them have no shop or café, only a church. I take Isabelle inside and light a candle for her future. She loves to watch the flickering circle of candles. In the bigger villages we can go to a café. Sometimes I am lured by thoughts of the dear comforting pâtisseries, but I have to save, I have to get out of here. Every cake means another day in the chateau. Sometimes I bring biscuits from the cupboardful and have them with my coffee. A bit of sweetness is all that matters.

They know me now in the cafés. They gurgle over Isabelle and string out adjectives about her like washing on a line: how she is sweet, pretty, delicate, *mignonne, gentille, gracieuse*. I like people in the street to think she's mine. If they say she looks like me I do not deny it.

I try and imagine what Isabelle grown up will be like. I imagine her like me, not like her parents. I hope she will rebel against them. I hope she runs away and does all the things that will shock them most. Philippe hopes she'll work in the bank with him. He said so one day. But she will never work in a bank: I'll infiltrate her.

*

A ROOMFUL OF BIRDS

Once a week I have my day off. Or so they say. I still have to get Isabelle up and give her some breakfast because Fabienne is never awake early enough. Afterwards I hand her over to her mother and go back to bed and maybe read the paper. Philippe gets the *International Herald Tribune* delivered: he likes to think he is being broad-minded and intellectual but in fact the English is too much effort for him and often it lies unfolded and unread in the kitchen until I devour the back copies on my day off.

What Fabienne does on the day off is take Isabelle to some friend's house to show her off, or into town to buy baby clothes for her. She can't imagine a way to amuse a person except to buy them things. She wouldn't think of showing her the colour of a buttercup or blowing her a dandelion clock. Instead she goes to these incredibly expensive children's clothes shops the French have, where a tee-shirt for a two-year-old will cost you fifteen pounds and a pair of designer baby-gros thirty. That's the kind of stuff she puts Isabelle into.

So they go off designer shopping and I lie in bed dozing and reading. Then I go downstairs and fix myself a lavish breakfast with no interruptions. By the time I've eaten it, they're back for lunch and Fabienne gets out the pretty little carrier bags of clothes to show me.

'Won't she look adorable in this?' or, 'Could you put her in this tomorrow for when these people come over?'

I stay in my room over lunch, or else she'll say, 'Could you just hold her while I make a phone call?' or, 'I think she might need changing – could you do it while I make some coffee?'

So I keep in my room, luxuriating. Days off. They're like your arms stretched wide in a meadow, one of the meadows here that are so full and high with flowers. Days off are so spacious: I can stretch myself right out.

A malingerer, Fabienne calls Philippe. He's so fussy over his food and forever worrying that he might be getting stomach ulcers or gallstones or kidney failure. He'll never go to the doctor though, just buys up pills and vitamins that he doses himself with before and after meals. Fabienne has more the air of someone living off a banquet, buying half a dozen different cheeses every week, more if they're having company, and always new varieties of cake or brands of biscuits, or some specially imported wine. But Philippe sticks doggedly to his favourites. And everything must be plain for him because of the possible risks of his possible health problems. He admonishes Fabienne when the food is too rich, though he will allow himself a little of the fatty creamy delicacies at the end of the meal before his tisane of fennel. He has his rules: never cook with butter, always peel an aubergine because the skins are no good (I love the way they go soft and wrinkled and black like some kind of velvety cloth), never drink coffee after 3 p.m., always wash apples (it is not enough to polish them, green skin against a pink tee-shirt, as he caught me doing). He never drinks tap water, only bottled. There are battalions of bottled water in the cellar, for we must never run dry.

He enquires too after Isabelle's food, although they never eat together because the mess distresses him. But he likes to know, 'Is the soya powder organic? Which shop did it come from, because that one near the station is no good? Has that avocado been mashed thoroughly enough for her?' Never, 'Is Isabelle happy?' or, 'What has she discovered today?' He is obsessed with what she eats. I can foresee she will be forbidden a childhood of coke and crisps.

He said it yesterday evening as he was coming in from the canaries.

'You're looking very attractive tonight.'

I stood rooted to the steps of the chateau and felt a cold mistral wind blow over me.

I do not believe it. I refuse to believe it. I cannot imagine Philippe knows what attractive means, so asexual is he. I cannot believe him capable of feeling for another human person. He is cold and sleek as an anchovy. I shut myself in my room and do not dare to go downstairs even for a cup of tea, though that is what I desire most in the world. I go and look at Isabelle sleeping and cannot believe how such a cold monster can make a living gurgling thumb-sucking child.

A ROOMFUL OF BIRDS

I try to make his words a dream, words that were never spoken. I will them away. Let him forget he ever spoke those drunk-on-sunset words. Don't let it be the same, age-old story. Master and servant. Employer falls for au pair; hurt wife; confused child. No, that can never happen here. Not to me, quiet, creeping unobtrusively about the old house, childminding, never a whisper of flirtation in me. And not Philippe, so arid, so unsensual, who exudes nothing but wealth.

Fabienne only likes him for his money. That's what she married him for. She told me so herself. That is what passes between them, he giving, she receiving. Nothing like love. She will have an affair I suppose. Some man will like her for her glamour. Philippe is indifferent to it. Attractive? How can he say I'm attractive when he lives with Fabienne? I'm skinny and bony, lank-haired, pale, un-French-looking. I don't tan coffee-coloured in the sun like Fabienne, I go redfaced and blotchy. I get spots from all the cream cakes I eat. I think Fabienne chose me on purpose because I was ugly so I wouldn't be a threat to her. I think he only sees me like the sheep and the canaries: a new obsession. Some perverse flirtation as a new hobby for when he comes home from work.

I suppose Fabienne was that once. A glamorous addition to the chateau. They ignore each other now. They have separate lives, they sleep in separate rooms. There are so many rooms in this place it is easy to avoid each other. They have their own bathrooms too. I cleaned them when the cleaning lady was away at her aunt's funeral. Fabienne's is pink and the shelves are like the toiletries counter in some department store, arrayed with jars and bottles of liquids and perfumes. I spent a long time trying out the smells of everything. Philippe's was dark green, probably because he thinks that's the colour a man's bathroom ought to be. I cleaned it very quickly, not thoroughly at all. It gave me the creeps to think of him in there attending to his skimpy body.

I begin to plot strategies. I count my money every day like a miser. I will stay one more month. I will leave at midsummer, before it gets too hot.

But Isabelle . . . sometimes I feel I *am* her mother, that to leave her would be to abandon her in a cardboard box at the door of villains, her parents. Sometimes I imagine being here for years, being her mentor as she grows up. But I know I cannot stand it much longer. I cannot bear having to be so furtive and so secretive, plotting my days to avoid Philippe. He is a person of habit, so it is easy enough to know where he will be when, and to be somewhere else. But this spy-life is abnormal, it cannot go on. Money is no longer a reason to stay on. There will be other jobs. But Isabelle . . .

I had a dream last night where it seemed as though a part of me – my sanity, my self – was in a little cardboard box like a cake box, and I had to open the lid and let it out. Sometimes it is as though I *am* diminished to the size of a cake box. My self has grown so small here.

OK. Midsummer. At the end of May I'll tell Fabienne. The hardest part because she's very persuasive. It will be like running away for an endless day off and she'll say she won't be able to cope. And Isabelle will become the blackmail piece. How she'll suffer without me . . . But I am resolute. I begin to compose resignation letters in my head as I walk along the lilac-edged lanes.

But it happened on a warm evening before the end of May and I gave no notice. I was in the kitchen feeding spoonfuls of mashed banana, her favourite, to Isabelle, when the phone rang and Fabienne, glass of wine in hand, answered it. It was for Philippe. She asked if I could run outside and fetch him from the bird house.

He was in there, pottering about with birdseed. I gave him the message and he said, 'Perhaps you could finish off the feed? There's only a few more to do.' He had demonstrated before how it was done: a certain amount of seed in each container, depending on how many birds were in the cage. And for the orange ones the special powder added in. He went out, closing the door so that the smell was unbearable, all that birdshit. I went round the cages he'd pointed to, pouring little heaps of birdseed from a plastic jug which he kept for the purpose. The canaries fluttered and squawked and gaped their horrible little beaky mouths open. I fixed my eyes on the colours of their feathers, the pinky golds and lemony yellows, to make it bearable.

The door opened and Philippe was back. I told him there were two more cages to be done and handed him the jug, half-full of seed. But he laid it down on the shelf, and it was so quick, he had his back against the door and his arms round me so tight I thought of the word clamp, a clamp, a vice: and his mouth trying to kiss my face: sweaty smell of his shirt and slimy silk of his tie: Isabelle, the way she moves her whole head when she doesn't want something in her mouth: smell of birdshit and the canaries screeching and chirping in their cages: he saying over and over, 'My little canary, my little canary, my little canary': everything in me stuck and slow: no voice: no movement in my arms or legs: brain very slow, thinking, 'It's happening, it's happening, I should have known, I should have known, au pair, au pair, it always happens: Fabienne, wine glass: Isabelle, mushy banana: Philippe, Philippe, creepy Philippe': 'My little canary, my little canary' over and over and trying to rub his face in my shoulder: my slow brain tells me out of a dream, 'Get him away from the door.'

Twist myself round so my back's against it, get hold of the handle, and he mumbling and fumbling doesn't see what I'm doing, doesn't know my dull clamped body-brain has suddenly gone sharp and fast, and opened the door and I'm out, gasping the air so fresh, so fresh after the bird-smell, his smell, gasping air and running up to the house, glancing behind to see if he's following but he's still in there with his canaries.

My bed, my blue room, its thick walls, sky ceiling, lilac smell. Chair against the door. Breath coming heavy, tears down each side of my face on to the covers. Isabelle's bedtime. Get up. Wash. Don't let Fabienne see you shaking.

*

Morning, very hot and still. Bluebell scent as we walk down the lane. I tell it all to Isabelle because there is no one else to tell. We sit for a long time watching the cows, Isabelle laughing when they moo. I hold her very close, my face in her babysoft hair, her baby smells. We go past the apple trees and I pull down a bit of blossom for her to look at. 'I'll miss you, Isabelle,' I tell her as her brown calf eyes look up at me and I kiss her blossomy face.

At night I pack and write a note for Fabienne. It's not the eloquent letter I had composed. I do not tell her why I'm leaving. Let her guess or let him explain. Then she can warn the next au pair.

It seems sad, my final evening: I feel there should be some farewell. But this is the only way to go: no explanations, no more chances for Philippe. There is a flaming anger in me that burns out all desire for reconciliation.

I'm up at dawn, long before he'll leave for work. I blow kisses, so as not to wake her, to Isabelle, asleep and perfect in her cot. Don't wake up, Isabelle, not yet.

I leave the note for Fabienne on the kitchen table.

Out of the back door that doesn't clank when you open it.

Finally, the bird house. The smell makes me want to be sick. I take the packet out of my pocket, the rat poison Fabienne uses in the cellar, ground up very finely. The exact amount of birdseed in the jug, just enough for them all, and a touch of the fine blue powder, like poster paint, mixed in.

Wash your hands under the tap, wipe them dry on your jeans, then off down the lane for the last time, down to the main road, no pram this time, thumb out, into a VW heading for Paris, long before they're up.

I worry about Isabelle. But they'll have found another au pair by now. Plenty of young British girls eager to practise their French and live in a chateau. I hope she's taking care of her, whoever she is, I hope she's showing her interesting things and teaching her English words.

Sometimes I dream of dead canaries. All the soft and

beautiful colours of their feathers. I have never killed anything before: it is a strange and horrible secret inside me. But I got myself out and I have to keep believing that I am more important than a roomful of birds.

CLUB LES ANGES
William Boyd

'None of these girls is French, right?'
  'No . . . But they're European.'
  'Not the same thing, man. French is important.'
  'Right.' I'm not sure if I know what he's talking about.
  'You know any French girls?'
  'Yes,' I say. It's almost a lie, but it doesn't matter.
  'Well? I mean well enough to ask out?'
  'I don't see why not.' Now this is a definite falsehood, but I don't care. I feel good, quite confident today, so I think I'll allow this lie to germinate for a while.
  I am standing in a pale patch of March sunshine talking to Preston, my American friend. We lean against the wall of the *Centre Universitaire Méditerranéen*, our temporary alma mater, waiting for our classes to start. In front of us is the small cobbled courtyard and beyond that, over a low wall, is the Promenade des Anglais. Nice's traffic whizzes busily by. I can just see the Mediterranean. The Baie des Anges looks grey and grim. Old water – ashy, cindery.
  'We got to do something . . .' Preston says. I like the 'we'. He scratches his short hair. 'Now I've gotten this new apartment.'
  'Oh yes?'
  'Wanna come by tonight?' Preston shifts his big frame. He pats his pockets – breast, hip, thigh – looking for his cigarettes. 'We got a bar on the roof.'
  This sounds intriguing. I explain apologetically that I can't make it as every Monday night I have a regular appointment for dinner with a French family – friends of friends of my mother.
  Preston shrugs, then finds and lights a cigarette. He smokes an American brand called 'Picayune' which is made in New

Orleans. When he came to France he brought two thousand with him. He never smokes anything else, he insists.

We watch our fellow students saunter into the building. They are nearly all strangers to me, these bright boys and girls, as I have only been in Nice a few weeks. To be honest, Preston is my only friend, so far. Slightly envious, I watch the others as they chatter and mingle. Germans, Scandinavians, Italians, Tunisians, Nigerians. We are all foreigners, trying hard to learn French . . . Except for Preston, who makes no effort and can hardly speak a word.

A young guy with long hair rides his motorbike noisily into the courtyard. He revs it unnecessarily a few times before switching it off. He is English, and, apart from me, the only other Englishman in the place. I think his name is Tim. One day, I imagine, we might be friends. We'll see.

Monsieur Cambrai welcomes me with his usual impossible geniality. He shakes my hand and shouts to his wife over his shoulder.

'*Ne bouge pas! C'est l'habitué!*'

That's what he calls me – *l'habitué. L'habitué de lundi*, because I am invited to dinner every Monday night without fail. He almost never uses my name. Sometimes it's a little wearing: '*Salut, l'habitué*, '*Bien mangé, l'habitué?*', and so on. Never uses my name. But I like him, and the Cambrai family. In fact I like them so much it makes me feel weak, cowed.

Monsieur and Madame are small, sophisticated and nimble, both dentists, it so happens, who teach at the big medical school here in Nice. They have three daughters – Delphine, Stéphane and Annique – all older than me and all possessed of, to my fogged and blurry eyes, an almost supernatural beauty. These are the French girls that I claimed to know, but 'know' is completely the wrong word: I am a votary, frightened and in awe of them, unmanned by my astonishing good fortune.

I am humbled further by the family's disarming kindness. When I arrived in Nice they were the only contacts I had in the city. I had been told they had been apprised of my arrival so I duly wrote to them citing our tenuous connection via my mother's friend. I was promptly invited to dinner and invited back every Monday night. I realise that I myself would never be so hospitable, not even to a close friend. I know of no one else who would, either. So I cross the Cambrai threshold with a cocktail of emotions gurgling inside me – shame, guilt, gratitude and, of course, lust.

Preston's new address is on the Promenade des Anglais. The 'Résidence Les Anges'. I stand outside the building, impressed. I have passed it many times before. It is hideous and vulgar, a modern square of coppery smoked glass with gilded aluminium balconies.

I press a buzzer in a slim free-standing concrete post, and speak into a wire grille. When I mention the name 'Mr Fairfield' glass doors whisper open and I am admitted. In a granite lobby a taciturn man in a tight suit shows me to the lift.

Preston rents a small studio apartment with bathroom and kitchenette. It is neat, grey and efficient. On the wall are a series of prints. Exotic birds: a toucan, a bateleur eagle, something called a shrike. I think of my mean room at Madame d'Amico's and a sudden hot envy rinses through me. I half hear Preston telling me how much it costs a month; that to get it he had to pay a fee *and* a quarter's rent in advance; how he raised this by cashing in his return fare to the States (first class). He says he has cabled his father for more money.

We go up to the roof, six storeys above the Promenade. To my vague alarm there is a small swimming pool up here and a large glassed-in cabana labelled 'Club Les Anges', furnished with a bamboo bar and a few modern seats. A barman in a cerise jacket runs this place. He is a plump pale-faced fellow with a poor moustache. His name is Serge. Preston jokes patronisingly with him. Already it is quite plain to me that Serge loathes Preston and that Preston is completely unaware of this.

I order a large gin and tonic from Serge – I don't know why – and for a palpitating minute I loathe Preston too. I know better, of course, but for the time being this shiny building and its accoutrements will do nicely as an approximation of the Good Life for me. As I sip my sour drink a sour sense of the world's huge unfairness crowds ruthlessly in. Why should this guileless big American, with his two thousand Louisiana cigarettes, and his cashable first class air fares have all this while I live in a thin frowsty room in an old woman's bathless apartment? And, to make matters worse, because of an interminable postal strike in Britain I have to husband and hoard my financial resources like a neurotic peasant conscious of a hard winter lowering ahead. Where is *my* money, I want to know, *my* exotic bird prints, *my* club, *my* pool? How long will I have to deny myself . . . ? I allow this unpleasant voice to whine and whinge on in my head as we stand on the *terrasse* and admire the view of the long bay. You shouldn't resist these fervent grudges. Give them a loose rein, let them run themselves out. I find it's usually better.

In fact, I like Preston. He is tall and powerful – the word 'rangy' comes to mind – affable and not particularly intelligent. To my eyes his clothes are so parodically American as to be beyond caricature: pale-blue shirts with button-down collars, old khaki trousers that reveal his white-socked ankles, big brown loafers. He has fair short hair and even unexceptionable features. He has a gold watch, a Zippo lighter and hairy forearms. He told me once, in all candour, that he 'played tennis to Davis Cup standard'.

I always wondered what he was doing in Nice, studying at the *Centre*. At first I thought he might be a draftee avoiding the war in Vietnam but now I think – based on some hints he's dropped – that he has been sent off to France as a family punishment of some sort. Certainly, he has no interest in his classes – which he attends less and less frequently – nor in the language and culture of France. He talks a lot about his eventual return to the States – and of how he will force his father to buy him an Aston Martin. The Aston Martin really seems to keep him going.

Soon I find I go to the Résidence Les Anges most afternoons, after my classes are over. Preston and I sit in the club – or by the pool if it is sunny – and drink a lot (it all goes on his tab).

I am usually fairly drunk by sunset. We chat about all sorts of subjects but at some point in every discussion Preston reiterates his desire to meet French girls. He suggests I ask them to the club. I say I'm working on it. Steadily, over the days, I learn more about him. He is an only child. His father is a millionaire – real estate. His mother divorced him recently to marry another millionaire. So between his two sets of parents Preston has a choice of up to eight homes to visit in and around the USA: Miami, New York, Los Angeles and a ranch in Montana. Preston does nothing.

'Why should I?' he says reasonably. 'They've got enough money for me too. I don't see why I should bust my ass working.'

'So what do you do all day?'

He thinks. 'All kinds of stuff . . . But mostly I like to, ah, play tennis. And get laid, of course.'

I can't help myself. 'Why did you come to Nice?'

He grins. 'I was a bad boy.' He slaps his wrist and laughs. 'Oh naughty, naughty Preston.'

He won't tell me what he did. I press him.

'Well,' he says. 'You know I told you my mother remarried? It was to this older guy, Michael. He already had a family, all older than me, a boy and three girls . . . Well, I dropped out of college and started to spend a lot of time at their house.'

He exhales. He eats an olive. His face goes serious for a moment.

'You should have seen those girls,' he says. 'Man . . .' He grins, a stupid gormless grin. 'I was nineteen years old. I got three beautiful girls sleeping down the corridor from me. What am I supposed to do?'

'You mean . . .?'

'Yeah. Sure. All three of them. They were real happy about it.'

I think through this. I imagine a big silent house. Night. A long dark corridor. Closed doors. Three bored stepsisters.

'What went wrong?'

'Oldest one got pregnant, didn't she? Last year.'

'Abortion?'

'God no. Anyway she was married by then.' He spreads his hands. 'Her husband doesn't know a thing.'

'The, the child was born.'

'Haven't seen him yet.' He turns and shouts for Serge. 'That's why I'm here, keeping my head down. I'm not too popular back home.'

It is Spring in Nice. We start to get a little bit more sun and whenever it appears, within ten minutes, there is a particular girl out lying on the *plage publique* in front of the *Centre* sunbathing. Often I stand and watch her lying there alone on the cool pebbles – the only sunbather in the entire bay. It turns out she is well known; this is something she does every year. By early summer her tan has a head start and she is very brown indeed. By August she is almost black. Her ambition each year is to be the brownest girl on the Côte d'Azur . . .

I watch her lying there. Even in my jacket and scarf I shiver slightly in the fresh breeze. There is something very admirable about such single-mindedness.

Eventually I take my first girl to the Club Les Anges to meet Preston. Her name is Ingrid. She is in my class, a Norwegian, but with dark auburn hair. I don't know her well but she seems a friendly, cheery soul. She speaks English, French and German.

'Are you French?' Preston asks, at once.

Ingrid finds this very amusing. 'I'm Norwegian,' she says patiently.

I apologize later when Ingrid goes off to change into her swimming costume. Preston says not to worry, he likes her. We sit in the sun and Serge brings us lots of drinks. Ingrid, after some prompting, smokes one of Preston's Picayune cigarettes. The only flaw in the pleasant afternoon is that as Ingrid drinks more so her conversation becomes dominated by a French boy she is seeing called Jean-Jacques. But Preston is the acme of good manners. Later we play poker, using cheese biscuits as chips. Ingrid in her swimming suit – she didn't swim – is somehow plumper than I had imagined. I decide that the adjective I would use to describe her is 'homely' . . . except for one detail: she has very hairy armpits. Later Preston confesses that he found this quite erotic. I am not so sure.

The next girl I take is also Scandinavian – we have eight in our class – but this time a Swede, called Danni. Danni is very attractive and vivacious, in my opinion. Straight white-blonde hair, tall, full-breasted. Unfortunately she has one slightly withered leg, noticeably thinner than the other, which causes her to limp. But she's admirably unselfconscious about it.

'Hi,' Preston says. 'Are you French?'

Danni hides her incredulity. *'Oh oui, monsieur. Bien sur.'* Like Ingrid she finds this presumption highly amusing.

Danni wears a small cobalt bikini. She even goes in the pool, which is freezing. (Serge says there is something wrong with the heating mechanism, but as we are – as usual – the sole patrons of the club I suspect he doesn't switch it on deliberately.) I sense that Preston is quite taken with Danni. He asks her what happened to her leg and she tells him it was polio.

'Shit, you were lucky you don't need a caliper.'

We got noisily drunk that afternoon, much to Serge's irritation. Danni produces some grass and we blatantly smoke a joint. Typically, apart from faint nausea, the drug has not the slightest effect on me. As Serge clears a round of glasses away he says to Preston,

'Ça va pas, monsieur. Non, non, ça va pas.'

'Up yours, Serge,' he says amiably, but I can see he's very angry. I realize the relationship has changed between him and Serge. Serge's truculent deference has gone; the dislike is overt, almost challenging.

After we have said goodbye to Danni, Preston tells me about his money problems. The club bar bill is now over 400 dollars and the management is insisting it be settled. His father won't acknowledge his telegrams or return his calls and he has no credit cards. He is contemplating pawning his watch. I buy it off him for 500 francs.

I look around my class at the girls. I know most of them by now, well enough to talk to. Both Ingrid and Danni have enthused about their afternoons at the Club Les Anges and I realize that to my fellow students I have become an object of some curiosity as a result of my unexpected ability to dispense these small doses of luxury and decadence – the exclusive address, the club, the endless flow of free drinks . . .

Preston has decided to abandon his French classes entirely and I am now his sole link with the *Centre*. It is with some mixed emotions – I feel vaguely pimp-like, oddly soiled – that I realize how simple it is to attract girls to the Club Les Anges.

Annique Cambrai is the youngest of the Cambrai daughters. She is only three years older than me but looks older than that. She has strangely mature good looks – dark, with a strong attractive face. She is studying law at the University of Nice. Her English is good, but spoken with a marked American accent. One day when I comment on this she explains that most French universities now offer you a choice when you study English – you can develop an English or American accent, whichever you think is more useful. Like ninety per cent of her fellow students she has chosen American.

One Monday evening after dinner I diffidently ask her if she'd like to come to the Résidence Les Anges to meet an American friend of mine, and perhaps try her new accent out on him. She's delighted to accept.

The next morning on my way down the Rue de France to the *Centre* I see Preston standing outside a pharmacy reading the *Herald Tribune*. I call his name and cross the road to tell him the good news about Annique.

'Finally got a real French girl,' I say.

Preston's face looks odd, caught in a sudden spasm of disappointment.

'That's great,' he says. 'Wonderful.'

A girl steps out of the pharmacy and hands him a plastic bag.

'This is Lois,' he says. We shake hands.

I know who Lois is. Preston has often spoken about her. 'My damn-near fiancée,' he calls her. It transpires that she has flown over spontaneously and unannounced to visit him.

'And, boy, are my Mom and Dad mad as hell,' she laughs.

She doesn't care, and I quite like her for that. Lois is a pretty girl with a round innocent face completely free of make-up. She is tall, even in her sneakers she is as tall as me. She has incredibly thick, dense brown hair which for some reason I associate particularly with American girls. I feel sure also, though as yet I have no evidence, that she is a very clean person – physically clean, I mean to say. Everything about her, even her worn college-girl clothes, exudes freshness. Somehow I can never imagine Lois – nor Preston, come to that – with greasy hair.

I walk with them to the Résidence. Preston confides that the main bonus of Lois's arrival is that it has temporarily solved his money problems. They have cashed in her return ticket and paid off the bar bill. Preston buys his watch back from me.

Annique looks less mature and daunting in her swimsuit, I'm glad to say, even though it is a demure one-piece. The pool's heater is fixed and for the first time we all swim – Preston and Lois, Annique and me. I feel strange seeing Annique so comparatively unclothed, and even stranger as we lie side by side sunbathing. Serge serves us drinks.

Lois obviously assumes that Annique and I are a 'couple' – a quite natural assumption under the circumstances, I suppose. Normally, this would thrill me, but I keep catching Preston gazing at Annique. A mood of frustration and intense sadness seems to emanate from him – of which only I am aware. A peculiar exhilaration mounts slowly within me: I know, now, that I have succeeded. Finally, I have brought Preston the perfect French girl. Annique, by his standards, represents the paradigm, the Platonic ideal for this American male. But he can do nothing, and what makes my excitement grow is the realization that I *can*. I think for the first time in our friendship – perhaps for the first time in his life – Preston envies another person. And as the knowledge dawns so too does my impossible love for Annique. Nothing will ever happen – I know that – but Preston doesn't. And somehow the love affair – the love affair between Annique and me – that will carry on in Preston's mind, embellished by his disappointment and lost opportunity, will be more than sufficient for me.

CLUB LES ANGES

Now that Lois is here I stay away from the Résidence Les Anges. It won't be the same any more, and I don't want to taunt Preston with the spectre of Annique. But one day my curiosity gets the better of me and I decide to call round. Preston opens the door of the studio.

'Hi, stranger,' he says. 'Am I glad to see you.' He seems sincere. I follow him into the apartment. The small room is untidy: the bed unmade, the floor strewn with clothes. I hear the noise of the shower from the bathroom.

'How're things with Annique?'

I look at him. 'Good.' I let the pause develop. 'No, they're good.' His nostrils flare. He shakes his head.

'God, you're one lucky – '

Lois comes in from the bathroom in a dressing gown, towelling her hair dry.

'Hi, Edward,' she says. 'What's new?' She sits down on the bed and begins to weep.

'It's nothing,' Preston says. 'She just wants to go home.'

It turns out that neither of them has left the building for eight days. They are completely penniless. Lois's parents have cancelled her credit cards and calls home have failed to produce any response. Preston has been unable even to locate his father. His stepfather still refuses to speak to him and although his mother would like to help she is powerless. They have been surviving on a diet of olives, peanuts and cheese biscuits served up in the bar and, of course, copious alcohol.

'Yeah, but now we're even banned from there,' Lois says, looking pointedly at Preston.

'I beat up on that bastard Serge,' Preston explains, with a shrug. 'Something I had to do.'

He goes on to enumerate their other problems. Their bar bill stands at just under 300 dollars. Serge is threatening to go to the police unless he is compensated. The management is hostile and very suspicious.

'We got to get out of here. I hate it,' Lois says miserably.

I turn to Preston.

'Can you help us out?' he says. I feel the laugh detonate inside me.

I stand in Nice station. I hand Preston two train tickets to Luxembourg and two one-way Iceland Air tickets to New York.

'You've got a six hour wait in Reykjavik for your connection,' I tell him, 'but there's no cheaper way to fly.'

I bask in their voluble gratitude for a while. They have no luggage with them as they could not be seen to be quitting the Résidence. Preston says his father is in New York and he'll send the money he owes me the day he arrives. I have spent almost everything I possess on these tickets, but I don't care. I am intoxicated with my own generosity and the strange power it confers. Lois goes in search of a *toilette*. Preston gives me a clumsy hug.

'I won't forget this,' he says. We celebrate our short but intense friendship and affirm its continuance. All the while I'm waiting for him to ask me. Through the crowds of passengers we see Lois making her way back. He hasn't got much time.

'Listen, did you and Annique . . .? I mean, are you . . .?'

'We're looking for an apartment . . . That's why you haven't seen much of me.'

'Jesus . . .'

I see the blow tremble his body. He turns away for a second.

'What's up?' Lois asks.

Preston gestures at me, as if he can't pronounce my name. 'Annique . . . They're moving in together.'

Lois squeals. She's so pleased. 'No? Isn't that great? Way to go!'

Preston has calmed down by the time I see them on to the train. More farewells, more gratitude. Preston looks around the station.

'God, it's too bad,' he says. 'I know I could've liked Nice. I *know*. I really could.'

'Yes,' I say. 'It's a shame.' I smile at him. 'I like it here. A lot.'

THE TRADER
Michael Cannon

Time was when I travelled to the city up from the south. Always at this time of year I've made the journey, and always I've sold whatever I had. I've trafficked in most things, in anything that will sell. Anything will sell there, this week, at this time of year. I've sold cloves and wine and figs and olives; I've sold cloth and oil and sandals. I've sold grain that the rats have been at and I've sold woven baskets that will burst half-filled the day after I've gone. I've sold good wine dear, and when it's scarcer and nearer the time that it's needed in the week, I've adulterated it with cheap wine and sold it dearer. I've watered wine and unloaded it on anyone stupid enough to buy: anyone who can't discriminate wine from wine and water deserves to be used. If people are made to want whatever they get, however pitiful, then they're more likely to get what they want. It's as old as the market and that's older than us. It's commerce and it can't be stopped. I know the world. I've sold doves for immolation and I've sold them to the foreigners too. They say they eat them. Strange people, these foreigners.

Let it be realized though, I'm not complaining. They say that before the old king's time you couldn't travel half a day's walk without giving some portion of your purse to some lout or footpad. It was either that or a stick over the head – and they might not stop at that neither. Make an example of the bastards I say; put out their eyes and chop off their hands and let them smell their way to perdition.

These foreigners, they understand that. A few executions posted up like signposts – like scarecrows: quote the law and the prophets all you want, a man breathing his last at a junction for ten hours does a lot more good than telling these louts to stop it for the good of their souls. These foreigners understand trade. Look at the roads they make. Nothing stops trade. Trade sends armies out from their capital cracking pavements across the world with the weight of their money.

I didn't stand to make much money this trip. When I used to come up from the south, up through Idumaea, I'd stop off at the bazaar at Beersheba and pick up anything worthless that would sell. I made lots of money then. I'd stop off at Hebron and hire the local wanton and have her wash my feet first. If you want something more exotic you have to go up to the city. One of them in the city told me she takes in more money spending that whole week on her back than she can hope to make in any other ten weeks. Nothing exotic about her – cheap though. It's like anything else, you get what you pay for if you know the merchandise. Time was when I'd beat the animal to get me to the city faster. Time was when the thought of those wantons made my blood riot. Good money I've paid for a sweat and a surge. Not now, though. I'm older now and feel the cold. The desert nights seem longer now and worse than before, when just the memory of a harlot kept me warm. When it's very cold I make the boy lie at my feet and rest the soles on his belly.

Time was when I made more money without the boy. So it seems. If things don't change I'll send him back to Joppa to beg with the string of other bastards his mother drops. Picked him up for a song and paid good money for him because I thought he'd bring in more. Eat! You've never seen the like. And no sooner had I taken him off their hands than his brother's bursting out between his mother's legs. These people, they're animals – feckless animals. Child after child – where's the profit in that?

He can handle the animals though. That's why I sent him on ahead. We came down from Caesarea and I went over on my ankle outside Antipatris. Soon as the innkeeper realized I couldn't travel he doubled the price. So it seems to me. I didn't want to send the boy on, not with all the goods, but I didn't want to pay double board for both of us either. I wanted the boy to sleep with the animals but the innkeeper wouldn't have it. The thing is, most of these goods are perishable, so the choice is made for you. Better a small comeback on something than sitting with a cargo of stinking fruit and dead doves. So I sent him on. I kept the doves myself though; they die easily with the jostling or if you're careless, and he doesn't seem to appreciate the cost. I told him if I wasn't at the gate by Tuesday at the latest to pick a good spot and sell what he could, and to come to the gate every morning early and check till I came. He's nearly a man and he's watched me trade before. Before I was fourteen I'd sold my weight in salt in a day. Don't go to bed without a profit I told him, and if you do don't sleep. So I stayed.

Eight days. Eight days in a rat trap paying good money for six feet of floor to sleep on that I get for nothing in the desert, and for food that uncircumcised swindlers wouldn't fatten their pigs on. Eight days. And all the time this trickle of fools coming through on their way south to the city, all saying the same thing, looking for the same man.

He's a charlatan or a fool this Nazarene, or both. Probably both. I've only heard fragments, and half the time it's fifth-hand hearsay obtained from people coming north, but it disturbs me because I can't work out what's in it for him. Perhaps he doesn't stand to make anything. If so, he's insane. He can pick his marks though. I see them passing through, wide-eyed, credulous, hopeful – looking for something. They're the type you pray for to come and barter with you when you see them loiter at someone else's stall, and then they come across and look at the merchandise and you let them beat you down to only five times what you paid for it, and you look crestfallen till they've turned the corner. I've seen the type. I know the world. And there they were, begging to be fleeced, and there I was with an ankle like a full wineskin and my merchandise days away. Don't look to the world for any favours. I know – I know the world.

Love your neighbour, they say he says. Treat your neighbour the way you would want him to treat you. It's obvious the man knows nothing about trade. Everyone wants to make a profit – everyone. And no one wants to be taken a loan of. If he keeps on this way he'll run up against the laws of economics. And economics kill. I told that to one of them passing through and I told him this Nazarene is probably bankrupt. Talk's cheap, I said, and it's easy to talk about distributing your goods when you don't have any. He thought about this for a moment and then he said no, it was me that was bankrupt. Me! But that's not the whole extent of their folly. They say he says you've got to love your enemies. Crush your enemies, take from your enemies, aggrandize yourself on your enemies, make your enemies pay reparations before they do these things to you. If you love someone how can they be your enemy? It's a contradiction in terms. And anyway, who really loves anyone in this world? The word's a convenience for the poets. Scratch a poet and you'll find a fool; starve a poet and you'll find he's just a whingeing belly with some ancillary limbs and no more notion of love than a camel. I know the world.

They say he beat traders out of the temple – claimed they were defiling his father's house. I don't waste my time on sympathy, but if I'd had any for him it evaporated on hearing that. It makes me wonder at the arrogance of the man – trying to stop commerce. He can't do it, the world will crush him. He disregards money. He's a heretic. There are too many people with vested interests to let him go on like that.

Eight days of sitting and scratching and wondering what the boy's made. The innkeeper beats his wife, a fat stupid woman who lumbers about in unlovely woe. I asked her to put some cloths in a bucket and let them down into the well, down deep where they will take the cold. I was going to wrap them round my ankle to lessen the swelling, I explained. She asked me how much I'd pay and I said I'd let it hurt. I'd beat her too if she were mine. I tore up the boy's other shirt and limped out to do it myself.

Eight days and I could stand it no longer. The longer I waited the less money people would have left to spend in the city. I limped to the donkey and beat the stupid animal all the way to Jerusalem. The doves didn't take kindly to the jostling. A trickle of the hopefuls were still making their way south, along the same road. A lot of them were marked, or born wrong, or crooked, or scabious, looking for help from the

Nazarene, for some panacea. If I'd known I'd have concocted something and sold it along the way.

I found the boy at the gates as I'd told him. I asked him what he'd made and he held out his hand with a small purse. He said that was all. I slapped him and told him he was a bastard son of a bastard, told him he could go and fester without me. I told him how much I'd have made, his age at Passover. I looked at what he'd given me and did a quick subtraction. I said the difference was coming out of his food till he'd made it up. He said it wasn't his fault and muttered something about trouble and the Nazarene. Some people wanted him silenced. I told him I could have told him that for nothing and that news of some zealot running foul of the authorities didn't make me any profit. I asked him what he had left and he said he'd take me to it. We started into the city.

There was a press in the crowds like you'd never seen and people were agitated in a way I'd never experienced any other Passover. Sometimes, this late in the week, they're jaded, but there was something neurotic about them now, like a child who's fighting sleep. There were some people looking like they'd give you all their money or stab you in the face and it didn't matter much to them either way. It felt like it took two days to get where the boy was leading, it felt hot and I had a headache, what with my ankle and the daylight wasting and them still with money in their purses. Tomorrow was Sabbath, and if they hadn't spent everything by then they'd keep what they'd salvaged.

He was staying at a place Caesar wouldn't have been ashamed of, three times the size of the place I'd just left, though this room had a big pile of rotting oranges in the corner. Don't tell me, I said, the animals are downstairs supping Cyprus wine out of a jewelled goblet. He just looked at me with that big stupid face and I gave it a slap. He still had two jars of oil and more skins of wine. Wine! On a Friday! I told him he was a fool with no more chance of becoming a businessman than he had of becoming tetrarch. The crime of it was that there was no time to adulterate the wine. Luckily, the innkeeper hadn't seen us come up, so I told the boy to pick up the rest and leave the oranges as rent. He told me he'd paid in advance and I cursed as I bundled him downstairs. By the time we made the street half the morning had been wasted. My headache was worse.

We went to three places where I'd kept a stall in past years, good places that stick out into the thoroughfares, where people have to filter past and can't ignore you. I thought I'd have to haggle or bribe, but the places looked like the day after, with one or two dispirited types browsing with no intentions and no money. All the other passers-by were on their way to somewhere else with that annoying preoccupied look that means no sale. I tried to arrest the attention of one or two but they just waved me away. One of the other stallkeepers told me it was no use, and that the execution had taken half if not all the business. I've never understood the point in watching people die: there's no money in it. Once you've seen one execution you've seen them all. I told the boy to go and find out what was happening and he came panting up and said the Nazarene was to be crucified. I could have told him that from Antipatris a week and a half ago. Business can build you a house or nail you to a plank. One good thing though, a crucifixion meant a crowd, a crowd outside the walls where there were no stalls, and on a day like this they'd be thirsty. And I still had wine. Don't look to the world for favours, but don't look away when one presents itself.

The boy told me where the procession had set out from and we headed to intercept. I sent him to store the oil in a place I knew, and took one of the wineskins from him. He was to catch up, bringing the donkey with the rest of the wine and the doves. I stood at the top of the lane and watched the column come into sight below me. The lane was steep and narrow, the noise considerable. The sun must have been practically overhead, because I couldn't see any shade and the heat pressed down on us. My head beat like a hammer and there was lots of dust. There were hundreds and hundreds of people lining the street, or craning from the flat roofs. I had to stand in the path of the procession to get a clear view. As it approached I could see the soldiers at the front pushing people to left and right with their shields.

There was a sort of bow wave of lamentation or derision always breaking over the head of the column. People seemed to want either to cry or spit. I'd never seen this before. The street was so narrow that the soldiers had to stay up front, clearing people out of the way, moving forward almost in single file, with no one flanking the prisoner. I could have reached out and touched the Nazarene as he passed. By the look of him it was obvious he wasn't going to last long on a cross, so I thought I'd better start selling soon. The crown of his head and forehead looked like a bloody paste and he was spattered with blood and gobbets of saliva. Small red gouts dotted his coat, reasonable looking cloth, so I suppose they must have flogged him. The soldiers didn't appear to want to do anything about the spitting. His face was streaked and I couldn't get a proper look at it. He was limping and they'd given his cross to someone else to carry. I was in a quandary whether or not to unload some of the wine now. The longer these things go on the thirstier people get, but they lose interest also and start drifting away in ones and twos. Besides, as I said, he didn't look as if he'd last.

I'd a cup with me to dispense, and I started shouting 'Wine! Wine!' but I could hardly hear myself with the noise of the rabble. They were an ugly crowd and looked too sad or angry or intent to notice whether or not they'd be thirsty yet. I decided to give it time: there was nothing else I could do. I tried to stop some people one at a time, but I'd have been as well trying to sell wine to the Jordan in spate. Someone told me there were thieves to be crucified with the Nazarene – Roman efficiency puts our parochial administration to shame. They'd have to be quick though, the Pharisees would want the criminals down before dark. They'd probably smash their shins to get them dead and off the crosses before Sabbath. Jehova doesn't like to see dead bodies on his day of rest. You can't work on the seventh day and it's ill-mannered to die then too.

The boy found his way to me with the animal through the press of the throng. People were nudging the cages all the time and another of the doves was dead. One of the remaining three looked still also, its movement having as much to do with the jostling as its own intention. I don't know if I could have managed any better with the crowds and the heat, but there's no point in spoiling the child. I pointed to the dead dove and told him that was coming off his food too. We steered the animal round and followed the tail of the procession.

I don't suppose he was in any hurry to be crucified, but if the Nazarene had been going any slower we'd have been going backwards. That wouldn't please the Pharisees who just wanted him dead and bundled out of the way in some hole. It didn't help me either: no one showed any inclination to drink, and the day was getting on without my purse getting any heavier. What with the heat and noise and the press and the dust, and me with a swollen ankle and a head that felt like it was going to burst from the inside, I thought the sooner they're dead and it's all over and done with the better.

When we passed under the shade of the gate to go outside the walls, my ankle felt so bad I had to rest out of the sun for a while. I waved the boy on with the animal and said I'd catch him up. They didn't take them far, just to the usual little mound where they display malefactors, and I could hear the hammering from where I sat. It beat in time to my headache – either that or the noise of the banging started a rhythm in my temples. Pain's a useless waste of effort. I knew if I didn't get started I wouldn't feel like moving, so I hoisted myself to my feet and started up the hill.

By the time I got there they'd already fastened the Nazarene down and were hoisting his cross vertical. It shuddered into its slot with a bang; I could feel the tremor through the bandages of my foot. Then they started on the other two. One of the thieves had watched the whole thing and now he started to cry. I looked for the boy.

He was on the periphery of the crowd with his face pressed into the donkey's flank, hands cupped over his ears to block out the sound. Not the best marketing posture. When I spun him round his face was like whey, and I could see he'd been crying. Perhaps he'd seen a few corpses before but not how they got that way. This must have been his first execution: some people go like that. I could see he wasn't going to be much use – people would be less inclined to buy from someone snivelling over his wares. A slap wouldn't dry his eyes so there was no point in beating him. I told him to stay where he was and took the wine from him.

Aside from passers-by, I've noticed there's usually only two types who loiter at the foot of a cross or around executions: the curious and the bereaved. You can usually make more money out of those with the macabre streak. The rest are usually too sad, or feeling sorry for themselves, to dig into their purses. This time it was different.

Certainly there were bereaved, but there were still a lot of shouting angry people about, just like on the way up, and the soldiers had cleared a ragged semi-circle about twenty feet wide round the foot of the Nazarene's cross and were pushing back deriders and mourners alike. They allowed some doe-eyed woman, his mother I suppose, through the cordon, and a young man slipped between the shields to stand beside her and hold her up. One of the guards turned towards the boy, but the Centurion gestured him back to his position. Between bouts of trying to sell I caught sight of her in snatches. She just kept gazing imploringly at the Nazarene and he seemed to be trying to talk to her. When I looked later she was back on the other side of the cordon with the young man, who had his arm around her shoulders. Whether she'd gone of her own accord or been told, I don't know.

It was different this time because there weren't many loiterers – or any I could find to sell to. None of the curious macabre. There were still just the friends and relatives, and the mockers. None of them wanted anything to drink. Even one of the thieves, both of them hung up now and flanking the Nazarene, joined in the ridicule – you'd think he'd have more to think of, it getting prematurely dark already and someone coming up the hill before sunset to break his legs. The Nazarene just hung, too busy dying. The soldiers posted a notice above his head saying that he was the King of the Jews. That didn't please most of the onlookers. There was too much turmoil to sell. The soldiers were playing dice for the Nazarene's coat. As I said, it was reasonable looking cloth, but maculate now. I thought of asking how much but thought better of it. Although it was getting dark the stultifying heat of earlier still remained. If no one was thirsty I was. I joined the boy and sent him for some bread, sat down beside the animal and took a drink.

When the boy brought the bread back I realized I didn't really want any. I could have slept but there was still jeering going on. The sound of the derision grew like a murmur, far away and insignificant, like the sound of a fly hovering, or water lulling you to sleep. I was drowsy and on the point of closing my eyes when a voice, high and desperate, cut through my tiredness. It was the Nazarene, shouting on his father or something. It startled me, like gulls rearing out the cliffs when I was a boy, stealing eggs. In my start I moved my position and a searing pain shot like a bolt driven home through my ankle. I cursed and hobbled to my feet. I'd give it one last try. I took the wine and left the boy.

This time I didn't try to sell from person to person, I was too near the extreme of fatigue for that, I just walked up the hill, as near the top as I could get, and held the wineskin above my head. The crosses were at the very summit, so I stood with my back almost pressed against the cordon of shields. Even though the sun was away, the sweat trickled down my forehead and stung my eyes. My arms grew heavy and my breathing laboured. I thought of money till my arms couldn't take the strain any longer. I'd given the whole thing up as a bad job, and was lowering the skin when the voice behind me shouted, saying he thirsted. It was the Nazarene. Whether he was addressing me or it was just a general observation I don't know. I didn't know either how he proposed to pay me. I don't look to the world for favours, but there's almost a conscious irony in the fact that my only customer that day was a crucified pariah with no purse and no way of dipping his hands into it if he had.

The Centurion gestured me to come through the cordon. As I approached he threw me a piece of silver and kicked the helmet at his feet towards me, telling me to fill it. He didn't make any attempt to conceal his dislike of me, but then his currency's as good as anyone's, he did pay over the odds and it was the only sale I had had all day. One of the soldiers picked up the helmet and I filled it half-full. I would have left it at that but for the look on the soldier's face, so I filled it almost to capacity. That done he ignored me, and I watched them dip a sponge in the wine and pass it to the Nazarene on a rod. One of the soldiers at the shields grasped me by the coat and pushed me back into the crowd. I almost went over on my ankle.

I'd had enough. A swollen ankle, a bursting head and my only customer almost extinguished. I looked at him as he craned for the sponge. His breathing was torturous and his ribs looked as if they couldn't keep his chest moving much longer. Once he'd drunk he hung in that resigned way. It was a bad day for us both – both out of luck. I'd make good the loss, but he wouldn't get better. His body was broken now, a thing, and no good to anyone. At the foot of that cross though I felt more sorry for myself than for anyone else. I suppose he did likewise. Concern goes inwards. It's all a question of perspective.

I went back to the boy who hadn't moved and hadn't stopped crying. When I prised his head out from the donkey's flank his face was mottled and his eyes swollen almost to closing. My ankle throbbed, so I loaded him with all the wine there was and climbed on the animal myself. When I looked at the cages I saw only one of the doves was still alive. There was no profit in cursing, and I felt too dispirited anyway. I threw the dead birds out and balanced the cage with the remaining live one across the donkey's back. We started down the hill.

When we'd descended some way, I spotted, sure enough as I'd predicted, a soldier coming up towards us with the iron club balanced across one shoulder – climbing the hill to smash their shins. I was curious about him: his expressionless face, the purpose in his stride and the way he seemed not to care at my looking at him. We had almost drawn abreast when that same cry, high and desperate, startled me. I sat bolt upright, and the suddenness of my movement caused the donkey to break into a canter. I clutched wildly, trying to regain my balance, the animal was slipping on the declivity and the broken scree, and I tumbled backwards still clutching the cage. I landed on my back, winded and stunned, too breathless to shout at the searing pain from my ankle. When I looked up, the first thing I could see was the soldier bearing down on me, still expressionless, gazing ahead. I fancied for a moment that I was the victim of his intention. I lay across his path and he showed no inclination to change course. In panic and despite the pain I rolled over. My left ear was to the ground, his foot inches from my face as his stride grazed me. His sandal was robust and worn, his foot ponderous and sinewy, exceptionally powerful, as he crunched up the hill. I rolled on to my back taking great gulps of air, my pulse throbbing in my ears. When I opened my eyes the boy was bending over me.

He helped me to sit up. The cage lay three feet from where I'd fallen, the other side of the soldier's path. The lid had come slightly ajar; the bird was straining at the gap. I shouted and reached towards it. As I grasped the cage another surge of pain in my ankle caused me to give an involuntary shudder. The bird slipped through the gap and between my straining fingers. We watched it, the boy standing and me sitting, a splash of white against the sky till it spiralled up and out of sight into the gloom.

The boy gave me some wine and helped me to my feet. I placed one arm on the animal, the other across the boy's shoulders and we started down into the city. It was beginning to get very dark.

NO NEW HEROES
Felicity Carver

'TELLIN – CARPET SHELL – COMMON WENTLETRAP (CLATHRUS CLATHRUS).' The self-conscious Latin, suggesting dreams of scholarship in unsteady capitals, made Kevin smile. There were careful divisions in the box that held the shells, made with pieces of card painstakingly Sellotaped to the sides. He picked out a limpet, roughened and grained like old bark on the outside, the interior silk-smooth and feminine. He thought of the day when they had gone to the seaside, when he had suffered the empty yawning feeling of car sickness while crouched in the back seat, when the roar of surf and shingle on an Atlantic beach had almost deafened them, and his mother had complained fretfully of the cold. He found it difficult to visualize her now. They had not realized then that the cold she complained of on the beach would not be cured by the heater in the car or the loan of an extra jacket. He could not recognize her in his own or his brother Michael's face. The only picture was a watercolour, framed, and hanging in the room downstairs.

It seemed wrong not to be able to remember in a place that had survived on memories. His father had lived on them finally, other people's rather than his own, immersing himself in Irish history like a convert to a new religion, talking endlessly of Connolly and Pearse to anyone he could trap into listening. There were still exercise books in the drawers of his desk, full of poetry his father had tried to write, ballads on Kilmainham gaol and the Easter Rising. As the scholar in the family, Kevin had been asked to approve and had been embarrassed because they had seemed naïve. He was ashamed of his father for having written such bad imitative verse. It had often seemed as though the people in the poems were more real to the old man than himself and his brother Michael. As the eldest, Michael had taken over the running of the farm long before their father had died, though they pretended he was still in charge and reported back to him about the harvest and new calves, and consulted him on what to plant in the long field. The old man had not tried to pressure them into his beliefs; he had not thought it possible for the two of them to feel as strongly as he had. There could be no new heroes, only the old ones.

Apprehension stiffened Kevin's fingers. He dropped the shell and grovelled on the floor, inhaling carpet dust as he searched under the bed. Bella and the Hoover never penetrated this far. There were old papers, festering socks and other clothing he didn't recognize, black seed-like mouse droppings and a couple of paperbacks. The mice had eaten part of the mattress, also some of the paperbacks; there were small chunks of foam spat out in heaps of beige confetti.

Why had he ever asked Alison to stay here? It wouldn't work, it couldn't. It had seemed so possible in his room at university where he spent some of his days and occasional nights with her. There, his home was what he described to other people, something mildly quaint and Irish; dangerous too, he'd made much of living on the border. Now he was faced with discovery. He should have known she would accept; she was interested in politics, going to meetings, sometimes chairing them, coming out enthusiastic, full of what had been said about the troubles, the solutions. She had adopted Ireland a while ago, needing a cause to fight for, having none of her own. He thought it was probably why she had taken up with him in the first place, though he didn't share her convictions. When Kevin went to a meeting he felt like a man outside a television shop watching the screens without the volume – only in a meeting it was the volume without the action, hollow palms clapping, the beer-breath of students, cigarette smoke shrouding their faces like the aftermath of a bomb.

'You're so negative.' It was one of her words that term. She picked up phrases and discarded them later like old clothes. Involvement's something else where I come from, he thought.

Where the past is a soft peatbog trembling under your feet. They were all caught up in it, his brother, his father.

Waiting for Alison to come, he took up his part-time job at the hotel where they greeted him with friendly suspicion.

'You won't want to be talking to us any more, not with all that education.'

'All those exams and still working in a dump like this.'

'You're the bright one, maybe you can tell us how the wiring works. The fuse is gone again.'

And when he couldn't tell them, they were happy because it proved that practice was better than theory, wasn't it? Or there was Joe who had been at school with him, earning money as the barman, dextrous with glasses and different drinks and girls. Smooth-talking Joe would never need books to get where he was going.

'What's the point in going that far away? You can do well enough here, can't you?'

'There's Dublin for you, surely to God it's not that bad.'

Watching their small interests, the farms, the businesses, what won at the Curragh, the border patrols. Everyone in and out of each other's thoughts. And Michael, his brother, apparently content with the land.

'You must be having a great time of it over there. All those demonstrations, and the parties.'

'Oh yes.' He had given up saying he worked a long time ago, they didn't want to hear it, he had to live out their fantasies. They knew, they read the papers, watched the telly. What could he tell them?

'Don't put those crates there, not now, we want them over this way where Joe can get at them easy.' Jackson fussed, cleaning his hands on the towel tied round his waist. 'What's your brother doing now? I hear he was in the north last week. Is the meat in the cold-store yet, the day's too hot for it to stay out long. Quite a man now, Michael, isn't he?'

There were long afternoons on the farm turning the straw in the warm wind, driving alongside the combine while it spewed out a stream of corn into the trailer. When he stepped out of his clothes at night, grain fell from his pockets, chaff and husks from the folds, gritting underfoot like shingle. Dust shook from his hair, the pillow grew blond with it.

The Aran sweater bought in a tourist shop was too thick for the September afternoon. There were small beads of moisture on her nose, and the high-heeled boots wobbled on the rough tarmac by the bus-stop.
'I didn't think you were coming.'
'I sent you a postcard.'
The day brightened for him, he seized her bag and threw it into the van with a feeling of ownership. He found himself talking all the way to the farm, pointing out landmarks like the tinkers' caravans parked on the old roadway, wondering at his own volubility. He took her into the house through the kitchen, noticing Bella hadn't cleaned it, realizing too late it was her day off. The place was crowded with clothes hanging like flayed skins from a pulley near the ceiling, while a frying-pan full of solidified fat rested on the stove with a weird Hallowe'en-mask design etched on its surface. He made coffee and they sat drinking it. Her eyes were half-covered by the dark curling hair. She's here, really here, he thought, absently picking pieces of dog-meal out of the fruit bowl.
When Michael came back in the evening, Kevin was nervous, hoping for his approval, angry with himself for needing it.
'I've heard a lot about you,' she said. Michael was wary of offending because Kevin was there watching.
'No good, I'll bet.'
'Not much,' Alison laughed, and Kevin was sure he could hear what Michael was thinking. Why couldn't you find someone of your own kind? She's English, isn't she? He could feel the unspoken phrases in the way Michael put down his glass.
Next day he phoned the hotel to say he couldn't come, there was too much to do on the farm, listening happily to the annoyance at the other end. Then he found Alison an old pair of wellingtons, and they went out walking over the small fields, past the broken-toothed walls, the hills fringed with rough woodland. There had been talk of selling the farm once, when a developer was looking for land nearby, but the thought had

seemed like a betrayal and they had left it, the new houses being built a couple of miles away by the village.

A helicopter surfaced briefly above the trees like a submarine coming up for air, hovering beside a church, then plunging down with the speed of a pheasant avoiding the guns. There were small figures moving over a field a long way off.

'Soldiers.' He pointed. She followed the line of his hand. 'That's the north over there.' What your political friends talk about, he thought.

'Is your brother with the IRA?'

'Why should he be?' He was aware the question wasn't an answer.

'I saw the books on the shelf in the kitchen. The ones about the Rising, Irish history.'

'They were my father's books. You should have met him, he was the keen one.'

Somewhere in the distance there was the spitting sound of a ricochet. 'Probably a rabbit,' he said. 'They get bored.'

She wasn't afraid, though.

There had been that other day, hot and thundery, the scent of cut grass heavy on the air. A large white house with wide windows that stared defiantly out over the countryside near Drymen, with Alison's parents, middle-aged, middle-class, sitting at a wide table trying to discover a mutual friend who could provide a reference for the strange young man their daughter had brought home.

Afterwards, Alison and he had walked by the burn at the end of the wood, past a paddock where ponies stood in the trees' shade. A black and white spaniel frolicked in front of them, then began digging at the bank in frantic haste. It yelped suddenly and rolled on the earth, biting furiously at its sides. Alison had run forward, had brushed the angry wasps away and pushed the dog into the water, submerging it in the pool, scraping the insects from her own clothes, while the dog pawed at its face and whimpered, eyes swelling.

Kevin had been unable to move; when he had read *Nineteen Eighty Four* he had known it would be wasps or bees waiting for him in the cage, not rats, that he would yell, 'Do it to her.' Then Alison had shouted at him to help, and he had heard the scorn in her voice and had come up too late to be of use. Later he had bathed the lumps on the back of her neck with vinegar, her mother's remedy, and kissed the small swellings that whitened under the pressure of his fingers, inhaling the sour smell of her disfavour.

At lunchtime in the kitchen Bella came in and slapped the plates of food down, great humpbacked potatoes swimming in a sea of gravy, and left a bowl of fruit reduced to some unrecognizable pulp on the side.

'She doesn't approve of you,' said Kevin.

Alison was dissecting the meat, trimming the fat off it. He caught Michael's eye and looked away. Then he cut the fat off his own so that she wouldn't be the only one, and scraped the plates into the dog's bowl when they'd finished.

'I'll be away now,' said Bella. 'Maybe you'll manage the supper. Perhaps she could heat it up.' The third person reduced Alison to an indeterminate status, like someone who is mentally handicapped.

'I'm sure I can, it's kind of you to leave something.' Bella wasn't to be won over. She put her hands by her sides like a drill sergeant and turned away.

'What did I do?'

'You're here with the two of us. Competition. That's enough for her.'

It was the horse that helped Alison and Michael to understand each other. He had found her looking over the loose-box door and asked if she could ride.

'Of course.' Kevin remembered the ponies in the field at Drymen, fat and idle in the sunshine.

The long-legged four-year-old was awkward as a teenager, lumbering out of the stall, scraping the flaps of the saddle on the door, staring intently into the distance while Michael gave Alison a leg-up. Then they were out in the soft earth of the field, hooves cutting great scars in the grass as the horse plunged, humped his back, and exploded into bucks, great wild leaps that took him off down the slope with the girl balanced on his back, her long legs reaching down and holding his sides, laughing as she turned him at the far end and made him circle, wheeling and twisting until his back flattened out again and he dropped his head and with heaving flanks floated over the grass to the gate, looking like the horse he would be one day. There was a red mark on Alison's cheek where a branch had caught her, an exhilaration in her face which Kevin hadn't seen before, and her eyes were full of the space of the sky and the swooping horse.

Michael was smiling with her. 'I thought he'd have you off.'

'No bother, he's great.'

Kevin grudged their excitement, he didn't share their admiration for the sweating animal, the hair ruffled with sweat on the shoulders, the hooves shifting restlessly. He had endured ponies for a while because there had been no option, but later his ability for schoolwork had let him become a different person and given him an alibi. Alison's hands were darkened with the grease from the horse's mane, he could smell it on them still when they were in the house afterwards. When she rubbed her fingers together it flaked off in small curls like shavings from a rubber.

'Don't you ever ride?'

'Not now. And never that one, he terrifies me, he's only half-broken. Weren't you frightened?'

'I like being scared.' He looked at her and didn't understand, and was afraid suddenly at the gap between them.

That evening he went out with Michael to the barn to help with hay for the cattle who stamped and moved in the straw, a few beasts being kept in till they calved. Their breath was warm in the half-darkness; he could smell muck, clean fresh hay, and the sweet reek of last year's silage.

'I'll be away tonight.' Michael was leaning over the old gate they used as a partition. Kevin felt his stomach tighten as he stood on the concrete passageway, hearing the rustle of rats in the straw.

'All right,' he said.

'Enjoy yourself then.'

Kevin swore softly, aware of Michael grinning, feeling himself dismissed like a child.

When he lifted the latch on her door later and slipped in, she was still awake.

'Where was the car going?'

'It was only Michael.'

'What's he doing?'

'I don't know myself, he keeps it that way.'

The sheets were cold at the side of the bed. He shivered beside her, nervous at being with her here in the house.

He knew Michael was back when he went to shave in the morning. There was already a rim of dark hairs and soap round the basin, blood-flecked foam from tooth-cleaning. Michael always had trouble with his teeth. Kevin scrubbed at the basin, suddenly fastidious.

Michael was frying eggs in the old grease of the pan. When Alison came down there were all kinds of questions in her face, and something of the reverence of a small boy meeting his football hero. Kevin tasted hot fat, blistering his tongue, watching her eyes on Michael's unresponsive back.

'What was it?' she asked him later, washing the plates under the tap.

'Don't know. Smuggling maybe.'

'Is that all?'

'There's money in it.'

'It's not just for money, though, is it?'

He wanted to say, don't glorify it, don't make him into something he isn't. He's my brother, he's a chancer, he takes risks, they all do. And if you quote all that Marxist-Leninist stuff at him he wouldn't know what you meant, the theory doesn't bother him, that isn't why he's in it. He was born into it. The day he accepted the farm he inherited the old man's dreams. He didn't have to find his war, it was on his doorstep, and I didn't realize what it meant to him then, not till a couple of years ago.

In his own room later he turned on the radio and listened

to the news, but there was nothing about the north, only the visit of some minister from London.

Alison rode the horse again the following day, cantering easily round the field while they watched from the gate, and when she came back he saw her face was alive as it had been the previous time. Flecks of foam danced off the bit, caught on their shirts, spattered on the ground as the horse sidled through the gateway.

'He's got quality,' said Michael. 'So have you.' She smiled and Kevin turned away as she slipped down off the horse.

He took her out for a drive later. He would show her it all, why not. She wanted to see for herself, that's what she'd said. They crossed the border with only a perfunctory search of the car, and he drove to one of the nearby towns, where they bumped over the ramps in the road outside the police station, the barbed wire high on the walls. Armoured vehicles moved swiftly through the streets, heading for sanctuary. They left the car and walked into the centre, and the shops were like any high street, full of people and children.

'I could be at home,' she said, disappointed.

I am, he thought.

He did not like to ask how long she was staying, he didn't want to put dates to it, limit his fantasies. Instead, she wanted to try and help with the farm; he drove the baler and took her on the tractor with him, standing behind her while she tried to steer it, his arms round her waist. They cleaned up the fields for Michael following with the plough, seagulls wailing round his head like new-born babies, the machine stuck to the grooves like an old record. She made some kind of cake that he hadn't eaten before, with cinnamon and ginger stolen from Bella's cupboard on her day off. Another time they burned the old stubble in the field down by the wood, and had a job to put it out at the far end, beating furiously with bundles of branches ripped from the trees after the wind changed, winning finally when a gust diverted the flames, giving them time to stamp it out. They collapsed exhausted, smelling the smoke on their clothes and hair, laughing, their energy spent, the prickling stubble scarring the backs of their necks. He had rubbed his eyes with his hands, and dark specks had floated over the sun when he opened them.

Other days she went riding, with Michael walking beside her. And then Kevin became aware when he woke in the morning that she was down in the kitchen early, when Michael got up, making the tea, grilling bacon because she wouldn't let them eat all that fat. Helping out, she said later when Kevin asked. I want to be useful, not just a guest. But he knew she listened like a dog for the steps on the stair and began to watch her, wondering why he had asked her to come. When he went to her room one night she was cool, pleading stiffness after the riding, and his hurried assertive movements were clumsy because he was afraid, giving her the excuse to avoid sleeping with him. He had gone back to his own room holding the hurt like a drawing clasped to his chest so that no one could see it. He knew that Michael had no interest – she was Kevin's friend from college, that was all – and could not bring himself to end what little was left.

When the message came he was outside, carrying a bucket full of water that slopped into his boots when he opened the door of the stable and the horse pushed its nose at him. He shoved at the animal. 'Get over you bastard,' he said with affection, and the horse blew at the water, snorting, turning its reflection into a monster.

He didn't hear Alison until she spoke. 'That was the phone. A friend of your brother's.' Something in her voice made him look round.

'Something up?'

'They didn't have time to say much, it was a call-box. And the accent, I didn't get all of it. A place, a crossroads, they want you to pick him up.'

Damn him. Oh, damn him. He didn't want to get in the van, to go out and drive into whatever it was that Michael was involved with.

'You'll have to go,' she said.

He was driving one fist gently into the other in his desperation. 'I suppose so.'

'For God's sake, he's your brother. I'd go but I don't know where it is.'

'What makes you so righteous?' They glared at each other over the roof of the van. If it wasn't for her pushing him he'd be away already. It wasn't her business, was it? 'It's not a game.'

'I didn't think it was. Are you going then?'

He was back in the kitchen at Drymen, inhaling vinegar, hearing the scorn in her voice.

'Of course.'

'I'll come with you.' She was in the front seat before he could stop her. 'It'll look less suspicious anyway.'

They crossed the border on the same road, but this time the guards went through the car and made them get out.

'Panic on?' He wanted to provoke them, his powerlessness annoyed him; if he was being dragged into their war he would fight it.

They didn't answer, just waved him through.

With the aid of an old frayed map they waited at the side of a narrow road, a high bank protecting them, watching the crossroads a couple of hundred yards beyond. Rain streamed down the windscreen, and water had leaked through the rubber seal on the door, flooding the pocket and creating a sodden mass of old rags and petrol-station coupons for glasses.

'I never imagined being involved, not like this.'

He slid his arm across the back of her seat and put it round her shoulders, settling himself, but she began to talk.

'You and your brother, you're not really that alike, are you?'

Do we have to be, he thought. 'How?'

'I'm not sure. He's different from most of the people I've met, like someone who's been abroad for a long time, who's travelled to places I'll never go.'

'He hasn't been away much, mostly just the north. And once to London.'

'I didn't mean that.'

He didn't want her to work towards it, he tried to change the subject, but she wasn't to be put off.

'It's as if he's done something that changed him. Like a long illness or being in a war. Another country where the rules, the way things are done, are different; ours don't apply. Except the other day, he was like anyone when we were down in the field trying to put out the fire. But sometimes I feel he's not there at all, he's living somewhere else.'

'A different reality.' He wished he hadn't found the words.

'You do understand then.'

'Oh I understand. But I don't want to go there.'

'I do.'

'You like being scared.'

'Is that wrong? It's so safe where I live.'

His fear was something that seemed to move in the rain by the crossroads, a feeling he recognized from other times, like the day he walked into a Belfast pub with Michael and realized they were in the wrong territory, seeing the glasses stop halfway to gaping mouths. Like a drug, he had seen Michael high on it, and Alison too the day she rode the horse. But you didn't have to go looking for it, did you? He had the taste now, a sickness in his mouth as he peered through the windscreen at the road, sensing movement. He wound down the window.

'Why does she have to talk about him all the time?' he thought. His feet were growing cold; he pushed them against the pedals, listening to the rain. He should have brought some whisky. It would have helped with the waiting, the darkness.

The noise was like hailstones pattering on the tarmac, it took him a moment to realize what was happening.

'Jesus, let's get out of here.' He let off the brake and rolled the van down the hill without lights, turning on the ignition, letting it jerk into life, rubbing the misted interior, huddling against the wheel.

'You can't go, not yet.'

'We can't stay, that's for sure.' Something hit, scraped along the flank of the van. 'They're shooting out there for God's sake!'

'But Michael.'

'He's late, he won't come.'

'He asked you to wait!' She was clutching his arm.

'He's got more lives than a damn cat, that one. Can you see him?'

She peered through the back windows, then opened the door and leaned out.

'Be careful, you don't know who it was back there. See anyone?'

'No.'

'Well then.' He changed gear.

'We should have waited.'

'What for? He may be back by now anyway.' She grabbed at the steering-wheel but he pushed her away.

'He asked us.'

'If we crash it'll be no good to anyone. Forget your bloody boy-scout loyalty.'

'Suppose he's hurt.'

'Did they say so?'

They crossed into the south on a small lane little better than a cart track, driving through a farmyard to reach the road the far side, and got back to an empty house and the dogs leaping at them in welcome. He tried to kiss Alison in the passage outside her room but she made it clear she didn't want him to. 'Wait a minute, look,' he said, but she shut the door.

Michael came back at midday; the dogs heard him first and slipped out of the barn, then Kevin went, afraid of what he might see, but Michael was only tired. 'Thanks anyway,' he said, and they laughed with relief and opened cans of beer in the kitchen in celebration, while Alison who had expected anger and recriminations looked on with incomprehension.

'She doesn't understand anything,' said Bella cheerfully, slicing apples into a bowl. 'She's packed. I didn't think she'd stay.'

When she came downstairs Kevin took the bag from her. 'I'll drive you to the bus station.' She didn't acknowledge his offer, but she climbed into the van.

On the way he said, 'We did the right thing, he wasn't coming anyway.'

She was staring out of the window, watching cloud shadows race over the fields.

'Did you know that in 1916 when they had printed copies of the Proclamation they couldn't put them up because they forgot the glue?'

'What's that supposed to mean?'

'It seemed significant.'

'You were going to leave him, weren't you?'

'No,' he said. He heard the lie in the small space of the car, against the rattle of the broken exhaust. I left him because you liked him, not because I was afraid. 'Do it to him,' that was what I had thought. Bella's right, she doesn't understand anything.

And he was happy because she was going and there would not be another betrayal.

TODDLE-BONNY AND THE BOGEYMAN
Douglas Dunn

For the sake of a conversation with Frank Irvine, it wasn't uncommon for Keith McMinn to pay his newspaper bill daily.

'I'll no' go bust because you don't pay me on the nail, Keith.'

'It was on my mind that I owed you for the paper, and, och well, I was passin' . . .'

'I've customers who pay their accounts when they feel like it – and I mean *seldom*. But even quarterly's all right by me. I'm an obligin' sort of man, Keith. How about weekly?' It was easy to feel exasperated with McMinn, harder to allow yourself to show it. 'I mean, I've known ye let it go the four days. Fortnightly? The perfect arrangement. Monthly's the average.'

Eight years ago, a few days before she died, McMinn's mother made a list of what he should do to fend for himself. He was to stick to Fraser for fish, Armstrong for butchery, and Logie the grocer. Sorrow before the event bestowed on her advice an almost luminous privacy. 'I hate to think of you living on your own,' she'd said. Her uncertainty at whether he could cope was matched by McMinn's dread of independence. 'If it comes to the bit where you can't manage,' she said, 'then talk to Dr Broadie. There might be a vacancy somewhere. We haven't had to even think of it, but there could come a time when there's nothing else for it.' She spoke with difficulty, as if summarizing a subject that was too complicated for both of them. He often remembered that afternoon. 'I want you to try,' she said.

McMinn reproached himself for falling short of his mother's instructions. His meals began as raw produce, but ended up undercooked, overcooked or as blackened disasters. From time to time he examined the frozen food displays in the supermarket that Logie's had become since his mother's death. He resisted their packaged blandishments and thought that those who didn't ought to know better. When he passed the Chinese carry-out he stopped and looked in through the plate-glass window, disapproving sternly.

For eight years his mother's list weathered the steam and fumes of the kitchen as it hung on the same nail as his calendar. It was a yellowing relic; it was also authoritative, admonitory, maternal and tender as it stated the memoranda of his life.

Anything that happened in Antynth was McMinn's business. He was that small town's classic pedestrian. With his mind fixed on its innocent disdain, he was an encyclopaedist of its trival alterations and momentous changes. His gait was one of a depressed jauntiness. Children imitated it. He was unaware of the impression created by his clothes that looked as if another outing would see them fall apart.

'They tell me that girls are drinking pints now!' McMinn complained to Frank Irvine.

'Is that a fact?'

'Pints! Young women!'

'Don't tell me you've taken to visitin' public houses?'

'Me? No! Never!'

'Not a drop 's crossed your lips? Do I believe you, Keith?' Irvine was teasing him.

'Only that once – the Labour Club's Burns Supper, nineteen eighty-three.'

'Will I ever forget it?' Irvine's eyes twinkled with kindly mischief.

'I'd no' blame ye if ye held it against me. I'll never live it down. I was a disgrace!' McMinn said.

'Don't say that, Keith. I mean, I'm no' a hypocrite. Once in a wee while I get plastered.'

It was McMinn's turn to tease, and Irvine was conscious of having placed the opportunity before him. 'Once in a wee while, Frank?'

'Maybe once a month,' Irvine conceded.

'More than that, though, if ye could get away wi' it! Once a month?' he said with broad disbelief.

'Credit me wi' a spark of responsibility, eh? I've a business to run!' Irvine said, exaggerating his defence of his reputation.

A customer came into the shop and Irvine began to serve him. McMinn waited by the counter but the newsagent said, 'Bye, Keith! See ye later.' It was a decisive farewell. McMinn had no option but leave.

Joe Crossan said, 'It beats me how he manages. All on his owny-oh, an' big empty spaces upstairs . . .'

'Keith does all right. Not all there, but he gets by on what he's got, Joe.'

'It's more than a loose screw. He only has to breathe an' ye can hear the rattle!'

'Human nature's what ye might call a hobby of mine, Joe. Ye wouldn't deny that ye come in here once a day? What do ye buy? At *least* half-a-pound of Liquorice Allsorts. It's a lot of daily sugar. There are folk in the medical profession would say ye must 've the death wish. Ye make me feel guilty. Ye're a confectionary addict, and I'm yer pusher!'

'Ye sell fags an' all,' Crossan said accusingly.

'Why no'? I smoke as well. I'm no' pious. I'm pointin' out that when it comes to windy spaces upstairs, you an' me haven't a leg to stand on!'

McMinn was walking along Shields Street on an evening in late April. A Rolls-Royce approached him at a stately speed and went past in a mechanical hush. A Rolls-Royce was a rare sight in Antynth. McMinn would have rushed to Frank Irvine's shop to report the news, but when he'd passed it a few minutes before he'd noticed Velma behind the counter. Any time she served him it was with looks of distaste. Fifteen minutes later, on Baird Street, beside the cement mixer and bricks, where they were building a new bank, McMinn saw the same opulent black car. A chauffeur was at the wheel. Two men and a woman sat in the back. Its windows were tinted, but not so much as to make the occupants completely invisible. You could see them, but you couldn't see them. You could tell that they were men or women, but you couldn't identify them.

The light was fading but several boys were still playing

football on the waste ground beyond the broken fence that made Lawrie Street a cul-de-sac. McMinn spectated from the fence for a few minutes and then went through one of the gaps in its rotting posts on which black smears of municipal weatherproofing were still trying to fight off ruin. A close interest in local football was essential to McMinn's instinctive assessment of what Antynth was all about. He watched a thwarted dribble with his hands on his hips. 'Ach!' he said, turning his head away like a critical expert. 'Left foot!' he shouted. 'Try it wi' the left foot!'

'What 'd you know about it?' the player shouted back.

'Toddle-Bonny!' another yelled in retaliation.

Years of parental guidance came to his aid. Ghostly advice encouraged him to walk away, around the edge of the imaginary football pitch. He crossed the waste ground to the disused railway line and site of the old station. Green shoots of fireweed sprouted by the long-abandoned coal depot. Two young men were racing motorcycles on the loose gravel. They braked so that their rear wheels swung on the guided weight of their machines. Each skid sliced the gravel and threw up a shower of tiny stones that rattled off shrubs and sheets of rusted corrugated iron.

Soon he was back on Shields Street. Once again the Rolls-Royce went by. 'What the hell 're they playin' at?' He took off his cap and scratched his head, wondering at his own, spoken puzzlement.

Outside the parish church the car's brief halt seemed to indicate that it was taking a closer look. As it passed him, it slowed, and McMinn stooped to look into it. 'Who the hell do ye think ye are?' he shouted at the departing car, having failed to see its occupants. Its acceleration was virtually silent. McMinn felt himself dislodged by its power and glamour.

McMinn suspected his own opinions and conclusions. He acknowledged that his intelligence was slow. He resented the belief that the Rolls-Royce represented some sort of conspiracy. Pally Gray was among the few people to whom he could talk. He was in his early seventies and had been a close friend of

McMinn's father. McMinn saw him once a week in the rooms of the local Labour Party Club.

'Pally, am I right, or am I wrong? No one in Antynth drives a Rolls-Royce.'

'Is this a joke?'

'No kiddin'. I saw a Rolls-Royce the other night. Even I can tell a Rolls from any other motor,' McMinn said, inviting Pally to take him seriously.

'A ritzy visitor from the other world,' Pally said, 'but not from outer space. Not common on these streets, but there 're plenty elsewhere, and folks there go for drives, Keith. Keith saw a Rolls-Royce the other night,' Pally said to a man who came to the bar.

'Och, it would 've been mine,' the man said.

'A uniformed driver, two men and a woman in the back,' McMinn protested.

'Interesting,' the man at the bar said, meaning the opposite.

Holding his lemonade and a crude brown-paper parcel, McMinn headed for an empty table.

'They don't call ye "Pally" for nothin',' Curly Pond said. 'How ye put up wi' that half-wit . . .'

'Son of my best friend, Curly,' Pally Gray said, savouring Curly Pond's nickname. He was as bald as a plate.

'Everybody liked Tommy McMinn, but ye have to admit that Toddle's manner would drive a saint to pugilism,' Pond said, attracting the barman's attention. 'Anythin' for you, Pally?'

'No, nothing for me,' Pally Gray said quietly.

At their table, McMinn said, 'I don't rightly understand it, but there was somethin' about that Rolls that really bothered me. Ye could tell. Ye could just tell, Pally. It was lookin' down its nose at me. It gave me the creeps,' he said, imitating a shiver. 'Put the wind right up me, it did.'

'Ye're tellin' me the difference between thirty thousand pounds worth of motor car an' that pair of shoes ye're wearin'.'

'It was the car itsel',' McMinn said. He struggled with how to say what he meant. He seemed able to make the gestures that would have accompanied his explanation, but the necessary words eluded him. 'I don't know how to put it,' he confessed, his gestures now those of his disappointment in himself.

'Never mind, Keith. I think I know what ye're drivin' at. Contrast of wealth an' nothin'. Contrast of future wi' no future.'

'Maybe that, but no' just that only,' McMinn said. 'It gave me a very funny feelin'. Ye know, Pally, I think somethin' big's about to happen. Any rumours goin' the rounds?'

'None that I've heard,' Pally said.

'I might be wrong, then. It was just a feelin'.'

'What's in yer parcel, Keith?'

'Do ye think Rick would take a decko at this for me?' McMinn began to undo the string. 'It's my iron. It'll no' go.'

'Rick obliges everybody else,' Pally Gray said, leaving it unsaid that he didn't see why he shouldn't help out Keith McMinn.

'You ask him for me,' McMinn said with a persuasive grey twinkle in his eye. 'He an' me don't hit it off.' He handed over the iron on its bed of brown wrapping paper. 'String's handy stuff, eh?' he said, stuffing it into his pocket.

Pally Gray returned from the electrician's table after what seemed to McMinn a long conversation. 'He'll be over shortly,' Pally Gray said. 'Don't look so doubtful. Rick 'll do what I tell him.'

McMinn smiled as his father's best friend took a long pull of his beer. For a few seconds he looked around the bar with confidence. Pally Gray was the wisest, most respected man in the Antynth Labour Party. He had been a town councillor for years when Antynth was a burgh, before the reorganization of local government that absorbed it into the District Council. Pally Gray had served two terms as the burgh's provost. There were no suggestions of grandeur about Pally Gray, but McMinn basked in reflected glory.

'That Rolls-Royce,' McMinn said with a rush. 'It looked as if it owned the place. I'm rackin' my brains to tell you how . . .'

'What's the point, Keith?' Pally Gray said with a hint of impatience. 'I've told ye that I know what ye mean. A Rolls-Royce in a town that's got next to nothin' goin' for it can shock a man wi' a sense of the unreal.'

'As if it owned *us*,' McMinn blurted, as if against the obstacle of a stammer.

'I've been in a few Rollses,' Pally Gray said. 'The burgh's official car was never a Rolls, but always a very impressive ride. I'd find myself in other burghs, of course, and some used to run a Rolls-Royce. When a delegation of us went to Edinburgh, the Secretary of State had us met wi' a Rolls at Waverley station. By then we'd sold the burgh motor, so we went by train. Couldn't do that now. Heavy traffic all the way to St Andrews House. For all the distance, we'd 've been quicker walkin'. Not on, of course. Layin' on the big flash car 's a bit like linin' the palm wi' silver, or talkin' ye round to a wrong way of thinkin'. A touch of the high-class that makes a man think he's on the side of the big people. The Sunday-best every day for as long as it takes to say aye to the wrong ideas. It got to me, but it didn't change me. Unlike some I could mention. All of a sudden they even started to *talk* different.'

'It's a goner,' Rick Williamson said, putting the iron on the table. 'It's passed on to the heaven of the small electrical appliances.'

'No hope for it?'

'Not a snowball's, Pally.'

'Where's my brown paper?' McMinn asked anxiously.

'I chucked it,' the electrician said. 'It was *dirty*. I should've checked the stamps. They were probably two monarchs ago. That was very old paper, Toddle.'

'It was my last piece,' McKinn said, sinking back on his chair.

'I can do ye a reconditioned iron for seven quid,' Rick Williamson said.

'Make it five,' Pally Gray bargained.

'Five?' McMinn said, coming back from the loss of his brown paper to meet the consternation of a bill for five pounds.

'Any idea how *cheap* that is?' Williamson said incredulously.

'All right, I can manage a fiver,' McMinn said with reluctance. 'But as soon as ye can, Rick. Without an iron I'll look a shambles in no time.'

'Aye, I can see it's touch an' go,' Williamson said.

'I'll be sorry to lose it,' McMinn said, holding the defunct iron.

'The diagnosis is death. Everythin' wears out, Toddle. There comes a time when ye have to grin an' bear it, then buy another one. This is a very old iron. I'm surprised it's lasted this long.'

Pally Gray drove McMinn home after the meeting. A lift was a treat that McMinn appreciated. It amused Pally Gray to notice the self-importance with which Tommy McMinn's son settled into the seat beside him. Outside McMinn's door on Ingram Street, Pally Gray said, 'I wouldn't mind bein' asked in for a cup of tea, Keith. Now that I'm livin' on my own, I sometimes can't be bothered to boil the kettle.'

'Oh, sure. Only too pleased,' McMinn said keenly.

Pally Gray asked himself in to check whether Keith still managed to look after himself. It was part of a promise that he made to McMinn's mother eight years before. Every two or three months he was moved yet again by McMinn's imitation of his mother's way of keeping the house. Furniture was in the same place. McMinn brought the tea through from the kitchen on a tray set in the manner remembered from his mother's routines.

'Did ye get the gas fire fixed?'

'Gas Board did it,' McMinn said.

'I thought it had a healthier hiss. Social Security come up wi' the right contribution?'

'Aye. Took weeks, though. The man there doesny like me, Pally. No surprise to me if he's plannin' on firin' me off to a Home.'

'Ye know who to come to if he starts anythin' bureaucratic,' Pally Gray said.

'What Rick said 's got me all worried.'

'How come?'

'About everythin' wearin' out. I've a vacuum cleaner, a refrigerator, an' an electric kettle.'

'Aye, it's a worry all right,' Pally Gray agreed. 'You make a lovely cup of tea, Keith.'

'Are you managing all right? I mean, now that Mrs Gray's . . . Managing all right on yer own? Och, ye know what I mean . . .'

'Kind of ye to ask. I appreciate it. I don't do too badly. Aye, everything wears out, including me. Some mornin's I feel as stiff as a table. I'm havin' trouble wi' the waterworks,' Pally Gray said.

'The waterworks? Ye mean these plans for privatization?'

'My waterworks!'

'Oh, that! I thought ye were talkin' politics, as usual,' McMinn said, risking a joke. 'Oh, well, ye know where it is when ye need it.'

When he was upstairs Pally Gray admitted to himself that McMinn kept his bathroom tidier than he kept his own. He took a quick look at McMinn's bedroom, too. No clothes lay scattered about, the bed was made, and, as always, Tommy McMinn's presentation copy of *Labour Politics in Antynth and District* lay on the bedside table. Before coming downstairs he tried the door to what had been the bedroom used by Keith's parents. It was locked, as it always was.

After Pally Gray left, McMinn washed the cups and saucers, the plate on which he'd presented biscuits; he rinsed the teapot and put away the sugar bowl, the milk jug and the tray. He shook the tray-cloth, then folded its linen lines along the distinct creases made by his ironing. He pulled out the electric plugs in the living room, then switched off the downstairs lights. He undressed and put on pyjamas. He washed and brushed his teeth. Before he turned in for the night he took the key to his parents' bedroom from the drawer in his bedside table. Inside, he put the dead iron on their bed. Other things lay on the covers – a letter from his uncle in Canada to say that his aunt had died; copies of the local newspaper in which were reports that he knew his parents would be more than just interested in. Among these stories were the write-ups, lasting issue after issue for weeks, about the redundancies at the factory that made paper bags, where Tommy McMinn had worked almost all his life, and then its closure. Christmas cards from relatives, year by year, mounted up in a cardboard box.

'The iron wore out,' he said to the bed in the darkness of the room. 'Rick Williamson says everything wears out. He's getting me another one. Pally's all right. He's getting by, but he's got trouble with his waterworks.'

He left quickly, locking the door, and wondering, as always, why he made these reports to his parents, or kept the interesting numbers of the newspaper on their bed.

Among McMinn's outdoor routines was walking to where the road from Antynth feeds into the motorway. It was a weekly event. He visited McCluskey's snack bar in a layby just before the road ushered itself into two lanes before joining the north-south and south-north hurry of the thousands of vehicles daily for whom Antynth was a sign at the side of the road. It was three miles from the town. McCluskey's snack bar was a converted caravan.

'No one in a Rolls-Royce ever drives in here for a quick refreshment,' McMinn said to McCluskey. 'That's for sure.'

'This is a hygienic waterin'-hole. Tea I make's fit for *anybody* to drink,' McCluskey protested. ' "Freshly cut sandwiches" – that means what it says. No dirty tea-cups here. No unwashed spoons. I give a spotless service.'

'Occasional large cars, yes; but when did you last 've a customer in a Rolls-Royce?'

McCluskey looked amused and suspicious, as if McMinn was about to catch him out on something. 'Who needs a cheese roll when they can afford a Roller? It'll be the straw hamper on the back seat, caviare, smoked salmon and the cucumber sandwiches – brown bread, very thinly cut, quick stroke of best butter . . . And the wee mahogany cabinet, probably refrigerated, containing the champers an' glasses. Not my end of the caterin' trade, Keith.'

'I saw one in Antynth last week.'

'So what?'

'Ten-to-one it must've come off the motorway an' gone straight past ye. Seen any big black Rollses lately?' McMinn asked seriously, his features pinched and pouting, demanding an answer.

'Even if it was solid gold an' playin' "Annie Laurie", what's a Rolls to me unless it stops an' makes me an offer? What's botherin' ye, Keith? Why 're we talkin' Rolls-Royces?'

'I walk up here, buy nothin', an' ye notice *me*,' Keith said.

'How could I miss ye? Ye come up that road like a one-man hunger march. Keith, the sun's shinin'! Why the raincoat? It's cryin' out for a decent burial. Donate it to the raincoat museum!'

'It said on the forecast, "occasional sunny periods",' McMinn said.

'Aye, *sunny* periods!'

'What comes in between "sunny periods"?' McMinn asked victoriously.

'Rolls-Royces?'

'I saw one!'

'Big deal. Look, how long do ye plan on wastin' my time . . .?'

'It's no' as if ye're doin' a lot else, Jim.'

'That's right, hurt me. I tell ye what, Keith. As a matter of interest. Personally, I'd find it a fascinatin' statistic. Away to that footbridge over the big M and count how many Rolls-Royces go by in . . . in an hour. That's it, a nice, round time. There's a cup of tea an' a ham sandwich in it, on the house.'

'Ye want rid of me,' McMinn said peevishly. He thought about McCluskey's suggestion. 'I don't have a watch, Jim.'

'Doesn't have to be an hour, spot on,' McCluskey said.

'I've a watch, but it was my dad's. I keep it for special occasions. Forty years' service in the Pokey Works. Gold presentation pocket watch. Are ye havin' me on, Jim?' McMinn asked suspiciously.

'Me? No way, Keith.'

'I'm hopeless at time. I could be there all day an' I'd still think it was less than an hour,' McMinn said.

'Och, I'll tell ye how long ye've been there when ye get back,' McCluskey said.

Big transporters roared under the footbridge, leaving the scent of diesel fuel that added to the day's fumes. A little shower began then stopped before McMinn could decide whether to run for shelter. In the time he stood there no one else appeared on the bridge which carried an ancient bridle path over the gorge cut by the roadbuilders through the low hills. Steel netting restrained shale and boulders on the escarpments dug through the local ground. Cars, trucks, tankers, vans and a military convoy raced under the bridge. Toward the end of his notional hour he spotted a Rolls-Royce, but it was beige, not black. He crossed to the south-facing parapet and watched it draw into the fast lane to overtake. Very few vehicles turned off for Antynth. Just as seldom did a car appear from that direction to join the motorway, either to head north, or, once over the flyover, to melt into the traffic going south.

'One Rolls, beige, an' it rained,' McMinn said.

'Just the one, ye say? I'm amazed,' Jim McCluskey said. 'Only rolls I'll know 'll have ham or cheese in them. Bring on the tourist trade. Ham roll an' tea comin' up, Keith.' As he spread an opened roll, he said, 'So what was this Roller ye saw in Antynth?'

'Who knows?' McMinn said. 'It's a mystery.'

'Mr Mortgage, Lord Bank-Loan or Sir Humphrey Income-Tax,' McCluskey said. 'Read the papers. There's money everywhere except here. Mustard?'

'No, no mustard,' McMinn said. ' "Occasional sunny periods"? I told ye what that means!' he said, and McCluskey permitted him a moment of triumph.

A few evenings later, McMinn saw the black Rolls-Royce again. It drove past him on Shields Street and then stopped. McMinn hesitated, believing from how the car slowed, then drew to a halt ahead of him, that it was waiting for his approach. Its engine was still running. McMinn moved toward it carefully. By the time he reached it he half-expected a door to open and someone to step out with a full explanation. Sodium glow from a streetlamp prevented him from seeing through its yellow reflections and into the car. 'Who are ye?' he said to the window. He slapped the dark glass with his hand. A face, seen as if it were under water, looked out at him. 'Who the hell are ye?' McMinn asked angrily. He felt himself inspected. He was convinced they had stopped to look at him. Gleaming under

TODDLE-BONNY AND THE BOGEYMAN

the streetlamps with polished authority, the car drove off past Frank Irvine's shop and McMinn trotted after it.

'Before ye ask me if I've seen a black Rolls, the answer's yes,' Irvine said over a pile of unsold magazines that he was tying up. 'Tell me all about it, Keith.'

McMinn breathed hard after his haste to get there. 'I don't know, Frank.'

'An' here's me thinkin' that if anythin' happens in this town, then Keith McMinn's got all the answers.'

'Don't talk to me like that!'

'Like what?' Irvine said, matching McMinn's offended tone.

'As if I'm no' here! Ye talk to me as if I'm a lot younger than I am.'

Irvine hesitated over the half-tied knot held by his forefinger. He pulled his string tight. 'Tell me about the Rolls, then.'

'People that drive them cars don't answer questions from the likes of me. Or you,' he added.

'Can't think what I'd want to ask them,' Irvine said.

'First time I told ye about that car, ye didn't believe me,' McMinn said.

' "Mystery Rolls Seen on Shields Street." Sorry, Keith. It's in the same category as "Woman Gives Birth." "Keith McMinn's Iron Pronounced Kaput." '

'What?'

'Same category as,' Irvine said. 'It's not news. Its trivial stature 's practically momentous. I didn't disbelieve ye, Keith. I didn't think it mattered. I still don't.' He was annoyed. He threw the bundle of magazines on the floor.

'Somebody high an' mighty 's in that motor,' McMinn said, irate that Frank Irvine, like everyone else, shrugged off its visits to Antynth as of no consequence. 'I know what people say about me,' McMinn said.

'Oh? Sure you're no' imaginin' it, Keith?' Irvine said absent-mindedly as he measured more twine from a dispenser.

> 'Toddle-Bonny lives in a tent
> His bum's at the front, his legs 're bent

Toddle-Bonny's the bogeyman
An' 'e drinks 'is tea from an old tin can.'

McMinn drew back from the counter. 'I've been hearin' it since I was ten,' he said.

'*You* said *that* to *me*,' Irvine said. 'No' me to you. Remember that.'

'Ye'd heard it before, though,' McMinn said. 'I'm a decent, honest *man*!'

Irvine shook his head sadly.

'If you'd my life,' McMinn said, 'ye wouldny think it such a comic turn.'

'Mine's no' all that hilarious, Keith,' Irvine said. 'I'm tired. I've been on my feet since five this mornin'. Velma's got the 'flu. My eldest son's got a drink problem in Edinburgh, where I hope he'll keep it. Lorna's set her heart on marryin' a bloke wi' green hair, an' he wears so much studded leather it'll no surprise me if their kids turn out to be suitcases. Keith, look at these unsold magazines. Business 's *lousy*. What's this for?' he said when McMinn placed some coins on the counter, and began counting more.

'Newspaper bill,' McMinn said.

'Ye paid it this mornin'!'

On Wednesday evening at the Labour Party Club Pally Gray delivered McMinn's lemonade and said, 'All of a sudden the Ghost Rolls is no longer a subject to baffle the mind. It belongs to a man by the name of Mussonwell.'

'Mussonwell? Mussonwell?' McMinn said, repeating the name until convinced that he hadn't heard it before.

'A Midas of hard times. He's bought a castle not twenty miles from here. A man for whom "slump" means the crock of gold at the end of the rainbow. For us it's a bucket of somethin' else entirely, but for Mr Mussonwell it means labour desperate enough to come cheap, an' deals made wi' unions.' McMinn's aghast facial turbulence invited Pally Gray to say more. 'A man whose principles might have to be endured if his interest in Antynth comes to anything. I hear things on the grapevine. Not as much as hitherto, but I have my sources. I hear, for example, that our esteemed Tory MP is cock-a-hoop about Mr Mussonwell takin' over the Pokey Works as premises for a new enterprise of his. No doubt development grants 'll pave the way, to say nothin' of political jiggery-pokery – forgive the pun. Not paper bags, of course. Mr Mussonwell's interested in makin' deodorized insoles for footwear.'

'Pally, what's a pun?'

'Forget I even mentioned it. What's important is that Mr Mussonwell has mentioned the figure of fifty jobs.'

McMinn looked thoughtful. 'I don't like the sound of it, Pally.'

'Fifty jobs is fifty jobs. Fifty jobs is fifty wage-earners. This town's as poor as the tinker's granny. Five more years of bad luck and we'll live to see sagebrush blowing down Shields Street. I expect an acrimonious discussion at tonight's meeting.'

'I *knew* there was somethin' to that car!'

'Too true,' Pally Gray said. 'Fifty jobs puts jam on toast. Fifty jobs puts whisky in water. Mr Mussonwell's no philanthropist, but he comes bearing gifts. It'll be some meetin'. We've a hothead or two who'll see cause for a fight in this.'

'I don't like the sound of this Mussonwell,' McMinn said.

'You're no' too keen on his car, either. But the town needs a shot in the arm, and Mr Mussonwell owns the shot.'

'Right, Toddle. That's a fiver ye owe me,' Rick Williamson said, placing an iron on the table. 'You dig in to yer purse, an' I'll be back in a minute.'

'Are ye all right for money?' Pally Gray asked McMinn. 'Sorry I asked,' he said when he saw McMinn's expression. 'I understand how ye feel about Mussonwell.'

'What can we do about it?' McMinn said. 'Nothin'. I feel clean out of objections, because I know they count for damn all.'

'It's a question of takin' the bad over the disgustin',' Pally Gray said.

'Thanks, Toddle. Happy ironin',' Williamson said, picking up his five pounds.

'Cap*it*alist,' McMinn said, pronouncing the word the way his father used to emphasize it.

'Me?'

'Aye, you.'

'Pally, tell me – what've I done to deserve this?' Williamson said.

'Keith's a bit rattled over this Mussonwell affair,' Pally Gray said.

'All right, Toddle. I'm in business for myself, but that doesn't mean I'm anything *like* Mussonwell,' Williamson said aggressively. 'Call me a capitalist again an' I'll iron yer face so flat ye'd think it was pressed in a laundry! Understand, Toddle?'

'Uncalled for, Rick,' Pally Gray said.

The incident was beginning to attract an audience. Williamson said, 'Yer half-way to capitalism yerself, Pally. No' hard to guess what ye'll be sayin' tonight. The ex-Provost's analysis. Take the jobs and like them. It sticks in my craw, Pally. Our party's got the representation in Scotland all sewn up. But when it comes to exercisin' its muscle its power's about as nifty as a fused plug. Ten lousy Tories out of seventy-two MPs 've fused it! Aye, but yer a Westminster man, Pally. Ye'd too many pals in the House. Ye'll follow the party line till the day ye choke on it.'

McMinn suffered to hear Pally Gray spoken to as if he no longer counted. Voices muttered an agreement with Williamson's sentiments. McMinn, too, was inclined to agree with them, but they confused him; he wanted to be loyal to Pally Gray.

'We'll leave my thoughts on the subject until the meetin',' the ex-Provost said.

'You tasted power, Pally. It was local, but it was sweet.' Williamson noticed his other listeners and looked at them as well as Pally Gray as he continued. 'Ye got used to lettin' contradictions slip in by the back door. First time around ye probably sent them back. Second time? Maybe aye, maybe no.

But they were turnin' up every day. *Bound* to get in sometime.'

'Your attitude's destroyin' this party,' Pally Gray said, shaking his head at a younger man's political passion. 'I don't think ye know much about it. A wee industrial town like this, hemmed in by Tory farmers, lairds' tenants, bijou villages colonized by Yuppies, all voters natural to interests other than ours – we haven't a chance if what we're offerin' 's the folk-socialism of yesteryear. We haven't moved wi' the times . . .'

Williamson interrupted Pally Gray's account. 'He wants us to move with the times! They're Tory times! Our responsibility 's to contest them, Pally!'

'I'm a bit tired, Rick. I saw us win the seat in forty-five, and then again the next time. An' every ward in the burgh. Tasted the great party triumphs, ye see, Rick, an' for the past ten years I've watched the clock turned back. Or that was how it seemed. In actual fact, the Tories make time work on their side. I'm too old to sit down an' think how to capture the clock, Rick. Mussonwell's jobs, though, Tory jobs that they are, are first of all *jobs*. So keep yer eye on the immediate issue.' Pally Gray looked up from his chair in silent appeal.

'He's admitting that he's historically embarrassed by party failures,' Williamson said.

'Embarrassed isn't the word!' Pally Gray said vehemently. 'Nor 's failures! I'm heartsick of Tory successes!'

'Historically' was a concept on the edge of McMinn's intelligence, but he liked the sound of it. To him it carried the satisfactions of reading a page in the book he kept by his bedside. Still, it pained him to hear Pally Gray announce, 'If the people don't have work, I don't care who provides it.' Mussonwell was a cipher to McMinn, a token of the detestable. 'I'll take the jobs,' Pally Gray said. 'That's the way the biscuit breaks.'

'Our country's timid,' Williamson said. 'It's as simple as that.' McMinn felt the urge to speak. Once or twice he'd opened his mouth and gagged on silence. 'We've had Scottish Nationalism as an organized political movement for over sixty years,' Williamson said to his audience, 'and not one nationalist's died for the cause. It hasn't killed anybody either. I'm as much against violence as the next man, but the facts speak for themselves. Westminsterism's cryin' out for the bum's rush. But what do we do? We don't even take ourselves seriously. Only twenty-five per cent of Scotland votes Tory,' he said, as if it was hard for him to believe his own statistics, 'an' it's folk tryin' to be English who call the shots? It's out of order. Anywhere else we'd be out on the streets!'

'Calm down, Rick,' someone said.

'Give the man a pint,' said another.

'What's involved?' Pally Gray said. 'Think about it, then ask yerselves if yer willin'. I know politics. I don't know anythin' about guerrilla warfare, bombs in railway stations, or ambushes at the bridge. An' at my age, I don't want to know!'

McMinn anguished on his inability to force words from his mouth. He caught a glimpse of someone nudging his neighbour then nodding in McMinn's direction as if he noticed that something was wrong. What started as a heated conversation between Pally Gray and Williamson was now a general argument involving the entire bar-room.

'I say Rick's talkin' good sense. Lowers the spirits, maybe, but . . .'

'Away an' behave yersel'!'

'I'm no' arguin' for complete independence,' Williamson stated. 'Devolution, but wi' budgetary powers, would do for a start . . .'

'Fat chance!' someone shouted.

'Nationalism's just the flavour of the month,' Pally Gray said dismissively.

'Oh, aye? Nearly everybody here likes the taste, then,' a voice shouted from the bar.

'Is this the meetin'? Or are we goin' through?' a voice complained.

On his own initiative, the barman pulled the plug on the fruit machine. The man playing it stood back with affront as its merry sounds of musical paydirt faded to an electronic hum and then silence. Its lights flashed. He shook the machine, then kicked it.

'If ye don't keep your voices down,' someone shouted, in a tone of admonitory amusement, 'Special Branch 'll be all over us!'

'Face facts!' Williamson said loudly. 'Opposition should be *opposition!*'

Voices buzzed around McMinn: they formed an audible blur. His collar felt tight. Pally Gray was looking at him with concern.

'Independence would help this country to grow up,' a mild-voiced woman said.

'Add the word "democratic" before "opposition",' her friend said, 'and I'm with you all the way!'

'All right, Keith?' Pally Gray said to McMinn through the heated babble.

'The Union's a joke!'

'Pally's right, though. I don't see me as a plainclothes rifleman.'

'Civil disobedience!' another shouted, his intervention provoking more arguments.

McMinn thought his own independence a miserable state of affairs. He had something to say on the subject of independence. It was wedged at the back of his throat. Fantasy eloquence toiled in an effort to master his vocal chords. Pally Gray was looking at him again. Something was said to Rick Williamson, and McMinn looked at the electrician. Men nearby rose to their feet. Two women got up at another table. The entire Labour Party Club seemed closing in on him. Fingers not his own were working to loosen his collar. The lights went out.

He woke up at two in the morning wondering how he had got into his bed in the first place. He could hear voices downstairs and recognized Pally Gray's. He switched on the bedside lamp. His book got in the way of his fumbling hand and fell to the floor. He sat up, dazed, perplexed, recollecting the argumentative evening. He had heard ding-dong verbal battles there before, but nothing like as combative. Still, it had been building up for weeks. All it took was Mussonwell to light the blue touch-paper and stand back.

'Movement upstairs,' Rick Williamson said.

'Aye, well, we'll give him a minute,' Pally Gray advised. He tipped whisky into Rick's glass. 'Ever wondered which way Dr Broadie votes?' Pally said. 'I've asked him. Says it's a secret between him an' the ballot box. I've never liked it when I don't know a man's politics.'

'Maybe he hasn't got any. It's been known.'

'I've enjoyed this *quiet* talk, Rick.'

'Me, too, Pally. Hope Toddle doesn't mind my fag smoke all over his livin'-room.'

'I'll see what's doin' upstairs,' Pally Gray said.

'Should I slip away?'

'Don't be daft. I might need a runner. Mind what Broadie said. "If ye need me, call right away." I've too much drink taken to drive.'

Pally Gray climbed the stairs like the old man he was. McMinn was in his dressing-gown, shaking his head. 'I heard it was you, Pally,' he said. 'What happened?'

'One of these turns of yours, Keith. Feelin' better?'

'No' bad,' McMinn said. 'Who were ye talkin' to?'

'Rick. He kept me company. Broadie's been an' gone. Says there's nothin' to worry about, but if ye need him, ye know the way. I'll spend the night, if ye like,' Pally offered.

'No need,' McMinn said. 'Nowhere for ye to sleep, anyway.'

'I could sleep next door.'

McMinn thought for a moment. 'I haven't been in it, since . . . och, you know since when, Pally. I could murder a cup of tea. Would ye do the honours? Maybe Rick 'd like one.'

'We've been on the hard stuff,' Pally Gray said.

'Oh, aye? What about the waterworks?'

'I can see *you're* back to normal!' Pally Gray said. 'Down the stairs wi' ye. Tea an' a bite to eat 'll see ye right.'

Pally Gray and Rick Williamson left about half an hour later. When they'd gone, McMinn tidied away the glasses and tea-cups and placed what was left of Pally Gray's whisky in the sideboard – 'Don't be daft,' the old man had said, 'keep it for the next time I'm here.' He pulled out the electric plugs, then switched off the downstairs lights. Once upstairs, he washed: he brushed his teeth, rinsed the basin, tidied the towels on the rail. He unlocked the door to his parents' room. Inside, in the dark, he told them about Mr Mussonwell and the fifty jobs at the old Pokey Works that might soon be turned into a factory for the production of deodorized insoles.

'Big arguments tonight, dad. All about devolution, independence and where the Party's goin'. I don't know what to think,' he said. 'Honest, I don't know. Pally held his own. Rick Williamson went at it hammer an' tongs. I didn't know where I was.'

THE PILGRIM
Margaret Elphinstone

It is useless to recall what has been left behind. I was happy in Ireland, but not contented. When I remember it now, I think first of the green earth, the rich smell of farmland, and the beasts in winter brought inside the steading. Strange that I should think of those things first, that belong to the place where I grew up. When I left I scarcely regarded the land. I wanted to be a scholar. And so I became one; a theologian and an artist. I made a Bible, and it was taken on a pilgrimage to Rome. I will never hear if it reached its destination. What is more, I shall never see my own country again.

There is nothing to be done about that. I vowed it. Perhaps I was mad. Never is too long a word, and I wonder if I have broken my own heart. I have had too long to think during the calm, when even out at sea the breeze was so small I could not stop the sail from flapping against the mast. The swell was slow and easy, and it felt like being rocked in a cradle. But the sea changed again. The wind came from the west, as it should do in spring, and I set my sail to make it blow me north. Blow it did, until I thought that I should surely founder. The swell grew so great that in the trough of it I could see nothing surrounding me but water, grey walls of it high above my head. Every time I mounted the crest it was like a miracle, the boat seemed so close to going under. But each time I floated up like a lump of cork, and from the crests there was nothing to see but the rain coming in from the west in grey squalls, and the pale sky all around.

If I am meant to survive this voyage, I will be brought through. I have faith enough to know that, but even such faith as I have is enough to daunt me. If I place myself in His hands, then I am succumbing to no other plan than His. That is the uphill way; life being no more than a series of demands, test upon test, and only the fragile staff of my own faith to rely upon. Failure is damnation, and success is only the crown of martyrdom. Sometimes I doubt myself. It was easy to become a scholar, lured by the treasures of the mind; then an artist, seduced by the promise of earthly beauty. By my own happiness I discovered the snare that was set for me, and fled from such temptations. To be cast out from civilization, to disappear into the cold heathen north: I had seen others do that, and admitted at last that it was the worst fate that could possibly befall me. Thus I recognized my destiny.

I am bringing the Christ to the north. I have nothing to offer but His Word. I am in His hands, and today I saw land for the first time.

I think I have sailed further to the west than those who have left accounts of their journeys. I never saw the coast of Ringan's see, nor the outline of the mountains that lie east of the Holy Island. I have seen no land for so many days, I must have sailed far to the west of all known islands. And now I see land to the north, long and low, still blue amidst the spray and haze. Landing is the most dangerous enterprise on any unknown voyage, but martyrdom will not be earned so easily; I know that.

The landing was hard. I should not be afraid of any mortal thing, because I know that to die in such an enterprise, steadfast to my purpose, would bring me in one joyous flight to the very Throne of God. To be plucked from that icy sea into the court of heaven itself would be release indeed; and yet so perverse is human nature that when it came to it I fought for my life as if living in itself were precious. Am I still so attached to this earth that I do not wish to die? What do I care for this world of shadows, and have I not studied the Word ten years, since I was hardly more than a boy? Sometimes I fear the flesh could still entrap me, but surely there is no danger of that now, when I have left all soft things behind me.

As I approached the island I saw a place where the rocks seemed to fall away, where there were no cliffs. It was difficult to tell: the swell was confused by the currents off the land, and only when the boat topped the crests could I see round me for an instant. There was white water ahead. I furled my sail, until the wind could only catch one corner of it, tight against the mast. I knew there was death in the white water, and I did not mean to die. Then, in the place where there were no cliffs, I saw the waves were not breaking right across. I tried to steer for the space between them, but the water grew choppy, and my boat was torn this way and that. Small lumps of sea began to come aboard. I had to bail as well as I could one-handed, grasping the tiller with my right hand, my eyes always on that changing horizon, so that I had to scoop the water all by guess. I don't think I caught much of it.

The sea roared in my ears. I saw black rock where I thought there was a gap. I thought then that I was gone. I fought, forcing the tiller across, till I was almost over. There were waves breaking an oar's length away. I heard a sucking and a roar of water. Then I shot free, carried on a wave beyond the breaking surf. I had time to see a curve of beach, shingle below green grass. I even saw the noosts and low stone wall, which told me there were people. The wave fell away suddenly. I began to rise again. Then there was water breaking all round, a great crash and a flurry of white. But I did not go down. The boat jarred on shingle, knocking me over so I crashed down on the keelboards. The wave broke over me, and I struggled up, fighting for breath. For a moment the shingle was clear, and I was up and out, dragging my boat with me, out of reach of the hungry sea.

Two or three waves broke over me before I was free of them. Then I was standing soaked to the skin and winded, alone on a strange beach, with the island rising in front of me.

I knelt on the shingle, holding up my hands, both filled with small wet pebbles belonging to this new land. The ground seemed to heave in front of my eyes, as though I could not adjust to solid earth after so many days upon the sea. I realized that my hands were shaking. I held them up, and gave thanks to God for preserving me from the fury of the sea. I dedicated myself anew to His purpose, committing myself to His keeping, that I might keep faith in whatever trial he should have in store for me.

It is hard to describe the events that followed. I felt at first as if I had walked into a dream. No, more than that, if I am to confess the whole truth. It flashed across my mind that perhaps the sea had taken me, and now I was translated. I had not thought that dying could be so simple. And of course it is not. Salvation must be earned; it does not fall upon one like the sudden sunshine on a spring day.

But the sun did come out as I was going over the hill. I walked slowly among pastures. The sheep stared at me, but hardly bothered to shift themselves as I passed. One or two had lambs already. There was a dead lamb close to the hill dyke, its eyes already taken by the gulls. The cattle were herded together near the gate, still bare-ribbed and weak from the winter, as though they had only just been lifted. The grazing was still yellow and sparse, but there were new shoots coming through, gleaming wet in the sudden sun.

I crossed the hill dyke, and found myself in a field of young barley. I skirted it carefully, and reached a muddy track. There I fell in among the people.

Only for a moment did I think myself gone beyond the confines of this world, but even then the thing remained uncanny. For how could they have foretold my coming? And yet they lined the track in welcome, the crowd parting so I might walk between, and as I passed they threw down rushes and cloaks, so that I might be protected from the mud. They seemed to be dressed in holiday clothes, unless I had indeed come where every day was holy. They chanted and bowed before me as I passed, and I could make nothing of it. I prayed for my faith to be renewed, and touched the Cross that hung about my neck, to reassure myself. I thought then it must be the Cross they recognized, in which case this could only be a miracle, that the heathen should rush upon their salvation, without so much as a word being spoken. I had expected a greater trial than that.

For an instant I was tempted by Complacency, which smiled

and beckoned me onward, implying that my presence was all that had been necessary, and the conversion was already made. I recognized the Devil in the work, and at once she stood before me, in the image of a woman.

The crowd fell silent then. They stood a little back from her, as though their purpose were no more than to lead me to her. I stopped, frowning. The tests of faith are unexpected, and such a confrontation as this had no part in my expectations. I had been prepared for martyrdom or torture, for suspicion and negotiation, for demands or for misunderstandings. But never had I been warned that I should meet a woman with a golden image hung around her neck, signifying some matter that I dare not think of. She was not young, but certainly she had been beautiful, and I think she had not changed. She did not seem to be afraid of me. I realized then that indeed I had been warned. It was not a thing that I had thought about, but I think it was an image from a dream. I have forgotten it: it is hard to remember dreams.

I became aware that she was waiting for me to speak. I tried to collect my thoughts. She did not seem at all put out by my appearance, and at first it did not even cross my mind that I was not expected. I only discovered that it must have been so later, when I had time to think it over. But even then I am not sure. Perhaps she did know that I would come. Yet she knows nothing of the true faith, and therefore such knowledge can only be diabolical. The Devil can take on fair flesh, in order to deceive. I imagine she knew who I was very well. Therefore, being what she was, she must also have known that we were enemies. But at that first meeting she showed no sign of it. She watched me, and waited.

I prayed swiftly for inspiration, to guide me in a situation that I did not understand. Then I said, 'Lady . . .'

The crowd murmured a little, and sighed.

'Lady, I have made the long voyage to your island. I knew that I should find it, although some told me it was only the figment of a dream. I was told that, so far north, I would find lands where none dwelt but outcast spirits, and that if I dared to come ashore, I would not live one night among the devils that inhabit these places of desolation. But I have One in whom I can have perfect trust. He bid me have faith. Therefore I fear no illusions nor dread no evil. He has brought me safely across the seas, and is with me still. He will prevail against all the evils that lie within the boundaries of the world.'

'What is it that you fear?'

Her question startled me. It was so important to make myself clear, for upon my statement depended the whole opening of my mission, that I had not much leisure to consider what she might be thinking. I did not know what she was, and I certainly had no idea what she might imagine this was all about. In a way, it was not my problem. I was not here to find out what she thought, but to present her with the Truth. But I knew that I had not mentioned fear.

'Fear?' I repeated. 'I fear nothing. I have faith in God, who brought me to this place.'

'You describe it as a place of the dead,' she remarked, 'but then you say you're not afraid of that, because you don't believe it. Why come to a place if you don't believe in it? It seems an odd thing to do. You must have imagined there was something here, or you wouldn't have made the voyage. And if you truly dread no evil, why do you need to speak about faith?'

'I have come into the north,' I told her, 'bringing nothing with me but the Word of God. I have need of no other power, because the Spirit has sent me, and whatever happens to my body, He is with me still.'

'To your body?' she repeated, and looked me over curiously. I lowered my eyes. 'But you're wet through!' she said. 'Did you come to the South Voe? You were lucky the tide hadn't turned. Another hour and you wouldn't have made it. But this is our Spring Festival, you know, so I think you must be blessed indeed, to have fallen as you have into the very middle of it. I do not know your gods, which is not surprising, as you come from another country, but I think that you will find that faith is not your exclusive property. If a god has sent you, I assure you that I will thank him duly, and I promise I will not ignore what he has done.'

*

When I look back over my days here, I try to discern a pattern. Most of all, I try to work out what it is that God demands of me. How much easier it would be if I could suffer in the body! But this is not to be granted me. Apart from catching a chill that first day, which made me a little feverish, I have enjoyed good health, and I have been provided with food and shelter without stinting. They do not live well here; for my own tastes there is little meat and too much fish, and the barley bread is heavy on the stomach. Also, they have no wine. But that is no part of my purpose; I can only be glad that since I left the monastery I can commit no gluttony. But I had expected to be forced to eat shellfish and live upon a rock, and to build my own shelter out of driftwood and reeds. To live like this is disorientating, and upon the charity of a woman. It seems politic to do so, and I have already begun my mission, with some success. But it would be easier if things were different.

I don't care to repeat what they say of her. The place is given over to false gods. Either she is a frail woman possessed by delusions, in which case perhaps I might cast out the arrogant devil that dwells within her, and bring her to Christian repentance; or, she is a fiend incarnate, deliberately leading these foolish people into the darkness of eternal damnation, in which case it must be my part to exorcise her from this tainted earth, and cast her into the chaos beyond the waters that surround God's earth. But God forgive me, I am afraid that she is strong. With His help I know that I can do whatever is required, but faith has never seemed so difficult.

The trouble is, she seems to like to argue. She does not recognize, or she refuses to admit, that we are struggling for the possession of men's souls. She has no awe for the glory of heaven, nor terror for the iniquity of hell. When I speak of these things she even laughs, and there have been times when I expect to see her snatched from my presence by the Fiend her master, or for her to vanish in a cloud of fire. Levity in the face of God cannot be forgivable, but I tell myself that if she is human (which I do not know) she might yet be brought to look upon that Face, and be redeemed.

Meanwhile, she invites me to sit with her in the evening.

She pours me ale, and asks me questions. She asks about so many things, from the number of head of cattle on my father's farm, to why spirits should be of the male gender. She wants to know about writing, wheat, and transubstantiation. Sometimes I think she is doing it on purpose to confuse me. Her theology is not sound, but she has a genius for controversy that I feel can only be diabolical. Sometimes I wonder how she regards these matters. She does not say, but instead she questions me, and then twists my answers into unrecognizable shapes, and stands my proofs upon their heads, until reality itself seems to shift and tremble under my feet. I suppose she must have some explanations of her own. I could ask her, but that is not my purpose. I have not come to probe the heathen mind, but to bring them to the truth. But I would like to know what she takes seriously. That is a temptation, perhaps, that I should beware.

These are not even the greatest of my difficulties. I know quite well that women have no shame, and that their minds inevitably turn to things of the body. In their presence spirit recedes, because they cannot keep their minds on holy matters for very long. Since I was a boy I have had almost nothing to do with women. My mission has been with the Word unadulterated, and thus I have been blessed. I knew that if I came among the heathen I would have to go among women, for women also have souls, and it is my purpose to bring salvation to all, without prejudice. But I had not expected to be so tempted. For many years I have hardly thought about women at all. I could not say that the temptation had departed from me completely, however. Sometimes I have dreams.

It is the dreams that are taking me over. She is too subtle to say anything herself. In all our discussions she has never touched upon sex, and of course I have not. She has worked upon me for all that. She has forced her way into my mind so that I cannot rid myself of her image. I would give much for the chance to make confession, but that is not possible here. I am ashamed of my dreams. I am afraid she has cast spells over me, for how else could she have infiltrated so far into my thoughts? I pray for the ability to resist her wiles, for this is now becoming a severe trial, but God has not yet shown me the way.

I delude myself. I know quite well what I must do. I will not be troubled by the sins of the body. It is a long time since I renounced those lusts. I will fast and pray, and I will impose penance upon myself. A pilgrim in the wild must become his own confessor. I am strong enough to control my own thoughts.

In the daylight I am strong. But at night even the strongest of men has to sleep for a little. And when I dream – oh, I know too much about desire.

May my God forgive me, I have failed. I cannot accept it, cannot believe that so great a sin could be so easily committed. If what was done could only be undone! It almost seems as if that could happen. Today is not so unlike yesterday. Perhaps all could be cancelled that happened in between. If only it had not happened to me! Everything else is still the same. Why should not this be the same as well?

I know that I delude myself. Nothing is the same, nor ever can be. My mission is over, and I am damned. The very thing I thought to be impossible, the crime I knew I stood in no danger of committing: that is precisely what I have done. I did not know how close I was. I could not know how very nearly danger threatened. I thought whole seas lay between me and the deed itself, and when it came to it, there was not so much as a trickle of water, so that I would need to lengthen my stride to step over it. I still do not know how much a thing could be. I thought myself proof against their magic. Strange powers must have been practised upon me, for I was not in full possession of my mind. If I had faith, if I had watched enough, I would have been ready to resist. My conscience slept, and I never saw the danger till it sprang upon me, when I was already doomed. Yet I knew her for a devil, or a witch. They call her priestess. I knew her magic to be strong. I have committed the sin of Pride, in discounting the power of evil over me, a mortal man. I knew that a woman had practised upon me to desire her, but I did not know how strong she would be, when she set out to achieve her wicked purpose.

If I were at home now, and able to confess, I would have to say what it was that I did. I must try to do that now for myself, in my own head. Then I must find a penance for myself. It will have to take the rest of my life. This earth is a miserable place, and our part in it is only to suffer. For the rest of my life I must carry the weight of this sin upon my back, but if I can repair the fault, and hope for salvation at the end, the whole mortal world will vanish in a twinkling of an eye, and these wretched mortal days seem but an evil dream.

I still cannot work out exactly how she did it. She must have been planning it over all the days we have spent talking together. While I was thinking about her immortal soul, she was thinking about . . . that. I dare not think about it. Three nights ago, she did not invite me to come in the evening. I was surprised; I had grown into the habit of talking with her as the dark fell. For two nights I heard no word from her. I was uneasy. I am alone in a land of strangers, and I had no way of knowing what any of them might be plotting. There is no one here who would not do her will instantly, without question. I was aware that she held my life in her hands. Yet what is mortal life? Nothing – she had no power over my soul, or so I thought.

On the third night she sent the girl across as usual. I was beginning to grow alarmed. But the girl spoke as if nothing had happened; indeed, as if the two nights' silence had not even occurred. I went, and when I lifted back the curtain from across the door, she was sitting in her usual place by the hearth, piling fresh peats on the fire. I could not see her face properly. The smoke from the fire curled slowly upward, so that the peat haze hung in the room, in no hurry to seek the outside air. All I could see clearly was the floor. There were still patterns in the sand from the morning's sweeping, as if little had been done in here that day. That was not surprising. It had been a fine spring day, and everyone would have been out, it being the sowing season.

She called me over to the fire, so I came into the middle of the room, and sat down close to her, warming my feet on the hot stones. She gave me hot spiced ale, as if it were winter, and I was glad of it, for there was still frost in the evening air. I wonder now if that drink were drugged. It seems likely, considering what came later.

I am not very sure what we talked about. I do know that she questioned me closely about chastity. The miracle of the Annunciation seemed quite alien to her, and the logic of it too much for her woman's brain to encompass. In fact she said it seemed ridiculous, and when she laughed, I saw the shadows grow longer on the wall behind her, and a cold draught eddied, so that the curtain over the door swelled out like a sail filled by the wind. I shivered.

'But why?' she persisted. 'It seems so very unnecessary.'

The more I tried to make it plain to her, the less she seemed to comprehend. I felt like a man floundering in a marsh, seeking the right path while the dusk comes down, and the light begins to fail all round him. If such a man should seek his direction from the stars and look up, only to find that the mist had crept in from the sea, and all the sky was hidden, he must feel something akin to what I felt, when I tried to pray for guidance while she spoke, and received nothing in return, not so much as a glimmer of light through the swirling peat reek.

'You must live in Hell,' she said.

I jumped. Her words echoed my thoughts, and yet what could she have known of those? 'In Hell?' I echoed sharply. 'What do you mean by that? I am a man of God.'

'But a man,' she said. 'Yet you have convinced yourself that your own nature is a sin. What can you think of yourself? And what on earth do you think about us?'

'Us?'

'Me. Women. What about us?'

I was shaken right off balance, and it took me a moment to compose myself. My right hand went up to touch the cross about my neck, and as soon as I did it I saw that she had noticed. 'I know nothing about women.' My voice sounded sulky, even in my own ears. I felt hot and confused. It was becoming harder every moment to remember what I was doing here.

THE PILGRIM

I made myself breathe easily, and then I glanced up at her. That was almost my undoing. She was staring at me; maliciously, I can only suppose, but at the time she seemed to be incredulous. 'Nothing?' she said, her eyes wide. 'Ever?'

'I am a man of God.'

'You don't have to keep saying that. I believed you the first time. It's this other matter I don't understand. I thought you were some kind of priest?'

It seemed quite impossible to make her understand. 'I don't think you have any idea what I am,' I said almost despairingly, although I had known that all along, and it should hardly have mattered.

'I certainly never heard of an impotent priest.' She stood up. 'Will you come with me for a moment? I want to show you something.'

For some reason she had touched me on the raw. I wanted to explain myself, but that was a trap. The opinion of a heathen woman had nothing whatsoever to do with my purpose. I must keep faith, and have all my wits about me, especially as this was no doubt some new trial. Perhaps I should have refused it, but I saw no danger, so long as I was wary. I followed her through an inner doorway.

At first I could see nothing at all. She was carrying a tallow dip, which reflected back from curved stone walls. We seemed to be in a much smaller chamber. It was colder away from the fire, but not dank. A lived-in place. She carried her taper across to the far wall.

There was an image set in a niche, within the thickness of the wall. I will not attempt to describe it. In fact I wish it could be expunged from my mind forever. I never hoped to lay eyes upon a graven image. I was taken off guard, having seen nothing similar in all my stay on the island. It was a blasphemous thing. If one were to carve the eyes of the Spirit upon a stone image, they would be eyes like that. Yet it would be the sin against the Spirit itself ever to attempt such a thing, and upon such a figure as that it would be sacrilege. The thing had eyes like an angel, set within the image of a woman.

I cried out, and turned away, pushing her roughly out of

my path. She yielded under my hands, and the light went out.

It was pitch-dark. I felt with my hands, and found nothing, and then only the curve of the stone wall. It still held some warmth in it, as though there had been fire in here. I tried to feel my way along, searching for the entrance, but there was none, only the stone wall curving, giving me no direction whatever. There was something at my feet, and I stumbled. I fell on my knees, not on stone, but on softness that gave under my weight. I groped desperately with my hands, and touched fur.

I think I cried out again. I don't know. I couldn't think straight. There must have been fear within me after all; I felt it well up, putting all thoughts to flight. My one idea was to get out of that place, or at the very least, to find some way of telling where I was. I was ensnared by the Devil, I knew that. I couldn't trust my senses. My eyes were blinded, my ears stopped, and I had lost all indication of direction. The fur under my hands shocked me. It was like a live thing, but inert, meaningless, in that cell-like place. I thought myself swallowed by evil, as Jonah was lost to the deep and swallowed by the great fish Leviathan. I stretched out my arms, but hopelessly, knowing that help was far away.

My hands met hands. No devil's touch, it seemed then, but strong human hands that clasped mine, like a brother. I must have clung to her, hardly knowing what I did. I heard a sob, and I think it came from me. Then for the first time since I was weaned I found myself in a woman's arms, and in my delusion it seemed that she was there to comfort me.

What she did then, I cannot begin to think of. It was like drowning. I had never thought that such a thing were possible. I have heard that when you drown your life passes before you in a dream, going back to its inception. If that is so, then in that room I drowned, right to the very beginning, when I came naked from my mother's womb. Yes, she brought me back to that, and at the time I saw it as Salvation. The rest was all a nightmare that had never been, every trace of time expunged in the chaos of the deep. I did not try to make sense of it. Before I had a mind I had a body. I was losing myself, but it felt to me like finding. I plunged to the very depths, and there I thought I confronted my own soul.

I am damned, not by lust only, but by blasphemy. Could I say this, even in the Confessional? I think I could not. The truth is – and I must find words for it, though I am damned – the truth is that I worshipped her, and it seemed better than anything I had ever done.

* * *

I was expecting something to happen. The wind had veered from west to south, and suddenly, just before the Festival was due to begin, the sun came out. Everything seemed as right as it could be. The winter had been sharp, but not too long. Few had died, and those only the oldest and the newborn. The cattle were lifted and across the dyke, and the lambing had begun already. The young barley was showing in the fields, and there was a smell of new grass in the damp air. Of immediate importance, we had looked over the food that we had stored, and it seemed that this spring would not be too hungry. We still had flour and dried fish, although the meat and the cheeses were all gone. Already we were beginning to get fresh fish, from the fishing between the gales. I do not like it when food is low, and they are forced out fishing when the sea is dangerous. We have lost men that way before, but not this year.

There was nothing to overshadow our Festival, not so much as a cloud in the sky. It had rained in the night, and we could hear the sea heavy on the rocks to the west, but on our side of the island the swell was subsiding, and the water turning blue under the sun. Yet I could not rid myself of a feeling of foreboding. I spoke about it to one or two that I trusted. Perhaps it was as well I did so, for then the event itself was regarded by the people as a prophecy fulfilled, and so their faith was never shaken. They could not know how much I sometimes doubt myself. Not to do so would be arrogance, and that would be danger indeed.

Certainly I had no idea what I was expecting. The Festival

was all propitious. While we were at the Stones the sun shone down on us, and the omens at the sacrifice were unquestionably hopeful. Since we had counted all the stock only the day before, this was hardly surprising. We finished the ceremony, and the chosen children stepped forward to lead the procession. It was hard not to pay them too much attention. One was my own granddaughter, still very young to take such a part, but she did it well. I hope I did not seem to notice her too much.

The procession wound its way downhill towards the shore. At the back, I could see over their heads, for the slope coming down among the barley fields was steep. It was then that I saw the stranger.

He was alone, and he treated our fields with respect. He skirted the barley, and made no attempt to conceal himself. So this was not a raid. I did feel a moment's pang of terror, but I realized fast enough that whatever this might be, it was not material danger.

He had been seen. The procession wavered, and halted. I would have spoken, but it was done for me. A rock dove came flying low across the barley field, out of the west, almost over the stranger's head. It veered away from the knot of people, and disappeared towards the sun in the south. It was rare to see the bird here so early, though some nest on the cliffs in May. I heard a murmur of wonder from the people, and then the stranger stepped forward, and was engulfed by the procession, about a hundred yards ahead of me.

They were already exalted by the ceremony, and they accepted his coming as part of the magic of the day. Perhaps it was as well. We know how to show hospitality, but when we are afraid, we strike out too fast, and then find out afterwards whether there were cause. On another day, I might have been lucky even to be shown his body, and that only in atonement. I was not so sure of the magic of it myself, but it served the present purpose. I let them welcome him as if he were the son of a god; meanwhile I waited.

I only saw him properly when he stood in front of me, and my people fell back into a circle round us. He was very young. Later, I found that this was partly illusion. He had lived well, in a plentiful land, and had known little of the sorrows of this world. He had seen more years pass by than I realized at first sight. It is puzzling; he is rich in many kinds of knowledge that are unknown to us, but knowledge without experience is a curious thing. I could never decide whether he were wise.

He was hardly dressed for a festival, but the contrast was even more telling. He wore a long woollen garment stained by the sea, knotted at the waist with a piece of rope. His hair and beard were untrimmed, and tousled by wind. He was tall and well-made. Islands tend to be short of young men, because life is often dangerous. It was important to find out what he was, for good or evil. We had seen none of his kind here before.

I waited for him to speak to me. That gave me the advantage. Luckily I understood him, although his accent was heavy, and he spoke too fast. I say I understood him; I mean I knew the words. He seemed to think that he had arrived in the islands of the dead, but he described them as if they were a place of terror. I could understand it if he were here deliberately on pilgrimage. There have been other travellers from the east, not in my time, who have sought salvation by voyaging west. A depressingly pragmatic attitude, I find. The soul's journey is not measured in miles, and there are other ways of reaching that country.

He spoke about the god who sent him. He struck me as being possessive about this deity, and defensive too. Why should I not respect another person's god? Yet he was afraid of something, and not anything physical either. I began to wonder if he were perhaps possessed. I realized that I must go cautiously. If he had brought anything evil along with him, I would make sure he did not part from it here. We have enough troubles of our own.

I asked him what he was afraid of. His denial was spurious, and vehement. Again he insisted in his faith in the unknown spirit that drove him. It seemed to be not so much a matter of fact as a desperate wish. We seldom mention the things that we truly believe, because they are so obvious to us. If a man continually insists that the sun must rise in the morning, I doubt his hold upon this world, and so it was with this one.

He spoke about his Word, trying to convince himself, perhaps, that if he said the thing, it would become true. Children try to make such things happen, and those who remain innocent. The wise know that words are but the reflection of what is, and not the source. Sometimes I wonder why language has been entrusted to the young.

He was no coward, this young man. I think that if we had killed him then and there, in renewed sacrifice to the spring sun, he would have accepted it, perhaps too easily – he would have died with his eyes fixed upon the things that are to follow. Well, I agree with that, but also I admire it, especially in one who has most of his years before him, all being well. But his body, like mine, was not one that a person who enjoyed life would wish to part from.

I looked him over as I thought about it, and that seemed to discompose him. I found that curious. Young men tend to be conceited, and are usually glad to be admired. I noticed that he was soaking wet, and for the first time it dawned on me that he had come down across the fields from the hill dyke. He could only have landed at the South Voe. It was possible; I glanced out to sea. There was a line of white straggling across to the skerries, almost at right angles to the island. That meant the tide was at the turn. He had only just come in time, then. I wondered if he had any idea of that. To make such a landing, on an unknown shore, and to arrive in the middle of the Spring Festival – I felt a stirring of something close to awe. Perhaps there was more in this than I had thought. Lately they have accused me of becoming cynical, and though they laugh, I know they mean something by it, or they would not speak. But when the people took in the implications of where he had arrived, they would think him charmed. We live by the sea, and a lucky sailor is a powerful man. I realized that I must take care, for the people would draw their own conclusions soon enough. Meanwhile it was important not to make too much of it, so I gave him a light answer, and as soon as the procession was done, I saw that he was given food and shelter, and dry clothes.

*

THE PILGRIM

I begin to recognize a need within myself. That is dangerous. I am a woman who has been starved, a little at a time, over many years, who suddenly finds a feast spread before her daily. Until he gave me what I wanted, I never even knew I missed it. The lack had crept up slowly with the years. For children, there are always other children. For the young, there is always life, and love. I have never lacked companionship. I am among my own people, and so all my needs are met, all but one, and that has grown with the years into a gnawing hunger. I look forward, and see the pain of losing this gift again, and understand why I smelt danger.

He fills my mind. I have never left this island in my life, for why should a woman travel? We have more important things to do. Curiosity is not in itself destructive, but it demands respect, like fire. I want to know about those other lands. I have always wanted to know, but so few who have been there know how to tell. I am fascinated by what they do, how they farm, what they eat, what they talk about, what is in their minds.

There is a great deal in his mind. It is like exploring a new country. Everything is unexpected, and I have so little to relate it to, for it is not like any place that I was in before. I think I know where I am, and then everything is turned on its head, as though the northern lights should shine out one night to the south of us, or the moon turn backwards in its round. Sometimes his ideas appal me, but they excite me too, because they are new. I cannot make sense of it altogether, and I still fear that he may be possessed. I never encountered so strange a theology as his, but his knowledge exceeds all the resources that we have upon this island.

Also, we do not agree, and that is like drinking spring water after salt. Of late years people have agreed with me far too much. Probably that is bad for them, but necessary, things being as they are. For me, it is a slow form of torture. My wits grow blunt from lack of exercise. It was not always like that. My life has not been empty, and there has been so much else to think of. But what I am now . . . I have become the one who is supposed to think for the many, and that is painful. It is much more amusing when there are two, especially when they disagree.

He loves to talk about his god. Some of it is all too obvious, the same story dressed up in new clothes. The stories he has are the sort we tell, about sheep and crops and fishing. His attitude to women is quite extraordinary, and this is reflected in his theology. I cannot quite fathom it. There is nothing physically wrong with him, I am almost sure of that. He certainly hasn't been castrated, though I hear they do that to their slaves, down south.

I have formed the habit of sending for him in the evening, when the work is done, and talking with him. I find I look forward to that. It is like taking the shutters down after a storm, and looking out from a closed room right across to the place where the sea meets the sky. This is indulgence, and I know it. I cannot keep him here for ever.

I am beginning to be afraid. I did not send for him last night, and I will not send tonight either. I have allowed myself to be tempted, and I have ceased to be wary. This from one who must be vigilant on behalf of the whole people. It is very hard to give up my evenings of discovery, but I see that it must be done.

It was foreboding that I felt first, when I knew that something was to happen, and still I knew not what. I should not have allowed myself to forget that. I have been too sure of myself, and I have played with fire.

This faith of his is not a passing fantasy. It is not one man's dream, that will vanish with all the rest by the mere turning of the wheel of time. This man is dangerous. His faith is unbalanced, and, left to itself, it will tear this earth apart. He thinks that the Creator of this world was a mere man, who fashioned everything that lives with his own two hands, as a potter shapes the clay. That is sacrilege, to think that life was made by human hands. It is disrespect, and there is nothing more perilous.

He thinks that because one man has died, the rest of us may live for ever. That is arrogance. What are we, if we are not creatures of this earth, subject to birth and death like all the rest? If we were immortal, what powers would we take on then? Enough to destroy the whole, I fear. This Christ of his, who has apparently swallowed up both birth and death, will devour this whole green earth. He will certainly take Her no other way, for She would never submit to him, nor any man. His word is nothing to Her, because She is beyond language. If this man really believes he can thrust his word on to us without force, then he is mad. If he is deliberately deceiving us, then he is evil.

I see him watching us. He talks to the people, and he watches us as we work. Sometimes he helps, and his strength is appreciated. There is a great deal to be done at this time of year. But he is not one of us. He is close to nobody, and when the people draw together, he holds back, as separate as the Stones that stand upon the hill. To take one's own life is wrong, and, though he lives, I fear that it is a crime he has already committed. He has flung his part on earth away from him as if he were no more rooted here than the stars that wheel above us. He calls that 'salvation'. He denies his humanity, or else he would know that not one of us can stand out against the rest. We belong on earth, and the earth will absorb us all.

For the sake of my people perhaps I should destroy him. That would be easy enough. Yet I am tempted to take the more difficult way. Perhaps I can save him from himself. It will be a risk, but I know how to do it. If anyone knows how to bring a man back to his own nature, it is I. I will let him come again tonight, and if I can, I will prove to him that he is human, and one of us. More than that, I will give him cause to delight in it, so that he may rejoice in being a creature of the earth. It is lucky for him that I have the skill to do it.

I am afraid of what I have done. Never in my life have I encountered such fear as his. He hates himself. He hates his own humanity, and recoils from the mirror of it in another. Perhaps he was born into the wrong body. He thinks his place is somewhere among the stars, and is aghast when he finds himself a man. I even wonder if he is right, and there has been a gross mistake within Creation. That is blasphemy, and cannot be. He is a man, who is possessed by a demon that has taught him to despise his body. There is no more to it than that. But the demon is strong, and perhaps I have unleashed too much.

Having fixed my purpose, I sent for him, and began to question him again, not to satisfy my own curiosity this time, but to try to comprehend his fear of the body. He thinks that to love a woman is a crime. He postulates a world where there should be birth without conception. He would give all power over creation to women, and then say that men only are divine, and yet he sees no paradox. Procreation, he says, should ideally be the prerogative of women and of gods, yet it is at the same time bestial. He thinks that to abstain from sex is to escape death, and yet he knows that he was born. He speaks of spirit, and tells me that it is separate from the body, pure essence of being. Then he tells me that it takes the form of a rock dove.

'A dove?' I echo. 'Pure essence? Perhaps you should take up birdwatching.'

He said I was too literal.

I began to realize that he spoke not only from misconception, but from profound ignorance. Something he said even made me wonder if he had ever made love to a woman at all. Yet he calls himself a priest, so that could hardly be, unless he comes from a land where nothing grows, which does not seem to be the case. I could make nothing of it; we were using words to drive ourselves round in circles, so I cut the discussion short, and took him into the inner room.

I showed him something that I cannot name here, for it seemed to be necessary to take him to the heart of the matter. He screamed, and would have fled, but I was in his way. I was holding the taper, and when he fell against me, it went out.

It took me a moment to find him. He was kneeling in the dark. When I touched him, his hands clung to mine, like a man drowning. He had fallen across the bed, on the piled-up furs. I took him in my arms. He never resisted, nor recoiled. At last I understood his fear. He was a man: of course he knew desire, and of course it mastered him. Any man at war with his own body would need to be mortally afraid. I think he had never known peace before, for who could, if they had been swimming upstream all their life?

I pitied him, and more than that, I found that I had grown fond of him. It was his mind that made him exceptional to me, but there was nothing amiss with his body. It was not difficult to make love to him. I could have done it well if I had cared a good deal less. As it was, I surpassed myself. I knew that he deserved it. As for me – well, men need some education in these matters, and he had none, but I did not require more of him. My own needs are provided for quite well enough. I did not need him as a lover, unless to be needed is a need.

He only spoke once during the whole act. I couldn't hear him distinctly at first, but then he said it again. 'I think I am in heaven.'

I didn't answer that. Heaven is his idea, not mine, and really, I had nothing more to say.

In retrospect, I can see what it was I hoped to do. He had given me a good deal, and I liked him. I wanted to save his life. The only way it could have been done was to bring him back to himself, to reconcile him to his own nature. So long as he thought himself more than man, he was much too dangerous for this world, and therefore inevitably drew to himself his own destruction. I wanted to save him, and to achieve so worthy an object my body seemed a small thing to give. I hoped that he would sleep and wake, to find himself living in a different kind of world, where he could be content with what he was.

I reckoned without the power of possession. He is not reconciled; he is distraught. He seems today to be out of his mind. I have only seen him once. He pressed his hands to his eyes and cowered away from me. He called me devil, and tried to exorcise me, as if I were a spirit. Since I am entirely human, his incantations luckily had no effect. He could have cursed me, had he known me.

His ignorance appals me. Every child apprenticed to magic crafts learns first that all things must be identified, according to their nature, before anything can be changed. That is why we spend so many years acquiring knowledge, learning the nature of created things and into which categories they fall. In comparison, the actual learning of enchantments is a small thing. All he had to do was to identify me correctly as a woman, and then his maledictions would have been all too potent. But he could not see what I was, even after I had slept with him, and so his words never touched me. There is an object lesson for every child upon this island. But that is by the way.

I think I understand. He had convinced himself that his dreams were true. Yet, when he looked into the well of life, he saw no god, only the grey eyes of a mortal woman, who has some skill in love. I do not hate him for not knowing me. But his agony threatens us all. I am the guardian of my people, the Lady of this shrine. Even if I loved him I could not let him live. He is trying to destroy us with himself, to tear down the veil that separates one kind from another. If he had his way, terror would be unleashed upon a world that had no way to deal with it.

Clearly he must die. I do not want to do it, and yet I have done harder things. It is not difficult to offer him the cup that heals nothing, except life. He takes food and drink from us without suspicion. He is our guest, and treachery towards a guest is a crime against nature. But it was not I who first abused the law. He has already poisoned his own soul, and I merely enact it for him. He brought this upon himself. It is a crueller thing to be the judge than to be the victim. He can sin against the earth, and yet die in innocence. I have obeyed the laws of this world, and so I must have his blood upon my head.

I have called my niece to me and told her what to do.

No doubt he will understand when he knows what has been done. He appreciates symbols.

THE SIEGE
Ronald Frame

This afternoon she's a few minutes early and up in the bedroom she turns on the television set.

There's live coverage of a siege in an airline headquarters in Stockholm. Mug-shots of the five terrorists appear on the screen, then holiday snaps of some of the forty-two hostages. A reporter is asking people in the streets of wintry Stockholm what they think of this state of affairs, here in their own city.

She leaves it on while she slips out of her dress. It crosses her mind to put a call through to her office – she has left instructions about an important client – but she decides it would only take an over-inquisitive telephonist to throw an unhelpful spanner in the works of this weekly 'arrangement'.

He hears reports of the siege on the car radio. A spokesman for the terrorists is interviewed, on a telephone line from the airline building, then the hostages' relatives are asked questions.

Momentarily he catches sight of himself in the driving mirror – the image he has to adjust to every time: a man with thinning hair, blue cheeks, a thickening jowl.

He doesn't think to turn over channels to some music. He isn't really listening. He looks about him and is seeing the spot from the window of another car at the tail-end of the fifties. His father is driving and he watches him from the back seat, a man with thinning hair, blue cheeks, a thickening jowl. His mother sits beside him in the front. For some reason she has hardly spoken since they left home. This is his half-term from school and it's an excuse for them to spend a couple of nights in a hotel. But the mood doesn't seem the proper one, and he has a premonition that the rest of their weekend together won't be so very much different from this.

Then she thinks, why *shouldn't* I call the office? Why shouldn't I do exactly as I like? Why should a telephone operator decide for me?

But 'freedom', she is also aware, doesn't come free. It costs, and – if you're wise – you never stop paying for the precautions.

The irony is that he looks like his father when it was his mother he cared for.

Loved.

He'd cared for his father hardly at all. He was only the role model on which nature had predetermined he was to be based.

She sits at the window in her bra and pants and watches as the car covers the length of the driveway, to the hotel's entrance portico beneath.

She withdraws behind the curtain, not for modesty's sake, but because she realizes he will look up – their room is always the same one – and he will presume she is sitting there because she is waiting for him.

Along the ridge of the dunes grow the umbrella pines, looking like the serrated edge of a saw from a couple of miles away.

With the window open he can smell their tang.

Approaching the hotel he is making a dozen journeys, in dazzling sunshine and through a leaf storm and with snow dancing in the tracks of his headlights. The building appears as it always appears, seasonal embellishments apart, suns spinning in windows or leaves spiralling or snow frilling the balconies. It's an eccentric imitation of what was probably the architect's muddled memory of a Swiss or German spa hotel, with a high green roof and two gabled towers at either end (both towers have a clock, but each clock face tells a different time) and a fussily mathematical arrangement of balconies.

He studies the middle windows on the second floor, counting in from the fairy-tale tower on the left.

She pretends to be busy in the bathroom when he opens the door.

She sprays perfume behind her ear lobes. 'Amazone'. Not one of the perfumes *he* has given her. He can think what he wants to about that.

He looks out at the view as he undresses.

His work has taken him to most countries in Europe, to the States and Canada and the Gulf and Singapore. He has seen landscapes and skylines in their multiple variety, enough to sate him for views from windows. But wherever his journeys take him, it's the memories of other places, nearer and more familiar but long ago, which occur to him.

He daydreams them on taxi journeys and sitting waiting in air-conditioned company offices and eating solitary meals in hotel coffee shops or watching a girl undress in his bedroom, and even after the exhaustion of lovemaking in a foreign climate they can't be forgotten but return to him in his sleep. His wife's voice crackling across a couple of continents into a telephone receiver turns into something else inside him, a pain: not of guilt or remorse, but rather the ache of time forfeited and lost.

Standing in front of the bathroom mirror she pulls down the straps, undoes the catch, and watches her breasts in the glass as they fall out.

In the office the men clients' eyes drop to them, poised beneath her shirts and shifts. Sometimes the women's eyes look too.

She isn't sure what their fascination is with her breasts. She stares down at them. They are neither large nor small, but they sit pertly, invitingly perhaps. Her nipples are neat, compact, pink.

She's noticed how men go to her breasts first, after her mouth and neck. They have always seemed to her too practical-looking as objects and artifacts to be attractive, too much connected with babies and the act of suckling. How can men dissociate *her* breasts from their mother's?

But maybe, she has realized, that's exactly the point – they don't?

He had come here with his wife, once, before they married.

As they'd driven over, he'd been thinking, maybe it's the wrong place to be bringing her? He hadn't stayed in the hotel since those school-holiday weekends of forced politeness. He'd hoped his mother's presence wasn't going to get in the way, a memory clutching at him: a disabling hand on his arm, preventing him.

But maybe, he'd realized, that's the whole point, it's no accident that here we are, in the province of my past time.

She is listening to the news of the siege with half an ear.

At one time she mightn't have thought it possible for her to be in the situation she now is. The physical situation that is – alone in a room in a hotel, with a man, on a weekday working afternoon.

She doesn't believe it means a great deal more to her than that. She isn't defined by being in this situation.

She doesn't feel herself *obliged* to be here. She can walk out whenever she chooses to; she is a modern woman, all she has to do is put her clothes back on, pick up her bag, find her car keys.

But . . .

He watches her slithering out of her tights. He closes his eyes, he *listens* to her, through the words from the television set.

In the fifties women had a sound: the shimmering sibilants of silk stockings fastened to suspenders, thigh grazing thigh – rustling taffeta and crepe – thin, pointed, clacking heels – bangles jangling on wrists.

Being with him – *choosing* to be with him – what this is in fact is the very assertion of her independence.

*

No other woman has managed to sound quite like his mother, with that effortless harmony of parts he remembers her for.

She knows he's thinking of someone else. Someone he's known. She can tell, there's a look.

Too bad.

She lives in the present. 'Present*s*,' plural: different, simultaneous presents. The office – outside – the people in the next room – the people in the television studio – the citizens of Stockholm – his wife at home, Anna.

Other people carry the past like an anchor.

Her mother was broken by it, although she pretended it meant nothing to her. She'd never discussed it with her children so it had only lived inside her, festering there. 'I hate your father,' she should have told them, or, 'I love him still, I'd forgive him if he walked in that door.' Instead she'd kept it to herself and she'd died over with every new day that came to her.

He traces the perfume to the exact points where she has put it on.

The first time they came here together they went swimming.

Later, she smelt how the beach girls used to in his indulged, indulgent adolescence, burying him in sand, laughing and calling encouragement to each other, their hair falling down and covering their faces and tickling him so that it was no grave displeasure – none at all – to be buried in sand till only his head and neck were showing. That was the time of the group, when you didn't want to be apart from it, 'the girls' or 'the boys', dealing so tentatively with each other like two cautious, diplomatic armies.

Then she had tasted salty. He had licked the gritty flavour from her lips.

Things have got beyond that point now. Maybe it means their days – their afternoons – are numbered.

He isn't happy to think it, nor is he as sorry as he might be. He has refined his extra-marital emotions to the minimum.

Carefully, tenderly, he slips both his palms beneath her

breasts and wishes – as he always wishes – that these few moments in the routine might last until they've yielded all their pleasure of anticipation.

Other men have done exactly the same, but she doesn't think of them, not individually. It is a collective sensation. Sex is a collective, even abstract experience for her.

If she had roots in the soil, in the earth, if she felt ripe inside and had the conscious want of a child, then it might be otherwise. But she lives her life with steadying concrete beneath her feet, and children frighten her with their whelp cries and staring, remembering eyes.

It has almost ceased to matter, 'with whom': it has *almost* ceased to matter . . .

While he is kneading her, she tries to imagine his wife. Anna. Sometimes, in the dark, wives are clearer to her than their husbands.

This affair seldom encounters darkness. They eat afterwards and they drive home separately with the aid of headlights, but she knows she will look back on it in time to come – when and if she cares to look back – as 'the afternoon affair'.

One afternoon they heard the news of a siege on television, and did the necessary with the voices on 'mute' and the flicker from the screen patterning the ceiling and walls.

That afternoon when he caught sight of them both – his father and the woman, in a city street where they shouldn't have been – it was what he noticed about her, her breasts, supported on one of those superstructures of the time, shaped under her turquoise dress and pointing forwards like torpedoes. He stood watching them and wondered if his father did it like this because he was imagining how it used to be, walking the same street with the woman who would be the mother of his children.

This woman wore seamed nylons and kept smoothing her skirt. Her knight companion was holding her elbow.

His mother had brought up a family and didn't have breasts like torpedoes (if she had ever had them), but maybe this other woman in the turquoise dress wasn't supposed to resemble her very closely, she was to be something else, a kind of caricature of a woman, over-the-top and almost too much to handle. Almost.

The teenage boy stood in a shop doorway watching them passing in the glass, imagining those breasts out of their silos, how they pleased in the ample flesh.

He never complains about his wife to her, as she has known other husbands to do. Anna's being such a mystery fascinates her, makes her even more of a mystery.

Sometimes she thinks she herself is only the connection between the different absences and gaps of knowledge, like holes, in her own life. His wife is one of those voids.

They have their gender in common, but that is all. Anna took the traditional option: she went for the new.

Now isn't the time to ask him all about her, but she will.

'Tell me . . . tell me about Anna . . .'

So, why does she need to know?

Sometimes – it's crazy – it's as if it's easier for her to imagine she's one of those other women she knows so little about, than to be the harlot who takes their husbands in adultery.

She only has to remember her mother – one of the wives – to remember all that she isn't.

But her mother lost out in the end.

Maybe, subconsciously, what she's engaged in now is avenging that wrong her father did them both?

He stretches out on the bed beside her and covers her left breast with his hand. He massages it lightly.

In summer, in the dunes, his mother would wear a yellow swimsuit and for the rest of the year whenever she dressed up to go out with his father he would see the mark where her skin took its easy deep tan to, and no further. Dressed up and doused with perfume, swishing past in taffeta and French silk stockings, she fascinated him, she *inspired* him: if for no other reason than because she had survived the experience of them all, husband and children, and she was still looking as she did at the end of it.

It was only later that he discovered she'd also been doing it for someone else: a man she wrote occasional letters to, whom she'd known twenty years before, whom she'd turned down to marry the father of her children. By chance the man caught sight of her and recognized her while she was waiting in an airport departure lounge to fly off to meet his father and he was sitting beside her, the dutiful son, keeping her company. Somehow he immediately intuited the situation, and he thought, how odd if it had been like this, *this* greying, middle-aged man for my father instead of the greying, middle-aged one I have: and would I have been born myself, or someone else? The man was perfectly charming, he explained he was waiting for 'Joan' and the situation was only betrayed by his mother being able to say where his wife was – on her annual solo holiday in Portugal – without having to be told. But that was all, that was as much as had come of it, the moment was over and gone. Or so he'd always presumed.

As he climbs on top of her she's thinking of the company client receiving the instructions she's left for him in the office, and she's watching the colours from the television screen dribbling across the ceiling.

And then she's thinking of Anna at home. Doing what? Cooking, perhaps. But Fridays are her husband's business evenings, so she probably isn't cooking.

Doing the shopping for the house? Gardening? Repairing children's clothes?

She used to watch her mother and she would vow, '*Never, I shall never* . . .' Her mother had belonged to a generation which didn't have the opportunity. She had had the opportunity offered to her, on a plate, and she'd decided very early on, I was born for this. I don't let this one go.

Sometimes.
It's easier. Or not.
You have to make the going, that's the
Bloody shame of it.
The sweat.

The grind.
Sometimes,
Though,
It's like reaching beyond.
Everything meets.
Everything clicks.
The great *click*!
Love flows.
Flows.
Too much for himself.
For everyone.
All times, where they were,
Stranded.
Rescuing, saving.
Bringing back, bringing
Home.
Love.
Joy.
Stupid word.
Bloody stupid.
Joy. Sometimes
Joy flowing.
A stream to catch them
All,
Float them off,
Carry them,
Reach beyond.
Beyond.
To . . .

It's a nice room. Very nice. She can hear the sea, just, through his breathing.

The sea. Doing as it is wont. Humouring them today. The gentle, lulling, turning over of its waves.

But not freedom. What of the pull of the tides, the moon-power? The sea, contained by its shores. Repelled by its rocks, defied by its islands.

The sea. Freedom/not freedom.

He lay his head on her breasts, between her breasts, in the dip, the slide.

He lies there like a child.
 The only child she will have.
 She looks up at the drifting coloured light on the ceiling. Ripples of light.
 She won't say anything. He has never come to her private, secret place. That is out of his reach. It has been reached before by others, a few times. Just a few. They have come to it together, she and the intrepid, athletic explorers in her past life that she is so reluctant to consider.
 Reached that faraway land of tropical heat and waterfalls. The high cliché country. Ridden there on their splendid sex.

There was Sophie, there was his mother, there was Gill, and Viv, there might have been a sister if his parents hadn't decided that two sons constituted a sensible sized modern family.
 He hears them through the flesh of her breasts, through the bones of her chest, beneath his ear, in the running of her blood and her milk. Voices, giggles, the sounds of nylons, georgette, sateen, rayon, disappearing heels.

The sea.
 She turns her head and looks to the source of the outer light.
 She closes her eyes.
 The sea, the sea . . .

Later, he lifts his head.
 She is sleeping, in a different day to his, and now, he realizes, would be the moment to take his leave. But it would probably only be to return another time, with her or with someone else, to hear the sea, smell it on warm skin, taste it.
 He props himself up on his elbows, then eases himself off the bed.
 In Sheratons and Marriotts, plugged into the cable films, faxing facts back to base he is a late-twentieth-century hologram man, in as many places as he is required to be. From the

windows the view is different every time but really it is always the same, ring-roads and copper-tinted high-rise office blocks and the tough, resisting scrub that grows on the edges of deserts. Away from England he calls home and charges it to expenses: in the background – as if it's from the next room (except that the hotel rooms are sound-proofed to exclude intimate sonic intrusions) – he can hear children's voices, music practice, cooker alarms, even, once, a car back-firing in the road. But it isn't to that he is listening, not properly, not to the details: he is further away and longer ago, the house is a new one, the children are running through the echoing rooms, no cooker alarm goes off by mistake, his wife is exploring the kitchen arrangements with a shrewd, canny eye he hasn't expected in her, just as his mother stood in the kitchens of their different houses for the first time taking in the situation, calculating with the part of her brain that didn't have anything to do with the evenings of dressing up to go out and the quiet corners of afternoons when another man than her husband must have trespassed into her thoughts.

* * *

She wears a Japanese designer because she is the sort of woman who dresses as she chooses to.

He still wears his city suit, because in that he is most like his 'other' self – and because, in the event of anyone ever chancing to catch sight of him with her, he can argue the all-excusing claims of 'business'.

They might pass as a married couple, even early on a Friday evening, but she believes she doesn't have a wife's docility, and he knows he is more alert and wound up than he ever is with his wife. He has a habit of hurrying her about the foyer and public rooms with a hand placed on the small of her back and she wishes he wouldn't, but it is a manner of propulsion they have become used to and they can perform it – to all intents and purposes – like a marital ballet. He is comforted by that, while she has begun to blame herself for allowing him.

Sometimes they eat in the hotel. On other evenings they

drive in the car to an over-priced restaurant nearby, converted from an old barn. Tonight, on the evening of the siege in distant Stockholm, they eat in the hotel dining-room: at a different table from the last time, which was different from the one before. (They don't want to draw undue attention to themselves. And too much custom stales.)

Being shown to the table they hear two elderly women tut-tutting over the television news, asking whatever is the world coming to?

They sit down; the menus are handed to them.

She suddenly enquires.
'Is your wife a good cook?'
He raises his eyes. He looks puzzled.
'Or maybe you haven't thought about it?' she asks, in a voice that sounds sharpish to her ear.
'I suppose – yes,' he says, 'yes, she *is* a good cook. But . . .'
He closes his mind to it. It's not what he wants to think about, at this moment.

'Lobster,' he suggests, seeing the word on the 'à la carte'. He doesn't particularly like or *dis*like lobster, but the word instantly conveys a picture to his brain and from his childhood he remembers live lobsters crawling about inside wicker pots on a quayside, watching them as he stood with his parents – year after year – waiting for the little ferry from the town to the resort, to carry them through the safe channels between the sandbanks like whales' backs.

'Lobster?' she repeats. 'Is that what you're having?'
She doesn't want to eat the same as him, on a principle of sorts. She doesn't want to be *seen* eating lobster if he is to eat lobster.
'Lamb,' she says, for no reason.
'Do you think it would be good?' he asks. 'Maybe I should have that?'
Lambs, springtime, green grass, sap rising, hope on the wing.

'No. I'll take the – the sweetbreads,' she says. He has told her he doesn't care for offal. It seems the only choice she has, sweetbreads, so properly there is no 'choice' left to her at all.

'Oh no, not offal.' He shakes his head. 'No. *I* shall have . . .

He remembers the quayside and the so-so taste he didn't adjust to till he was in his middle thirties.

' – lobster,' he says.

Sweetbreads and lobster, they tell the waiter. With some chilled white wine, please.

While they wait they discuss what they see around them in the dining-room: the newly completed Fifth Avenue-chic decor (she doesn't like it, he doesn't mind), the clientele – a curious mixture of the staid and adulterous, and never the twain mixing – and, beyond the heads, the views of early dusk through the window.

When the food arrives, they eat gratefully. The lobster is salty-fresh and tastes of the sea; the sweetbreads have been cooked simply, with some sorrel, as she likes them best.

The lobster requires dextrous handling, she has a finicky side salad, so neither of them has very much reason to speak. He doesn't want another question about his wife, and he wonders – not for the first time today – why she is so interested, if she secretly hopes to be a wife herself. She doesn't want to have to answer another of his questions about her job, or the colleagues she works with: that life is separate from this one, and she wonders why he is so interested, when he doesn't really *listen* to the wary answers she gives him. Does he need to believe in their difference and apartness? – that it makes for some sort of danger to them both? Does he need the stimulus of an imaginary intrigue afoot? Oh Jesus God . . .

Leaving the dining-room they pass a news-tape machine. It announces that the siege continues, but they don't stop to read it.

They walk out into the garden.

'I have to go back,' he says. 'Anna is having a party for the children.' He smiles. 'Lots of washing up, I expect.'

She shrugs unsympathetically.

'Use paper plates,' she says.

'They'd probably just eat them!'

She smiles, relieved she'll never have children, so she will never know if he's exaggerating or not.

At least the children's party provides them with the excuses they require, to finish the afternoon and evening.

There is always a pattern; or, rather, there are two patterns. Sometimes he spends the night in the room, sometimes it is she – it is never both of them together.

Tonight *she* will stay and try to forget her important client and whether or not he received all the instructions she left for him. She will wake in the morning to a skyful of light and the distant rumbling of the breakers.

They walk along one of the gravel paths.

Neither of them speaks.

Their situation eludes them both.

He doesn't seek danger, but – instead – more security than he has: he is wanting to find in her, a stranger, his own past.

From her own experience she fears becoming anyone's wife – an abandoned wife like her mother, who had to bring her up unaided, without the help of any man – and she needs to remind herself continually of the strangulation of marriage.

He wants her to be an empty page for him, the silence of recall, and she tries to catch him glancing at his watch, checking that there are no give-away crumples in the creases of his clothes.

Neither knows how it will end, although it must. They each hope for a clean, very final conclusion. It's most unlikely there will be any anger. They may even arrange to meet every so often for lunch, to show there are no hard feelings on either side. For him the affair will already be a peripheral memory he is trying to recapture in another bed, with another woman, and on her part she will be confirming the wisdom and no-non-sense practicality of her own independence. He will always be a man at the sweet mercy of the women in his life, and she will always be a – considering, self-justifying – person apart, her own woman.

Or something like that.

She leaves the lights off as she watches his departure from the bedroom window. The television picture colours the room, and the words muddle about somewhere in the middle of the empty space.

The car radio, which he forgot to switch off earlier, crackles as he turns the ignition key. Voices come up. It's the news, that same bloody siege.

Coincidentally television and radio are both dwelling on the same aspect of the drama. The relatives are being interviewed again, or it's the two tapes being re-run: the interviewees sound tearful, hopeless.

They each hear, in the bedroom and in the car. *She* is embarrassed by the emotion in this oddly theatrical ritual taking place in a cold northern country, and she wonders what it is the gunmen are fighting for. The woman radio correspondent turns her attention to the 'freedom fighters' but *he* has picked up the word 'home' from a sorrowing Swedish mother and, in his head, he calculates how quickly he can get back to Anna and the children and the kitchen festooned, like a little Christmas in April, with streamers and balloons.

INCUBUS
Dorothy Johnston

Snow drifted past the window. Its white light bathed her face. She raised her arm and smoothed down her deep, full, black hair, which lay heavily about her shoulders. The fire whispered and crackled behind her, throwing shadows and flickering colour on to the back of her blouse and skirt. She stood, shimmering in the half-light, then turned to me and smiled. She knew me then.

* * *

Outside my flat it has been raining hard all day, endlessly, without remission, over damp blue-grey slates. Heavy clouds have suffocated the day, and the light is beginning to fail, but I have never before been afraid of the dark. Only now has its cold and sombre mood begun to touch me.

The dark and I are not strangers, although I was often unaware of darkness, even when I lived within it. It was as much part of the manse as dust and draughts and grimy windows. As familiar as the sight of her wandering from room to room, tearing her handkerchief, muttering about slights, about humiliations. I used to stay in corners, and she rarely noticed me through the gloom. When the day fell, and the light lapsed slowly into dark, she would begin to blend in with the house that she hated. Black was her colour. The colour of her hair, her eyes and the hollows underneath them. Her moods were black as was the shadow that hung over her. Her clothes were black for her brother who had been killed before the war.

She did not frighten me. It was her eyes which used to start in fear when I ran from one corner of the room to another.

'Jack?' she'd say. She gazed at his picture constantly, it was like a mirror image of herself. His eyes, like hers, were slanted, over high, sharp cheekbones, but unlike hers, were creased in a smile.

In winter, the darkness would precede Sara and Cambell coming home from school, but only just. She would stand at the door and watch them walk up the hill, through the gate, along the pathway. If they were late, even a few minutes late, she would begin to scold them with a low, soft voice at first, rising steadily. She would recall evenings waiting for them, filled with worry. Over an hour she kept them one night. Over an hour in the cold and dark and Cambell was afraid of the dark. He began to cry and she laughed and poked his cheek. He let his arm flail out in a faint attempt to strike her but she caught him fast and pulled him into the house. We heard short, sharp noises coming from the kitchen as she slapped him about the head. Sara stood with her usual glum, downcast expression, her eyes wary behind thick spectacles. She knew our mother would not hurt Cambell much. Her hard strokes were kept for Sara.

For my father she saved plates, and cups and pots. She sent them spinning past his head and smashing against the wall. He flailed around blindly, trying to catch them with his eyes closed, his spectacles askew. I too turned away. I could not bear to see him look a fool. I preferred to see him as he was on Sundays when I would look above, up to where he stood in his black robes, his head high and his arms outstretched, the cynosure of all eyes.

In the night if I could not sleep I would creep downstairs to his study. The light from his lamp would be visible underneath the door. In conscious imitation of a cat I would pad in stealthily and watch him sitting at his desk, writing. Then I would crawl up on to his knee and play with his stiff, white collar. I would see myself reflected in the thick glass of his spectacles. 'You should be in bed,' he would say, but his voice would be soft and a mild smile would play around his lips, as he'd plant a kiss upon my forehead. He'd carry me then, out of the study, telling me the story of a cowboy. Up the creaking, groaning staircase, always talking, quietly, softly. As the story ended he would place me in the bed with a sleeping Sara. He would kiss his own two fingers and place them on my temple. Then he would leave, as quietly and stealthily as I had approached him. And I would sleep, soundly, deeply.

'Where has he gone?' A voice shrieked inside my head on the evening of my nightmares. I had reached the study door but no light shone beneath it. I ran back up the stairs alone and crept along the hall. Behind the door of my parents' bedroom I heard them talking. 'Ye stupid git.' His voice sounded strangled, coming up from his throat, quite different from Sundays when it resounded around the church in rich booming tones. 'Can't ye see I've a position to keep up?' How different he sounded when speaking to parishioners, when he would drawl out his vowels, making them last as long as possible. 'Look at ye, look at yer hair, it's a bloody mess, and yer clothes are filthy.'

'I can't dress any better' – her voice was rough and ragged from too much weeping – 'without money, you never give me any.'

'Make yer bloody clothes then. Other women do.' The vehemence in these words frightened me and I ran back to bed. I pressed close into Sara's back but when I closed my eyes I saw my mother in bloody clothes. Instead, I stared at the threadbare curtains but there too, the blood-stained clothes appeared. At first blurred and indistinct but soon clear and bright and dancing before me, until I realized that they were only lights, red drops of light from houses in the village.

I squinted up into the sunlight. Summer sun as yellow as my hair. Mrs Patterson and Mrs McLeod were gazing down on me, telling my father that I had the loveliest hair they'd ever seen. I held fast to his hand, felt a squeeze around my fingers and knew that he was proud. 'Watch the wee one with that white skin in this weather,' Mrs Patterson told him, 'she'll be burnt to a cinder.' As she spoke, her eyes travelled over the flimsy, patched shift I wore. When we walked away I heard them mutter, 'Poor wee thing.' I smiled up at my father but his head was down and his cold, grey eyes did not see me.

The women in the village gave my mother cold stares in return for her greetings and gauche attempts at friendliness. She pretended to be angry and to hate them but it was clear that she was deeply hurt. Her feelings flashed across her face as she experienced them, which made her a bad liar, although it didn't stop her. She told lies as often as she told the truth. The looks the village men gave her were not cold. She was handsome, although her hair was bushy and unbrushed, her clothes shabby, for her skin was clear and the colour of old ivory. Her figure was long and slender, too slender at times but curvaceous still. I did not understand the looks men gave her. I could not understand why their eyes seemed to flicker, as if trying to see all of her at once, when in conversation. Her face would flush, her hands flutter. She might hold her hands clasped in front of her chest like a schoolgirl and gaze up at them from under her long black lashes as if she was Scarlett O'Hara.

Azure, primrose, violet. A riot of colours proliferated in the village gardens over summer. In many of the long evenings my father would be out visiting, and Sara and Cambell at cubs and brownies. I spent one of these evenings in an upstairs room used for old musical instruments, toys and other junk. I played first with a hula-hoop but it was too big, so I played with the dust instead. I scraped it from a shelf and made piles of it on the floor. The sun had illuminated a warm square in the middle of the room and that's where I sat, watching the dust rise and swirl in beams of sunlight. A dog barked. It stopped. It was completely silent.

I felt that I was alone in the house. I was not afraid but wondered where she'd gone. I looked out into the garden, around the stone wall which enclosed the lawn. At a neighbour's apple tree, the top of which hung over into our garden, I traced a long shadow and saw her there, half hidden by the penumbra. The father of one of Cambell's friends was with her. I screwed up my eyes to focus and see what they were doing. I thought he raised his left hand and laid it on her shoulder, but she saw me then, and jumped with fright. I ducked down below the window, and waited. It was quite still and silent for some minutes. Then I heard her laugh. It was light, and high, and almost as soft as the evening air.

It was bitterly cold in the manse that winter. I couldn't play outside and even the downstairs rooms were too chilled. The day came when I had to approach the fire in the kitchen, where she sat, rocking herself on the balls of her feet. She was staring into the fire muttering, and holding her arms outstretched to warm her hands. I sat on the stool opposite her, she brightened, and looked long into my eyes. Perhaps wondering at their pale-blue translucence, as cold and still as pond water on a winter's day. 'My father smashed my dolls,' she said and wrung her hands, her eyes raised to the sky as silent-movie actors do to signify despair. 'My father gave everything to Rhona, never to me.' It was a familiar incantation. She talked about the new clothes Rhona was given and her own cast-offs. The side of her face closest to the firelight was coloured with bright hues like the stained-glass windows of my father's church. Tiny reflected flames danced in her deep, dark, chocolate-brown eyes, eyes like treacle, lucid and limpid and moist with tears from a thousand sad memories and a million regrets. 'I didn't want to go into nursing,' she said, 'but my dad told me to, and in those days you did what you were told.' A flicker of light from the flames licked her lips and stained them crimson as they slid over her white, slightly prominent teeth. Her mouth curled at the corners always, as if nature had played a cruel trick and made her seem to be always happy. 'I never wanted to marry him – and if I'd known about his mother . . . She's an evil woman.'

She turned her face to the fire, her sharp, aquiline profile made a dark, jagged edge against the bright blaze. I looked into the fire and saw only the fire burning. She looked into it and seemed to see the dead, her mother, my father's mother, Jack. And the living too, her father, my father, grim-faced folk from her own village in the north and people from the village we lived in now. All rising up once more to accuse her, again and again. She turned her face away from the flames; in the watery-grey light from the window her staring eyes were coal black. 'Flowers,' she said.

We bought white carnations. First of all she found an old coat she'd left lying around and I found mine. She buttoned me into it, smiling gently into my face. 'We have to keep you warm, little ghost,' she said. It was a grey, stiff day and even the pavement beneath my feet felt harder than usual. When we'd purchased the flowers she held them in front of her, grinning triumphantly, her tousled hair and dirty old coat flapping about behind her. As we approached the school it seemed to set its dull brown facade against us. Its dark windows were like glaring eyes warning us off, but she carried on. I stayed at the door of Sara's classroom and watched my mother walk over to the teacher, who seemed frozen in her chair. Down into the teacher's hands my mother placed the flowers. 'From Sara,' she was saying, 'a present from Sara.' The sound of muffled laughter was rising like a rushing roar of water in my ears when I saw Sara as she lowered her head into her hands and buried it there.

In my mother's hands, over the table in the manse kitchen, was a swatch of gold material, while a tense Sara stood in front of it with a look of loathing in her eyes comparable only to my mother's when she looked at my father. Against the gold cloth she held red lace for Sara to see the effect. Sara was born on Wednesday, and Wednesday's child is full of woe. So it was her lot, she had no choice but to say she loved the material, for the dress my mother would make for her, to wear to the Christmas party. As she trundled away on the sewing machine in a corner of the parlour, in lamplight, my father stole up behind her to see what she was doing. His mouth dropped open as if in horror when he saw the material but he said nothing and left the room. He must have given her money to buy clothes for herself and she had chosen to buy this cloth instead. She was busy and happy, the manse was peaceful for a time.

At each fitting, my mother laughed and smiled, eagerly adjusting darts and seams. Sara said nothing and her eyes suggested that her mind was far away. On the evening of the party my mother popped the dress over Sara's head and buttoned her up at the back. Dutifully Sara twirled for us. Red lace adorned the neckline and spilled over on to puffed sleeves. Around the waist a tight red sash was tied above a wide skirt, pushed out by netting. A false scalloped hem ran round the bottom with red bows at the top of each rise.

When Sara came home, my mother brought her into the kitchen where we all waited. Sara was chewing her lip and I thought it might bleed.

'Well?' said my mother. 'Did you have a nice time?'

Sara attempted to smile and held on to the grimace that appeared instead. 'Yes,' she said, nodding energetically, 'yes it was lovely.'

'And,' my mother's eyes widened suggestively, 'did you meet any boys?'

'Yes, everyone said I was very pretty in my party dress.'

Cambell and I climbed on to Sara's bed and listened to her asthmatic gasping for breath as her body shuddered with sobs. 'I hate her so much,' she spat out. 'They laughed at me, it's a horrible dress.'

'It was a lovely dress,' my mother told me many years later. 'I ruined my eyesight making that dress. I worked all night with only a lamp because their father was so mean with the electricity. It was after that I had to start wearing glasses.' She sighed a deep sigh and shook her head. 'But she didn't appreciate it, or anything else I did for her. I've always been nice to people but I get nothing for it, nothing at all.'

She had kept her hair defiantly black, although the dye had made it dry and brittle. Her magnificent skin had stayed that way long after her hair had lost its real colour, but when it wrinkled, it was sudden and complete. In the midst of the lines her black eyes still glittered and she put her usual bitter emphasis into the words. 'I did everything for my children but they don't even bother to come and see me.' Her eyes were filling up with tears now, and so, for different reasons, were mine. I had developed an allergy to dust in adulthood. However, she kept the bungalow cleaner than the manse.

A silence had come between us, during which she gazed at the straining buttons of my jacket with severe distaste. The identity of her regular, fat, blonde visitor was a mystery she had no desire to unravel. I glanced at the clock to see if it was time to leave but, in the encroaching darkness and with my deteriorating eyesight, I couldn't make out the hands. I could only hear the clock ticking methodically as it had done that evening when we were all in the kitchen, reading and sewing, and listening to the wind . . .

The wind screamed above the roof and battered at the manse windows – at times it seemed to be in the room with us, as well as all around. But the faint, whining noise was not part of the wind's wailing but was Cambell trying to breathe, and wheezing. My mother's eyes darted over to him swiftly, every few seconds. Her hands were tensing around the needle she passed through the rough cloth, back and forth. Her shoulders had gone rigid. Her shriek was louder than the wind. Cambell ran but she was faster. He held on to a chair but she prised his fingers loose. She dragged him, his shoes scraping across the stone ground. With one hand she opened the door and with the other, threw him outside. She then calmly locked it, returned to her seat and continued to sew. My father buried his head in his newspaper and Sara stared at her book. I drew back, into a corner and waited.

I have no idea how long he sobbed and cried and banged on the door. He called to his father to let him in but no one moved. Only she could let him in which she did at last. He was soaked by the rain, she hugged and kissed him, then put him to bed where he stayed for many months.

Cambell cried louder at her funeral even than Sara. I knew how much they had enjoyed finding tight, black clothes to wear, since they suited them so well. My father and myself stood slightly apart from them, short and stocky both, but with our feet firmly on the ground. Swaying back and forth, a reed in the wind, Cambell wept, looking like Jack with his dark, shadowy narrow face. My father remained impassive. Perhaps he was recalling past decades. Perhaps regretting his decision to stop practising as a minister after only a few, short years. Perhaps wishing she had died back then, allowing him to keep his church. Perhaps wishing they'd divorced, but then again, he did not believe in divorce. He had laid many plans on regaining his freedom. He planned to visit Greece and the Holy Lands. Instead, he died, one year after her.

The house was left to Cambell. He asked me to go and clear out the attic of any important papers as he hadn't the stomach for it. I had to pull myself up into the attic and felt my eyes sting from the excess of dust, before I could see anything in the charcoal dimness. Lumpen shapes began to appear out of the shadows, old suitcases, toys, picture frames, lamps. Layers of white dust had draped themselves over everything, even the narrow skylight.

I searched for documents in suitcases full of paper but came across instead a batch of old photographs and became lost in reverie and nostalgia. There was Sara, in black and white, looking ugly with her hair swept back, holding me, crushing me it seemed by my expression. My father and Cambell standing where the apple tree leaned over the wall. My mother, Cambell and myself, on a picnic rug, faces blurred by too much light in the camera.

I picked up a larger photograph, the only one I had ever seen with both of my parents in it. It was their wedding photograph. This was written, with the date, on the back of it where their marriage certificate was attached. Even her lips were black in this photograph, open as they were in a big glad smile. Her eyes were mischievous under the net veil of a hat she wore at an angle. Her costume was a sophisticated suit, a fur stole draped confidently about her shoulders. He was much as I remembered him, albeit younger and possessed of a little more hair. His face, perhaps, was softer, wearing his habitual sheepish smile. He was dressed in black, other than his minister's white collar. She was not as slim as I remembered. I

THE HILL STREET PUBLIC CONVEYANCE
Frank Kuppner

The following account – taut, luminous, vivacious, perfect – which I hope follows, is based on an original in *Lord Halifax's Ghost Book* (First Volume: London, 1936). This is allegedly, or supposedly, or apparently, a selection of weird tales made by either Mahatma Gandhi or Charles Lindley (Viscount Halifax) from a lifetime's collection compiled by his late father, the Lord Halifax of the title. The latter gent was demonstrably interested in this and related topics in a mature, amused, and fundamentally gullible sort of way. He was evidently one of that appallingly numerous subset of people – the proof that it is not an infinite subset is quite easy, but I shall not give it here – who believe that when we are asleep we are asleep, and when we are awake we are asleep too. I think I disagree. So, I think, did Baudelaire. As if it matters. Let me open-heartedly ignore all this and start a new paragraph.

Nineteenth-century stairways, *moeurs*, moving hands and telephones are, of course, far more interesting, preternatural and frisson-inducing than their wan and ludicrous ghosts ever managed to be. Nonetheless the wonderful dreamlike narrative of one story, *The Bordeaux Diligence*, engenders an impressively convincing effect, which seemed to me, and also perhaps to the window-cleaner, to be traduced by its original ending. Therefore I have completely changed the ending. I found it ludicrously melodramatic. That's twice I've used that word – I really must try to be more alert in future. Not that I have any psychosexually rooted objection (in principle) to men being bitten by women. You would be quite quite wrong to suppose that – though possibly some people would find your naivety attractive. I will even confess that I am not hostile to teeth, albeit in an extremely amused, mature, not fundamentally gullible way. However, apart from that, I have made only minor alterations, *passim*, partly to sharpen the narrative (or so he thinks), and partly to cover the whole work in my fingerprints, so that it will be easier for me (who, after all, is not a career diplomat) to consider the work as being entirely mine. A pleasant if déluded fantasy! For I would not wish you to think of me as being a thief. Or, if you do, I hope at least you will not allow this to influence your actions. (I will gladly leave it to others – believe me – to call you a pervert and a hypocrite.) I presume you do know that a diligence was or is a public horse-drawn coach, do you? If not, I have just told you, with overwhelming but not (alas) utter accuracy, what it is. In fact, I have just told you *whether you already knew or not*. For such is my imperishable generosity of spirit.

I did indeed think (it is typically astute of you that you anticipate me correctly here) of changing that frankly obsolete term (i.e. diligence – a word which I trust you remember having encountered, possibly in Sterne, but anyway at a moment not yet irrecoverably subsumed into what it must already be rather difficult for you to avoid thinking about as your past, an august, thrusting and distinguished one though it no doubt is). I also thought – and please pay particular attention to this if you are real – of changing the titular destination from Bordeaux; to, say, Greenock; or even to Hill Street (intending, perhaps, the one in Roscommon in Ireland). However, in a curious way no such alteration will allow itself to be made. Some things must just stay as they are. And some ares must just stay as they thing – a statement which, alas, does not really make very much sense.

But it is not precisely for that reason that I at once subjoin a version of the narrative referred to above. Try not to fall too deeply, or even more deeply, asleep in the near future, I beg you. Thus. A Parisian gentleman, who had recently lost his wife and was still deep in sadness and misery, was walking down the Rue Keppler roughly towards the Anglican Church. He passed three men, who looked at him in a very pleasant manner. As he hesitated, uncertain perhaps as to whether he

THE HILL STREET PUBLIC CONVEYANCE

knew them, one suddenly pointed to a woman at the end of the street and enquired, 'Pardon us, sir, but would you possibly deign to do us a trifling favour?'

'Certainly,' he replied, without even needing to think.

'Would you mind, I wonder, asking that dark lady at the end of the street at what time the Bordeaux diligence sets off?'

He thought the request a little odd, but obviously harmless. So he quickly strode to the end of the street in question, greeted the lady, and asked: 'I beg your pardon, madam. But could you perhaps tell me at what hour the Bordeaux diligence starts off?'

She breathed in sharply, and glanced at him. 'Don't ask me,' she muttered. 'Go and ask that *gendarme* across the road. He's been doing nothing but look up at that window for nearly an hour.'

So he went straight over to the *agent de police*, smiled politely, and proceeded to put exactly the same question to *him*.

'What?' said the guardian of the law, his eyes widening.

'When does the diligence next set off for Bordeaux?'

Hearing this again, the *agent de police* snorted, turned briskly, and arrested his questioner without further ado, taking him straight off to the police station, where the man was forthwith ensconced in a modest cell. Eventually he was brought up before the magistrate, who asked him in a bored voice exactly what his crime might be this time?

The *agent de police* broke in and replied, 'He asked at what time the Bordeaux diligence starts off. He was also quite clearly in the proximity of possible government buildings.'

'So it's reached that stage, has it?' asked the magistrate, to the sound of sycophantic laughter. 'Put him in one of the lower cells. See to it immediately.'

'But,' protested the gentleman; 'but I only asked what time the diligence starts for Bordeaux. In order to oblige some chap. He asked me to ask a woman. She told me to ask the *agent de police*. Where is there any harm in that? Is this justice?'

'Better put him in the next-to-lowest cell,' was the only reply. He was led away.

Next day, the gentleman, slightly paler by now, was brought up before a Judge and jury. The Judge asked in a stage-whisper, 'What is this man accused of?'

'He came up and asked me at what time the diligence sets out for Bordeaux,' the *agent de police* quite openly replied.

'Oh, it's *that*, is it!' exclaimed the Judge. 'We need hardly go any further, I suppose you agree. Gentlemen of the Jury! Is the prisoner guilty or not guilty?'

'Guilty!' they answered at once, unanimously.

'Take the miscreant away!' the Judge ordered. 'Seven years hard, at Cayenne!'

So the criminal was taken out to South America inside a convict ship. He became a prisoner in Cayenne. After a dreadful time, he eventually began to strike up some sort of friendship with a few of the other prisoners newly arrived there. One morning, quite by chance, they had the opportunity to tell each other the real reason why each had come to be sent to that place. One said one thing, the next another, and so on, much of it already known or surmised, until it came to the turn of the very latest arrival. All eyes turned expectantly to him.

'Oh,' he said shyly, sorry to have to disappoint them by the external banality of his tale. 'It's quite simple. You see, I was walking down the Rue Keppler – I don't even remember why. I saw three men. They asked me if I would oblige them by enquiring of a lady at the end of the street at what time the diligence for Bordeaux would set out. So I did. It didn't seem important at the time. I went over and asked her. She told me to ask the *agent de police*. I could hardly refuse. However, when I asked him, he only snorted, smiled and arrested me. Then the magistrate; then the judge. And now here. I don't understand it myself. What do you think?'

There was silence. Utter silence. From that time forward everybody shunned him. Even in Cayenne there are hierarchies of worth. No one so much as looked him in the eye, except once or twice, probably accidentally.

After some time, there was a new regime installed. The Acting Governor of the prison came to investigate the cases of various prisoners, believing that many of them really ought to be let off with lighter or more appropriate work. At long last the Parisian gentleman was brought before the relevant official, who, doing his best to put his charge at his ease, asked him to tell him in his own words exactly what had been the nature of his offence. Intoxicated by relief, the wretched man repeated his story in the fullest detail imaginable, joyful that he would finally be allowed to witness the undoing, however belated, of a dreadful miscarriage of justice. When he had finished, he looked up at the Governor who ordered him to be taken away to solitary confinement and kept there until further notice.

Distraught, the poor man now applied for the ministrations of the chaplain. He arrived, but, on hearing what the crime was, he turned round instantly and left.

So the gentleman continued in unabated misery for seven excruciating years, until his sentence reached its end and he was allowed to return home. He was now without hopes, without money, without relations, without friends. Thus it was that one day, a month or so after his return, he thought he would or should walk down the Rue Keppler once again. As he did so he saw the same woman at the end of the street. She looked older now, but her eyes were as bright as ever.

He accosted her brusquely. 'You!' he said. 'You are the author of all my misfortunes – remember? I asked you seven years ago when the diligence for Bordeaux departed from here and you refused to tell me. Don't you remember?'

'But why would I do a thing like that?' asked the woman. 'The diligence for Bordeaux? One moment. Yes. It leaves at twenty minutes past nine every morning without fail, does it not? From that stop over there. Look. You can already see two or three people waiting for it.' Having said which, she walked unhurriedly away.

He never saw her again. He went over to the stop and stood there for a few minutes, before changing his mind and passing on. He now had other things to do.

STRAWBERRIES
Candia McWilliam

'Church or chapel?' would ask my nurse, and my parents would set their mouths. My nurse was asking if my high-church father or atheist mother would care for an arched piece of bread from the top of the loaf or a squared-off piece from the bottom. Whichever either chose, it would be buttered to the edge and smeared with fish paste. We were having tea in the white day nursery, which always smelt slightly of singeing. My parents did not care for each other, and they detested Nurse, but could not agree as to her disposal. I loved her.

As though massively exhausted, my father began, 'Nan,' (this was to convince himself that he had come from generations of people who had employed servants) 'Nan, no more can you impute the Romanesque line of that particular crust solely to churches than you can suggest that our friends the Welsh worship in boxes; or, if, by "chapel", you mean something more Romeish, while the Gesu in Rome could conceivably be considered squat, I cannot myself be sure that it might be seen as a square.' Did he talk like this? If not in fact, certainly in flavour. He never stopped, never definitely asserted, incessantly and infinitesimally qualified. He was an architect but however did he draw his straight lines? How, once he had begun it, did he stop drawing a line? He might continue, 'The fish paste, Nan dear, is, I must acknowledge, an apt touch for the believer when one brings to mind that ichthic idiogram for the name of Our Lord scrawled on the lintels of Byzantium or in the sands of Palestine; this reduction, indeed, of fish, this distillate of the deep, this patum of piety.'

Did he speak in his intolerable manner out of hatred for our unadventurous nursery world, the humiliating occasional necessity of spending time with the son he had somehow got on the stony woman sitting low in the nursing chair? I am certain he did not speak from love of words, for all his polylalia; he issued his words as though they strained the sphincter of his mouth, and sank, drained, whenever he at last completed a sentence. To ensure freedom from interruptions, he moaned at not quite regular intervals, as though his speaking mechanism were running down. He also breathed energetically and gobbled at his cheeks.

My mother in contrast was so quiet as to suggest illness. When she spoke, the remark would be of the sort that made me pleased I had no brothers or sisters. The thought of anyone having to hear the things my mother said made me embarrassed. Today she said, 'Did you know, my pigeon, the firescreen is worked in silk from worms which have eaten nothing but the white mulberry's leaf?' It was her overworked absence of banality which made me uncomfortable. I do not now think she was affected, rather, I think she may have escaped into willed eccentricity, which combined with an already eccentric nature. I have inherited her warmth towards esoterica; she had none for people, but she loved her dreadful facts.

Unlike my mother, I have always felt inhibited by the idea of displaying curious information in daily converse. I find it hard to imagine dropping into a free, swiftly moving conversation, odd bits of factual knowledge; they seem to choke the progress and clarity of the thing. I loathe those men who just happen to know about monorchitism in dictators or the curative properties of the toxic members of the potato family. I like best knowledge which comes from comprehension. I do not care for ornamental knowledge, as worn by my mother. Expository or even revelatory knowledge are what I like. Since I became an adult, the mathematics of space and time have been my particular weakness.

But then, on the rug of knotted grey and green cotton rag, concentrating on the knotting's soft randomness to drive time off, I was years from my final resting place, the study of finite dimensional vector space. I have mentioned that I was an only child. I had no friends. If you have bundled and divided the genetic fibres I have offered you, you will not be surprised. But I did have, on my father's side, some cousins, and I liked them.

We were to see them the next day, for the funeral of a great-aunt of mine and of theirs. She had died alone in her flat by the river. On my last visit before her death, accompanied by my mother and by Nurse, my great-aunt had been alert in her freezing flat. She was as sane as a horse and my mother behaved normally for at least an hour. Nurse was scandalized by the cold, and told my mother so. My mother replied, 'Cold is so very good for keeping the more highly-strung tropical blooms fresh.' There was a very small posy of flowers at my great-aunt's flat, and it was made out of wire and buttons. It lived in a vase with a blurry view of a castle painted on one side, strangely out of register, as though the transfer had been done by someone trembling badly. Beside this vase lived a photograph of my four cousins and me. This photograph pleased me in two ways, once warmly, for love, and once in a hot mean way. We were richer – in money – than they, and my coat, even in a photograph, was clearly better fitting, better cut, and of better cloth. I would be wearing this coat to the funeral.

Tea over, Nurse bathed me and read a story to me, a story too young for my age in order to foil nightmares. We also conspired to keep me a baby, so my parents needed her and she could hold my own helplessness against her dismissal, when it came.

My parents overcame their fraught lassitude for long enough to give me a goodnight talk on the warping of furniture ferrules in comparative latitudes (my father) and the lost-wax art of a man (am I tidying the past unmercifully?) called Gloss O'Chrysostom (my mother). If he had listened, and she had momentarily emerged from her hypochondriacal trance, they might have found one another quite interesting. As it was, he worked at home, there was not yet a war to take and glorify him, and she simply had too little to do. I, as a child, was not sickened by all that rich leisure, since that is a child's state, to judge its own circumstances the norm. And children have not learnt to measure time. Nevertheless, through observing my parents observe time and its passage (clocks, watches, timers, tolling, chiming, sounding, and the terrible mealtime gong), I was fast losing that innocence.

I said prayers to Nurse, having rescinded to my mother the elaborate pieties she knew I had enunciated to my father. My private prayers were simple, 'God bless me and God bless Nurse and God bless the Morton cousins.' Their Christian names were easier than mine, John, Bobby, Mary and Josephine. Noel Coverley was my name. I have two middle names which I will tell no one. They attest the intimate spitefulness of my father, who has ensured that I recollect his coldness and his pretensions every time I fill in an official form. Thus he has slung my adult self about with the unhappy overdainty child I was. My grandfather had been the brother of their grandmother. It was the sister of these two who had died in the cold flat by the river. Another thing I love about mathematics of the sort I live among is the way that they blunt the points of time's callipers, by stretching them so far apart, into other sorts of time. Families do the opposite, all the relationships marking time so clearly on that short wooden ruler.

She lay in her coffin and the flowers held out in the steady cool for the whole service, which was long, and presided over by Anglican nuns. My parents and Nurse and I (in the coat) were driven in our grey Morris. The cemetery was beyond Chiswick. The cousins and their parents had come in a car they had hired for the day. Our driver sat in our car. Theirs went for a walk and bought a paper and a bag of pears. Nurse, who was a thorough Presbyterian and averse to what she called 'smells and lace', shared the pears with him. She was partial to a little fruit.

It was my first funeral. Several things about it were unbearable yet intensely pleasurable. The only completely awful thing was the thought of a person in a box. The words of the service went to my head, so my tears were delicious. The 23rd psalm seemed to paint a nursery Arcady where a nurse and not a parent was in charge. We would all be good and fear would be cast out. For the duration of the funeral, I ceased fretting. I did not once look at my mother's defiant white cerements, her alarmingly druidical hat.

The mother of the cousins wore a woolly mulberry thing and she gave me a nice smile when the sermon was threatening to break the richly religious mood. Each of my cousins wore a navy blue felt hat. I had almost chewed through the elastic on my own hat. I could feel its petersham ribbons on the back of my neck. I was a skinny boy with blue knees and pale red nostrils. I had the strength of ten. I was always hungry, though I did not eat in front of my parents if I could help it.

We crossed the road that divided the church from the graveyard where my great-aunt was to be buried. I was prepared for this burying to be the most shocking thing I had seen, worse than my father battering on my mother's door, worse even than seeing a dog shot. So I was better off than Mary and Josephine whose faces crumpled as they saw the spadeful of earth land on that box containing a person. Perhaps they had suddenly realized that they might not live for ever. There was a wind, and while there were fewer motor cars in those days, the dirt from the Great West Road was worse. Our eyes filled with grit and our noses with the smell of cinders. John and Bobby did like men; they screwed up their faces so that no tear could possibly find its way out. I, being 'delicate', was expected to cry, and did so with unmixed pleasure.

The only thing which shook me was the presence of another, unknown, child at the funeral. She was standing with two adult people. She made them look ridiculously large. She might have been my sister, she was so thin. She had a smirk behind her becoming tears. Her mother and father looked sleek and almost impolitely well-groomed. The small girl was dressed in a blue velvet cape with white fur like a frosty Eskimo doll. From the blue velvet bag she carried she extracted, still crying with her face, a peppermint disc the size of a florin. I smelt it amid the wool and naphtha. I looked reverent and stared hard at her from under my lowered lids.

It was not only the mint of which I was jealous. Would this child come back to the cousins' house? Would she offer them more highly-flavoured snippets than I let them have from our different way of life? Was she related to me? Or to them, and not to me? I sent up a prayer which mentioned my great-aunt only incidentally. Its main petition was that my cousins did not, or would not, excessively care for this child.

My mother took my hand in her gloved one. The kid felt like the lids of mushrooms. I knew what she was going to say and had a pretty good idea what she was going to do. Piously, for health reasons, against burial, she was about to break a glass capsule of eucalyptus beneath her nose, and blow it loudly. It was only since I had become seven that she had ceased doing the same for me in any exposed place. She then said, 'While we have a moment of peace' (what a moment, our family at prayer in a windswept graveyard) 'my dove, just take heed of your mother when she reminds you simply to rise above the dirt and devastation at the house of your cousins, who are by no means as fortunate as you. Naturally, for reasons of politeness, we cannot fail to attend the proceedings, but I know I can trust you not to have any needs or to give in to any temptations you may encounter.' She meant don't go to the lavatory and don't eat.

One of the two lessons of that day was that death makes me hungry. It is as though food, the staff of life, were a spell against falling into dust.

The burial done, my parents and I joined Nurse. She had the sweetly acid smell of pears on her. Her grouse-claw brooch had already that day achieved much in the way of irking my mother. We all got into the grey car. It slunk through the small streets near the Morton house. The driver could not park in their street; he would have blocked it. We had passed on the way a vehicle as long as a lifeboat and red as a fire engine. Its chauffeur was upholstered in cherry red, with cavalryman's boots. A whip would have been unsurprising. My parents, who until now had exchanged no sentence, only my father's accustomed latent speech and my mother's dammed silence, looked at each other. That in itself was unusual. They spoke together, 'Victor and Stella.' My father continued, my mother no doubt wrung out by the effort of speech. 'And the odious child, a vision in coneyfur. I wonder they did not drown it.

Of what possible use is it to them?' My father was in this way approaching one of his favourite topics, the childrearing customs of the Spartans. He did that turn especially for Nurse, who could not control her outrage, even when she knew she was being riled on purpose. My mother remained silent, thinking no doubt of the struggle awaiting her in the Mortons' house.

Their father I called Uncle Galway. He taught history, cricket and Latin at a nearby school. Aunt Fan taught part time at the school, when she was not busy with her children. Her subjects were botany and maths. She occasionally taught dressmaking, though even the pancloths she knitted were out of shape.

Their house was attached to its neighbour. It gave the impression of being a big cupboard, perhaps because nothing inside it was put away. In the sitting room, the temperament and pastimes of the Mortons were apparent. The room was stuffed with books, rags, wools, jigsaws, a tricycle, a tank of tarnishing but sprightly goldfish, a cat on a heap of mending, jars of poster paint, a shrimping net and some wooden laundry tongs lying on top of a crystal garden in its square battery-jar of waterglass.

Upstairs, I knew, there would be clothes everywhere, in optimistic ironing baskets, over bedheads, stuffed into ottomans. Everywhere were clothbound books, yellow, maroon, tired blue. In the bedrooms there was a good chance of hearing mice; the Mortons were allowed food wherever and whenever they wanted it. They kept apples and sweets in their chests of drawers, where socks might have been in another house. They were a family which shared its secrets.

The sitting room went straight into the kitchen. Today both rooms were occupied by those who had come on after the funeral. Why were my family, with so much larger a house, not entertaining the party? Their sallow social tone might have been suitable to the decorous gloom conventionally required by a funeral. But they had not offered. It seemed better, at the end of a long life, that there should be not my parents' mean, ordered luxury, but what I saw spread out almost indecently in the kitchen, soft cheeses, deep pies, steaming fruit tarts, jugs of custard and of cream. Aunt Fan was dispensing the food with a battery of unsuitable implements, pie with an eggslice, trifle with a silver masonry tool, cheese with a palette knife, cream from an Argyll. It was a bright mess of colour and juice, squashiness and superfluity. Nurse and my mother stiffened, the one as she saw good food in quantity, the other as she perceived the prowling spectre of uncontrol with its attendant bacteria, spillage and decay.

My cousins fell on me, wagging like pups. Each of them held a thick slice of well-buttered black cake, so by the time they had greeted me I was an object of horror to my mother. She took a long look at me, winced, drew herself up, ruffled and settled her shoulders, and bent, in movement like a riverbird, to unbutton and remove my now Mortonfied coat.

Nurse fetched a plate for herself. My unspoken arrangement with the cousins was, as usual, to get myself upstairs unobserved. I think now that their parents colluded in this against my mother. The house's muddle was a considerable help. I now, too, surmise that my mother's desire to be free of me was even stronger than her dedication to germ warfare. And on this occasion it was clear that she could hardly remove her glare from the pair of grown-ups who must be Victor and Stella. They were tall and, separated from their curiously superior child, clothed in blatancy and confidence. My itch for vulgarity responded to those glittering froggings and facings.

But what concerned me was their daughter, now free of her velvet cape and revealed in a white cotton dress smocked in unfuneral red. The collar was embroidered with very small red strawberries, natty *fraises du bois*. The buttonholes down her back were sutured in the same bright red. Her hair was long, thin and white. She had no front teeth, just two gum spaces. This gave her a lisp. Bobby introduced us. She was Coverley too, her grandfather my grandfather's brother. How had my father overlooked, in his passion for overinformation, especially where it touched upon himself, a whole knot of family? My cousins obviously liked this girl. So I hated her.

'Hello,' she said. 'Is that woman your nurse?' I saw Nurse, for an instant, without love. She was piling a large plate high with food, all mixed up. Her skirt was wide as a fender.

'Yes, she is. And where's yours?'

'Left, they always have; can't bear it.' So she was one of those bad children who rushed through nurses and showed off about it.

'What do you do to them?' I asked, not in admiration as she might have hoped, but prissily.

'It's not me, it's my father, and I can't possibly say. I don't know exactly but shall soon enough my mother says. The last one broke his ivory hair brushes and tore up some of his clothes. My mama says it is something I shall learn all too soon. Men have a rolling eye, she says.' All this with the toothless lisp. In spite of her chilling self-command, something gave me a hint of fellow feeling.

'Is your mother mad?' I asked. From observing Aunt Fan, I knew that my own mother was not typical.

'Is yours?' asked the child. 'She looks it.'

'Come on, you two.' It was Mary. She stood between me and the other cousin, whose name was apparently Lucy, taking her left hand and my right. Mary was shorter and sturdier than we were. Nurse came over and blocked our way to the stairs. She did not mean to; she was just that fat. I looked up and saw she had two plates, spilling with good things, leaking over the edge. I read the names of the china in her shiny hands, 'Spod' and 'Crown Derb'. Her fingers covered any remaining letters. Each of the plates had been broken, at least once. Now they were riveted, and should not have been used for food. Where the cracks were, a deep purple was beginning to appear, the juice of black fruits.

Nurse was a small eater, but she heaped her plate at the Mortons' house.

'Just go and fetch a cup of black tea, dear,' she told me. She was not smiling.

'And would you,' she spoke to Lucy, 'get a slice of lightly buttered bread?'

Equipped with this thin meal, we returned to Nurse. She

wore her bowler-style hat indoors. She peered out from under it. The coast was clear.

She filled the narrow stairway as she led us up its druggeted steepness to the bedroom where our cousins had made a table of Josephine's bed.

'Pass me the tea, dear,' she said. 'And before either of you' – she spoke to me and to Lucy – 'starts on your meal, it's bread and butter. Sit down.'

We sat at opposite sides of the child's bed and she placed in front of each of us a gleaming incoherent feast on broken china. She looked at Lucy, who appeared less menacing up here. She smiled at her and the little girl smiled back, showing side teeth like buds.

Taking a white cloth from the holdall whose cane hoops lived at her elbow, Nurse said to Lucy, 'Lift up your hair, love, and Nurse will tie this round your neck. You don't want fruit juice on those smart strawberries. Eat the bread and butter, the both of you, then you can say you had bread and butter when you're asked. Church, Lucy. Chapel, Noel.'

I explained to Lucy what it was that Nurse meant. All those nurses, and she didn't know a single thing. Eating opposite me and bibbed up in the white cloth, Lucy became at once an ordinary little girl, hungry, skinny, released for an afternoon from the obligation to be odd. By the time we had finished our tea on the bed her untoothed gums were purple and I loved her.

Already equipped with the deviousness and instinct to flirt of a grown woman, she had been dissembling ignorance, she told me years later, when she pretended not to know what Nurse meant by 'Church and Chapel'. 'I was putting you at your ease,' she said. By then we were smokers, and, as I held up a light for her, we looked through the pale flame to the bright red burning tip of the cigarette, bright in the dark like a wild strawberry on dark moss.

SOME NOTES ON HIS DEPARTURE
James Meek

Sandy lay on the floor of the lounge, listening to music and looking up at the ceiling. The room was full of clutter, and the ceiling was empty, smooth. It would be good to walk around there for a while, the floor the ceiling and the ceiling the floor.

At that moment he fell from the floor and landed heavily on the ceiling, bruising his nose and winding himself severely. The furnishings in the lounge crashed around him. A soft thud on the floor suggested Mrs Dalnaspittal downstairs had suffered a similar fate.

Sandy stood up. He was not badly hurt. Betrayed by gravity, there was a turnup, it had always seemed too good to be true that even without special shoes there was no danger of falling off. A serious infringement of Newton's laws had occurred – and why trust an Englishman's guarantee of free gravity for life, no strings attached? Yet the Englishness of the man was not the issue, indeed he had seemed fine, clear-thinking; this shite about apples was typical of the couthy tales they told you to distract you from the nub, the nub of the nub. And here he was, standing on the ceiling. Nubs within nubs. How could Newton explain that? How could Einstein? If you couldn't get at Newton's nub for shite about apples there was certainly no way you could raise Einstein in conversation without some smartarse saying $e=mc^2$ and then slotting a pint in his thrapple as soon as you asked him what it meant. Edward McSquared, the inventor of Einstein.

Everything in the room was now broken. The television was smashed, the record deck cracked, the amplifier box spilling its guts out, the chipboard and melamine bookcases come apart. Total disaster and waste. No, because the books were

OK, and the records could be surprisingly tough when dropped. The worst thing was, the ceiling turned out to be all lumps and cracks, and besides it was white and there would be his dirty footprints all over it. He took off his shoes and looked up. The floorboards were solid, beautiful wooden things, daft to even consider leaving them.

So, the car gone too presumably, so much for the wheel lock, just dropped right off the street into the air without a sound, along with all the traffic.

The pros and cons of the situation. A lot fewer nuclear weapons for one thing, all the nuclear submarines falling out of the sea, and bombers being able to flip over maybe but finding it very difficult to land. A lot fewer people as well, all those folk shopping in the high street just plunging into the sky, the bowling club members observing that what Galileo proved concerning objects falling at the same rate regardless of size was indeed true as the position of the bowls relative to the jack remained more or less unaltered, raising among the more imaginative the possibility of one last game in three dimensions, if you happened to have a bowl close to hand.

Mandatory vegetarianism was inevitable. There, if anywhere, was a lack of foresight, or maybe it had been an injustice to farmers, thinking of them as possessive, conservative, cautious but, anyway, imagine not keeping the livestock properly secured to the ground against a gravitational lapse! As it was the fields would have been cleared in seconds, allowing for the odd cow getting tangled up in a tree. The sheep, inoffensive beasts, not fast moving, calm, were most to be pitied. Hurtling from the planet, still chewing grass.

A look out of the window was the thing. God though, imagine missing the exact moment, imagine not looking out the window at that particular time. More chance thus of a broken skull, but to have seen everything in the world that was not fixed or held down separating from the planet instantaneously.

What complacency! Just because the ground seemed solid, to think standing on a hill in the open air you could lift one foot, or stand on tiptoe, or even jump so you had no kind of hold at all! Given the number of people there were, some of them somewhere would have been trying to jump as high as they could. To reach the moment of achievement two feet above the ground, to make a supreme effort of muscle-power to lift yourself a tiny wee fraction off the heavy planet, and then to feel gravity snap like an overtight guitar string! An instant of ecstasy: you are flying! Followed by the pain, you are falling.

Sandy glanced at the window and looked away again. Moral cowardice. Make no move. What was the opposite of moral cowardice? Immoral cowardice. Therefore his cowardice was the better kind. It was entirely moral. To reach the doorhandle would be hard. Parochial Scottish architecture, just because gravity had always worked before, no provision had been made, i.e. having a handle exactly halfway between the floor and the ceiling. So much for David Hume, though at least he accepted nobody had read his book, let alone faced the consequences.

Sandy sat down on the ceiling and drew the cushions from the settee around him. He put one between his back and the wall and sat on another. What if gravity should return? He put a cushion on his head and the last one on his lap. A prudent measure, keep one step ahead. Was it just luck he had been in the house, or some sharp sixth sense he had, warning him not to go out? Survival of the fittest. Shame about the jungle creatures. Perhaps the big cats had managed to hang on, but for the elephants and the zebras there was no chance. The birds . . . fifty-fifty, though some of them could roost OK. But the fish! Jesus! Millions of mackerel and halibut spread out across the sky, another sight he would never see.

Gravity could come back at any moment. The ideal position would be to stand on his head, balancing all four cushions on the soles of his feet. Then nothing could happen to him. This was hardly practical. Better to sit as now, only with all the cushions laid along the length of his body. One way or another, when gravity returned, he would be ready.

Supposing he was the only one. Just him and his furniture somehow picked out. Suppose the thud he had heard from

SOME NOTES ON HIS DEPARTURE

Mrs Dalnaspittal had gone, there was every possibility that gravity had failed across the board. A short journey to the window would resolve the question once and for all.

Sandy lay down flat on the ceiling, rearranging the cushions so they covered his body and face in a continuous line. So, two kinds of people, those who had fallen so far and been stopped, like him, and those who had fallen into the sky. Which would be the better group, from the socializing point of view? To stay behind was the obvious choice. This would be survival. The food in the kitchen would last a certain while, and by that time, by signals, by careful trips outside, he would have made contact with others who had avoided tumbling into the unknown. They would band together and form a hardworking, democratic wee community that could fend for itself and knew how to deal with outsiders. After all, who had been cleared off the planet? Who was out in the open? Old women with shopping bags. Tourists. Travelling salesmen. Farmers. Lorry drivers. People walking dogs. Newspaper vendors. Policemen. Tough youths who hung around. Dossers. At the same time many of the old folk, the sick and the disabled and babies would have died like Mrs Dalnaspittal, or wouldn't last long. This would leave healthy working people to carry the torch for human civilization in a world without gravity.

Mind you certain of the indoor types were not so definitely good. Too many pale unmuscled people who did not like the fresh air and exercise. Agoraphobics. Besides, how could you rely on all the afflicted folk dying? Millions lying or sitting in rooms all day long, kept in the one place by terrible inheritance of wasted limbs, incomplete brains, excess weight. Excess weight! A joyful release. One by one, chocolate bar in hand, the refugees from the fat farms and slimming clubs squeeze out of their windows and vanish without effort into the void. What about the prisons? Convicts also to contend with. Plus the accountants thrown about their offices. There was in the end no telling who would be left to share the vicinity with. And in groups brought together by circumstance, how to maintain law and order? Put it to the vote was fine before, when behind the vote was a man and behind the man was another man and behind the other man was a big office and behind the office were a lot of heavies with big sticks. The same with the ordering around of many big strong men by a wee speccy man with Highers and a degree and a mode of language that enabled him to define the concepts by which he assumed authority and shared it with others of his kind. There you would be with the assorted remains of human kind, a dozen of you, and who would you be? Sandy; a pair of teenage casuals in labelled cardigans and moccasins; a recipient of care in the community; a very drunk man; a thin mother and a loud baby; a 10-year-old girl with pigtails and thick spectacles; a man in a raincoat buttoned up to the neck, holding a briefcase to his stomach; a tiny foreign woman who did not speak; a blind pensioner of indeterminate sex; and a night-club bouncer six foot high, weighing fifteen stone, wearing a large beard, who was good at shouting. The possibility did not exist of sitting round in a circle, reaching democratic decisions for the common good of the twelve. The bouncer did not care that the man in the raincoat was blessed with useful scientific foresight concerning the future of life in a world without gravity, or that the tiny foreign woman did not wish to have sex with him, or that Sandy for all his flaws and weaknesses was a good man who warranted protection and assistance. It would come down to single combat, Sandy and the bouncer wrestling on the oil-soaked ceiling of a derelict factory, the bouncer killing and eating him.

Who would have fallen already, fallen first, fallen ahead, if not hill-walkers? Then open-air swimmers, athletes, sunbathers, shepherds, explorers. The seas and rivers, the soil in the fields, the sand and pebbles on the beach, they would be falling too. Surely the air itself would drift away. Those who hung on would be lost, choking to death, and if they left it too late to leave they would fall out of company, in ones and twos scattered across the world, miles apart, people who thought about it too much. He had to go now. Could he take something, something to drink, and make his way through the air by flapping his arms to another late decider and share it with

SOME NOTES ON HIS DEPARTURE

them? If the bulk of the falling world was gone on ahead, they would have gone involuntarily, without control, without a decision, without knowing. Whereas his would be a definite act, a choice, an attempt at discovery, him and his companion. As for the falling, it was an attitude of mind, a mile high and the shape of the earth beginning to show and seeing the planet getting smaller and smaller, it would be flying, surely.

It all depended on the way the planets were set up, but if they kept getting faster and faster they might pass one of the big ones, Jupiter and Saturn, seeing the rings close up, curving from the centre of your vision to the corners of your eyes, if the air to breathe hadn't dispersed by then. The possibilities were endless the moment he stepped out of the window, which he would do very soon indeed.

WILLIAM
Willie Orr

William crouched like a spider behind the water tank in the loft. Fragments of web, suspended from the rafters and matted with the dust of two centuries, touched and clung to his hair. Above him, water hissed through the valve as the ball-cock closed. In spite of the noise, he could hear the others downstairs in different parts of the house calling his name. He felt safe in the gloom. They would not look in the loft. He removed his school jacket, folded it carefully and laid it over one of the beams so that he could sit comfortably with his back to the tank. He drew his knees up to his chest but winced suddenly as the pain returned. He had forgotten the gash on his knee, sustained as he scrambled through the trap-door. He explored the wound with his finger, trying to establish its extent. The blood was congealing, forming a sticky film on his knee. He moved his finger gently across the surface. It was not too serious.

> *I do not feel pain. I can pluck hot stones from the fire and carry them through the village. I can run through the desert, following the sun, from dawn to dusk without a rest. I have climbed the cliffs and stolen a feather from the eagle's nest. I do not feel pain.*

But he was afraid.

He heard his father's car leaving the garage and, as it passed beneath his refuge, he listened carefully to make sure that it did not stop at the front door. He was relieved to hear it accelerate. As the sound of the engine faded, he visualized its route down the long drive – past the monkey-puzzle tree, under the beeches and out past the gate lodge. When he was certain

WILLIAM

of its departure, he relaxed. If he was caught now, it would not be by his father.

He stood up and peered into the tank. He could not see the surface of the water in the dark so he lowered his fingers into the space to find it. Instead of the water he touched the ball-cock and the valve hissed angrily at him. Startled, he stepped back, lost his balance and, trying to keep his feet on the narrow beams, fell heavily across the rough timber. He could not suppress a cry of pain as his knee hit the wood but managed to lie quite still, listening, trying to discover if his fall had been heard.

The house was silent but for the scraping of a branch on the slates. Slowly he levered himself up to sit behind the tank again.

He heard the school bus passing the gate and imagined his friend, kneeling on the back seat and searching the long drive for his scarlet blazer and cap. He began to plan his day. If he could escape from the house and reach the safety of the rhododendrons without being seen by the gardeners, he could leave the grounds by the secret gate and go down to the canal. It was not really a secret gate but no one used the path now so it had been forgotten. Apart from the main gateway, with its ivy-clad, stone archway, it was the only gap in the high wall which surrounded the garden. He calculated that no one would see him as he left the grounds and followed the path to the canal. He would avoid the bridge, which carried the main road over the canal, and cross the water by the lock gate. Then he would be in the beech wood.

I can glide silently through the woods – not even the squirrels hear me. I can follow the track of the deer in the fallen leaves and smell the spray of a dog fox across a stream. I am the fleet of foot, the shadow, the hunter with the white bow.

First, however, he would have to escape from the house, avoiding his mother and the maid. He imagined his mother's fury if she caught him, her great bulk, like a galleon, bearing down on him, the veins on her temples pulsating and her small, fat hands twitching with the urge to hit him. Yet she would control the impulse, for, since his father's return, she had transferred the task of chastising him to her husband. He was still afraid of her when she was angry, remembering clearly the pain of her hand on his leg.

He held his breath and listened but he could hear only the blood pounding in his head. They must have abandoned the search. He crept across to the trap-door and slowly raised the cover. The sweet smell of hair oil rose from the bathroom and the light made him blink. The room was empty and the light-cord perfectly still, but the open door, which had provided his final foothold, was firmly closed.

The last time he had been trapped in the loft his mother had taken a bath. He had raised the trap-door and looked down on her as she lay in the water. He remembered the domes of her breasts and the shadow of her thighs beneath the surface. When he was younger, she had often joined him in the bath and held him between her knees as she washed his hair. He had been allowed to wash her back and she seemed to enjoy that but, when his father returned, the bathroom door was locked against him and he was banished from her bed. He could not understand the change. He had done nothing to deserve it. If she had seen him looking down on her on that occasion, he knew that the tranquil form would have erupted and thrashed about the bath like a squid on a hook. He hated the way adults could change so quickly from repose to agitation and wished that things would happen slowly to give him time to observe and respond.

He folded his jacket with the buttons inside and dropped it into the bath. It landed inaudibly on the plug-hole. Then he lowered himself slowly through the opening, holding the cover open with his head. As he hung at arm's length above the bath, with his fingers caught painfully beneath the cover, he realized that his toes were fully a foot above the towel rail on the wall. If he dropped on to the rail, it would certainly break free from the plaster and crash into the bath. If he just let go, he would fall into the empty bath and break his ankle. He swung round, first in one direction and then the other, searching for another foothold. There were none. His fingers and arms began to ache as he hung in the air. He could not climb back to the loft.

I am Kana of the Apes. I was reared in the trees. I am stronger than a lion and can fly through the trees like a bird. I am the king of . . .

He dropped into the bath, wrenching his shoulder as his arm hit the side.

He lay for a moment, overwhelmed with nausea, as the pain shot through his neck. He kept his eyes tight shut and his teeth clenched and waited for the shock to subside. As he waited, he listened for sounds of alarm downstairs. He was not sure how much noise his fall had made in the rooms below. He could hear his mother's voice at the other end of the building but there was no note of urgency and there were no footsteps on the stair. He opened his eyes, trying to ignore the pain in his arm, and removed his shoes, which, he decided, would make a noise on the stairs. He climbed out of the bath and stood for a moment at the door, listening. Only the murmuring of distant, indistinguishable voices and the usual creaks of the old house, as it adjusted itself to another mid-morning, disturbed the silence. Folding his jacket over his arm, he opened the door and peered out.

As he did so, a white cat appeared at the other end of the long corridor beside the main stairway. It noticed him immediately and trotted towards him, wailing enthusiastically.

'Go away!' he hissed, flapping his jacket to discourage its advance. It stopped suddenly, halfway along the passage, its back arched, its tail erect and bristling and its fangs bared menacingly. It was a massive cat and William was terrified by the transformation. He could not understand why his attempt to chase it away had provoked such a hostile reaction.

Then he heard the other cat. It had emerged from a doorway behind him and, as he turned, it flew past him, a dark streak under his jacket, and leaped at the white cat. Suddenly they were one animal, screaming, scratching, kicking, crashing from one side of the corridor to the other like an unpinned Catherine wheel, emitting a cloud of soft fur which settled slowly on the carpet. For a few seconds William remained transfixed, mesmerized by the ferocity of the battle, then, hearing his mother on the stair and catching a glimpse of red blood on white fur, he fled down the back stair, out the back door, across the gravel and through the secret gate. He did not stop till he could see the canal.

He threw himself down beneath the whin bushes, his favourite refuge, and tried to recover from his flight. His fragile rib-cage heaved spasmodically as he struggled for air and his breath whined in his throat. Nevertheless he altered his position so that he could see the house and the road, as he suspected that his escape had been heard, if not seen, by his mother or one of the staff. There was no one in sight yet. He felt quite safe in the whin bush, for, apart from the narrow entrance, the sharp spines reached down to the grass on all sides, forming a small, virtually impenetrable hemisphere, like a green hedgehog, on the hillside. Indeed, as he peered out through the opening, the bush seemed to close round him, shrinking to form a second skin.

If they find me here, I will curl up and fire spines into their eyes. When I move through the jungle at night, the black panther cringes as I approach. When I shuffle through the dead leaves on the forest floor, the lion whimpers.

Beneath him, the sheltered valley lay motionless in the morning sun, bisected by the glistening strip of water, which stretched into the distant marshes as straight as a railway track. On his left, about half a mile from the whins, tall lime trees, swollen with sap so that every leaf oozed and stretched with quivering vitality, completely concealed the house. Beside the road, which crossed the valley between neat, hawthorn hedges, the smoke from the forge curled reluctantly into the hot air. He could imagine the ring of the smith's hammer, as he beat the red-hot strips of metal round the horn of the anvil to make a perfect curve, and the sharp smell of singed hoof as a hot shoe was pressed on to the foot of one of the massive cart horses. An acrid scent, quite unlike the sweet, heavy smell of whin flowers, which filled the bush.

He listened for voices calling for him in the garden but only the quarrelling rooks on the tall trees disturbed the silence. As he listened, however, he heard another sound, which made him swivel round and face the canal – the distant throbbing of a barge engine. Horse-drawn barges were a common sight and he had often plucked grass from the canal bank for the great horses to nibble through their soft, felt lips, as they waited on the towpath for the locks to fill; but there was something exciting about the smell of oil and the powerful thrust of an engine, churning the water as the barge surged forward. The approaching vessel was the only motorized barge on the canal.

He knew some of the bargemen and had travelled with them for several miles, but the master of the diesel barge had taken him right up to the mill town, allowing him to hold the tiller on the long strait. He remembered his waistcoat, worn and shining round the pockets, with silver buttons stamped with anchors, and the smell of his pipe as he leaned across occasionally to touch the tiller. The man rarely spoke but, when he did, he spoke of whales and harpoons and flukes bigger than bridges and icebergs taller than trees and, when he described these scenes, his eyes, gazing into the distance, seemed to see every detail moving before them. He smelled of sweat and oil and tobacco and William wanted to be a man like him. He wanted to sit close to him and be his friend, but always some slight defect in his appearance deterred him from expressing his feelings – last time it had been a drop of amber saliva sliding from the corner of his mouth into the grey stubble on his jaw. Besides, his face sometimes twitched and trembled with fearful energy, as if, beneath the weathered skin, opposing forces were locked in combat like gladiators in a net. Sometimes the movement became so violent that William thought that the flesh might melt and flow down his face like wax to reveal a hideous skull. Sometimes his whole body trembled, as if the fragile nature beneath could no longer sustain the powerful frame. As quickly as these spasms came, however, they departed and the man resumed his usual profound tranquillity.

William watched the bend of the canal under the beech wood but there was still no sign of the barge. He calculated that, if he could reach the bridge without being seen, he could leap from the canal bank on to the deck of the barge as it passed. He turned to make sure that there was no one on the road.

She was there and, with her, the maid and the gardener. He cursed, using words which would have shocked her. The trio were staring in his direction, the gardener pointing towards the whins. Instinctively William lowered his head and crawled backwards into the middle of the bush till he could no longer see them. The throbbing of the barge engine echoed in the beech wood. It must have passed the bend. Four hundred yards of open ground lay between his refuge and the canal but, somehow, he had to reach the barge. He was bound to be discovered in the bush. Had he been able to swim, he could have crossed the canal and escaped to the beechwood.

He crawled forward again, the gash on his knee stinging painfully as it rubbed in the sand. They had left the road and were hurrying towards the whins. He imagined his mother's wrathful face and the smirk in the eyes of the maid. Then he remembered the ditch. The whin bushes reached across the ridge behind him to the big meadow, where a drain led to the canal. He looked back. The cattle had gathered in the shade of a heavy chestnut tree, flicking their ears, quivering their hides and swinging their tails to disperse the flies. He did not want to enter the meadow, as he had seen the somnolent herd spring to life and chase his father along the canal, hoisting their tails, bellowing and kicking their heels in the air, obviously enraged by the tall fly-rod which swung above the fleeing figure as he ran. William had avoided the field since then. The ditch, however, was beside the fence. He crawled quickly through the whins, a shoe in either hand, sometimes having to push his way through the sharp spines. Behind him he could hear them calling his name. He reached the ditch undetected and began to follow it to the canal.

It was not as deep as he remembered so he had to crawl

again to keep his head below the bank. Pools of stagnant water lay among the king cups and black mud clung to his ankles. A snipe shot out from the weeds ahead of him and, startled by the crash and the rush of its wings, he flung himself flat in the mud but, hearing the barge, hurried forward, his legs, short flannels and grey shirt caked in slime. To his consternation, the ditch opened out near the canal so the only hiding place was the canal bank or the last hollow in the ditch too far from the water to reach the barge.

He raised his head high enough to see the whins. His pursuers had not reached his refuge and the barge was still some distance away. He had some time to spare. He tied his shoelaces together and held them between his teeth to leave his hands free. Then he remembered his jacket. He had left it in the whins. He cursed again then, bracing himself, ran across the open ground and lowered himself into the canal, holding on to tussocks of coarse grass on the bank. He was safe.

The chickweed, which had parted as he broke the surface, closed again round his shoulders. Suspended in the dark water, his legs almost invisible in the depths and his face streaked with mud, he could hardly be seen from either bank.

The surface water was cool but, below his waist, it was painfully cold. However, it seemed to support him and he was sure that he could hang on till the barge arrived. But it did not come. He realized that it had stopped. He knew by the hum of the engine that it was out of gear. He began to worry about his predicament and studied the bank, hoping to find a place to climb out. There was none. He glanced across the canal and saw the steps. Between him and the steps, however, the black depths waited menacingly for him to attempt the crossing. As his arms tired, he tried to climb out but the bank was so undermined that he could find no foothold and he was quite unable to haul himself out of the water. His hands began to ache and, suddenly overwhelmed with dread, he began to whimper.

The bargemaster held his mug in both hands and, sitting on the gunwale, gazed along the glistening surface of the canal where the swallows swooped for flies, clipping the water with their wing-tips and leaving little circles in the reflection of the sky. He had edged the barge against the bank, disturbing a coot, which nodded away angrily to the other side. He stared across the meadow to the chestnut, where a herd of cattle were inquisitively following a group of three people towards the distant Georgian mansion. For a moment he thought he heard a cry from the canal ahead. He listened attentively but could hear nothing but the drone of the engine. Deciding that it was the coot, he set down his mug and retrieved his pipe. He was about to remove the metal cap, when he heard the sound again. He stood up and walked along the deck to the bow. Far ahead, the calm surface was broken by erratic ripples, as if an animal was in the water.

He hurried aft, set the engine in gear, and, as the water churned behind it, the great barge slid slowly forward. He stood in the stern and searched the banks ahead. The water was unusually agitated. There must be a beast in the water, right enough. Then he saw the child, thrashing weakly under the bank, its head only occasionally above the surface. Snatching the long boathook from its cleats and stopping the engine, he caught the child's shirt and, hauling it gently towards the barge, lifted it aboard.

William spluttered, coughed and spewed water across the deck as he gasped for air. As the man bent over him, words echoed in his head . . .

> *I am the Lord of the Jungle. I can kill crocodiles in the river, swirling in mortal combat below the water. I can swim faster than the water snake and the yellow fish under the falls.*

As he recovered, the man carried him to the cabin in the stern. He set him on the bunk and, removing his sodden shirt and vest, rubbed him down with a coarse towel. William began to shiver uncontrollably. The man placed a blanket over his shoulders and crossed to the sink to light a small paraffin stove under the kettle. A blue flame flickered silently in the gloom as the priming spirit burned until, with a roar, the paraffin vapour ignited. The man pumped up the pressure and returned to kneel in front of William. As he removed his socks, his large, clumsy fingers rolled the wet wool down his shins with remarkable delicacy.

William, still shivering, stared down at him. The edges of his peaked cap were frayed and, under the cracked peak, his heavy brows quivered. He had paused in his task and was gazing at William's legs; not at the gash on his knee, which was oozing blood once again, but at his white shins. William's mother had often said that his legs were like match-sticks. Obviously the man thought so too. Yet he was stroking the smooth flesh tenderly. His face was twitching again and, when he looked up, his eyes were so full of sorrow that William instinctively reached down and put his arms round his neck, feeling the stubble of his jaw against his face. For a moment they were still, the pale coils of the boy's arms wrapped round the dark neck and a drop of water from his lank hair sliding down the man's cheek. Then the man staggered backwards, pushing William away roughly.

'Christ's sake!' he snarled and turned away to wring out the wet shirt, vest and socks. Half turning from the sink, he signalled to William to remove the rest of his clothes.

Obediently the boy took off his wet flannel shorts and underpants, left them on the floor and wrapped himself in the blanket. He wanted to apologize but he was afraid to speak. He could not understand the man's reaction. He watched him collect the flannels, wring them out and disappear from the cabin with the bundle of clothes.

William moved back against the bulkhead and looked round the room. The port-holes, black with coal dust, admitted little light so it was impossible for him to see into the corners. Unlike his own home, the cabin contained no pictures and no books and the only china was piled, unwashed, round the sink. An empty birdcage hung from the ceiling beside a paraffin lamp. The sea chest beside the bunk was also empty, its lid hanging open from one hinge. The room was bare, except for the clutter around the sink, as if no one lived there. It reminded him of his grandfather's austere bedroom where he had heard the old man shout at God in the night, but his had been clinically clean and meticulously organized. This was like a cellar which someone had started to clear out and then abandoned. It smelled of tobacco and oil and socks. The kettle was blowing a column of steam towards one of the port-holes and he thought about calling the man but realized that he did not know his name. Suddenly he remembered his mother.

She was bound to ask the bargemaster if he had seen a boy or send the gardener to do so. His punishment would be much worse now, with his school clothes soaked and his shoes . . . he must have dropped his shoes when he sank in the canal. He would be beaten for that. He could not go home now. He would have to live on the barge. Just as he came to that conclusion the light from the windows disappeared altogether. They had entered the lock. He heard the creak of the heavy lock gates closing and the thunder of the sluice in front drowned the sound of the engine. If they cleared the lock and reached the open water, he would escape detection.

He crossed his fingers as the light began to return and the sound of the sluice faded. When the cabin shook with the thrust of the engine and trees moved across the port-holes, he lay back on the bed.

The bargeman returned to the cabin and, without looking in William's direction, lifted the kettle from the stove. William wanted to ask him if he had seen his mother at the lock but knew that such a question would arouse suspicion. The man put tea leaves in a pan, poured in hot water and brought it to the boil. Mixing the brew with a spoonful of thick tinned milk in a mug, he handed it to William and left the cabin.

William held the mug in his hands and was about to drink the tea when the engine stopped and he heard voices. He tried to make out the words but they were indistinguishable; even the tone was muffled by the thick hull of the barge. When the man's footsteps sounded on the deck above he decided that the gardener had found him but, when the bargeman appeared, he showed no signs of anger. Instead he handed him his clothes.

'Go now,' he said quietly, 'Get dressed and go.'
'But my clothes are still wet . . .' William protested.
'Go home and change. You will be alright. Hurry.'
There was no point in arguing. He put on the damp clothes which had been so firmly wrung out that they were nearly dry. Nevertheless, they were cold and uncomfortable and he began to shiver again. He did not put on the socks. The man took him roughly by the arm and led him up on deck where he discovered that the barge was pulled in against the bank and moored to a tree. Sitting on the grass was a stranger, with his cloth cap pushed to the back of his head and, between his boots, a green bottle. The bargeman lifted William on to the bank but held on to his arm firmly.

'Go home, boy,' he said, 'Go home and stay away from the canal. If I ever see you near the water again, I'll thrash you till you bleed.'

He let go and William staggered back, hurt and confused. He thought the man was his friend, that he liked him. He could not understand the change. He walked back towards the lock, expecting to see his mother waiting by the bridge.

'I hate you,' he shouted back, unable to see the men though his tears, but he did hear the stranger laugh.

'Bastard!' he shouted, 'Bastard, bastard, bastard!'

He started to run, throwing his socks in the canal.

I am the lone hunter. I am the fleet of foot. I am the hill-eater, trail-burner, comet-catcher. I need no one, no one, no one.

He ran along the towpath, under the bridge, past the locks and into the vast cathedral of the beech wood where the smooth, grey trunks curved sensuously upwards like long thighs into the skirts of the green canopy above. He ran until his ribs seemed to crack, until his legs sagged and he collapsed among the leaves.

He lay for a long time, a small, fragile figure under the tall trees. The wood echoed with the song of thrushes and the whisper of young leaves as a breeze moved through the high branches. When he had recovered, he climbed the steep slope towards the top of the wood, where the big boys had their swing. A stream had carved a deep ravine through a seam of sandstone and, above it, one of the trees stretched its limbs across the gorge. The boys had attached a long rope to the tree and were able to swing across the ravine. He had never been there alone and, when the boys were there, they would not allow him to try the swing, claiming that it was too dangerous for a small boy.

He found the rope and pulled it with him as he climbed the bank towards the stone that marked the starting line. For a moment he hesitated, knowing that once the run was started it was impossible to stop, but, dismissing the possibility of an accident, sprinted down the slope, swung out over the ravine, and, relinquishing the rope at exactly the right moment, executed a perfect flight and a relatively painless landing. He was delighted, clapping his hands and cheering until a blow on the head sent him reeling across the clearing.

'Stupid child! You could have killed yourself.'

The gardener caught him roughly by the arm and led him home.

His mother replaced the phone and stood with her back to him, glaring at the wall. He glanced at her but looked away quickly in case she turned round. His eye fell on the white cat. It was curled up on a velvet cushion, its tail over its nose. A single scratch on its ear was the only evidence of the morning's battle. William hated it suddenly and would have kicked it, had it been within reach. It was so content and so obviously part of the family, while he felt like an intruder, an undesirable substance smeared on the carpet. The room seemed to tower over him. Tall velvet curtains reached into the shadows below the cornices and huge portraits frowned on him from the walls. He looked down to avoid their eyes and watched his toes moving through the carpet like dolphins through the tide. He moved them separately to enhance the effect but nearly fell over when his mother shouted at him.

'Go and get changed!'

He hesitated. He wanted to tell her about school, about what would happen when he returned, but she turned and yelled at him, repeating the command.

He and the cat fled from the room.

He stood beside the headmaster on the school steps as his mother walked back towards the car.

'Thank you, Mrs Thomas. We will look after him.'

'I am sorry to have troubled you, Mr Wiseman. It will not happen again. Will it, William?' she asked pointedly as she opened the car door.

William said nothing. He was preparing himself for the punishment that would follow her departure. He was wearing his school uniform again – the grey shirt and silk knitted tie with flat ends and coloured stripes, grey flannel shorts, knee-length socks with red tops and black shoes. As the car drove away the headmaster caught him by the hair on his temple and guided him towards the study.

'I am rapidly running out of patience, Thomas. I am going to give you a lesson you will not forget.'

He guided William into the study and locked the door.

'Miss Stewart,' he said to the secretary, 'would you be kind enough to fetch the long ruler?'

She smiled as they exchanged glances, a strange excitement injecting unusual speed and efficiency into her response. She was not a young lady, thin and bitter, consumed with unfulfilled passions and the ineradicable guilt associated with them. She seemed to enjoy the misfortunes of others, as if, through their suffering, they bore the punishment for her iniquities. William hated her.

The headmaster seated himself on an upright chair, ordered William to take down his trousers and, for the third time that week, laid him across his knee. His tweeds smelt of camphor and tobacco, not the bargeman's tobacco but a sweet, exotic perfume. As he lay on the man's knee, he remembered the bargeman's face when he knelt in front of him to remove his socks and the short embrace.

'Pass me the ruler, please, Miss Stewart.'

William could see her pointed shoes as she crossed the floor. They remained under his nose as the instrument slapped down on his naked flesh. Suddenly, William was seized with uncontrollable rage and, turning round, dug his nails into the man's cheek, squeezing and gouging till blood ran down his fingers. He leaped to his feet and, pulling up his trousers, ran to the door, unlocked it and fled towards the school entrance.

I am the Great Bear, Earth-shaker, Tree-trembler, Wolf-killer, Man-slayer . . .

' . . . I am unconquerable!' he shouted, as he ran down the stairs.

ILDICO'S STORY
Peter Regent

She was not old, but the wind had seared her face till it was as wrinkled as a shrivelled apricot that had hung on the tree all winter. The wind that swept over the plains was as sharp as those marvellous blades from the East that slipped through flesh as if it were curds. It turned men's faces to dry rinds, and reduced their bodies to quiddities of sinewy endurance. Her own shape was harder than it used to be, and her skin was burnt gold – no trace, now, of the red that had danced on her youthful cheeks. But today there was no wind. It was hot. She undid her jacket and shouted to the maid to bring milk. *The* maid! That she, who should have had a hundred girls, and German men-slaves to run at her bidding, should be reduced to a single maid!

The girl brought the bowl of kumiss with lowered eyes, but there was a defiant swagger to the swirl of her skirt as she turned to go. The woman's lips drooped in wry amusement. She, too, moved with a free, hip-swinging gait; her father had always laughed, and said the girls of the horde learned their walk from the mares.

She drank the prickly ferment at the tent door, looking out over the plain that stretched away through a haze of dust and heat to the mountains at its rim. The stark expanse lay exposed to an enormous sky, in which storks circled far overhead. Sometimes clouds gathered to enact high drama over the plain. They reared like horses; swept in cohorts, with banners flying; heaved, broke and reformed like armies locked in battle. But today there was only the haze stretching into the distance and, near at hand, little twisting devils of yellow dust that whirled skittishly away.

She was tired of being here. Already the profile of the hills at the edge of the sky was a commonplace, and she did not like such ingratiating familiarity. She loved movement and a changing scene: new peaks marching at the edge of the sky as the unending plain reeled away under pacing hooves; the sudden alarms of the tracks through the forests beyond the plains; the grassy ways across the high pastures, where it was still spring when the plains were sweltering and breeding storms. She loved the moment of breaking camp into the freshness of early morning – the crescent of horses and riders dancing forward, the shouts and lowing of horns, the bright green of untrodden grass that was sprinkled with flowers like a carpet looted from the bazaars of southern cities; she recalled the fresh smell, and the way the taste of warm mares' milk persisted on the tongue. Then the heat and thirst of the long day, and at last, at dusk, the watering of beasts, perhaps even a perfunctory washing off of dust, and the smell of kebabs grilling.

But her husband was given to lingering. She had not felt the swaying of a horse-litter for nearly two years. This place was stale. There was a smell of rotting vegetables and ordure; of settled habitation. It was an alien smell. She was becoming that contemptible thing, a settler's wife! She was tired of being still; she loved movement. She was like her mother; she was a woman of the horde.

In the great camps her mother had whispered to her about the heroes that strode and shouted to each other among the tents. They had ignored her, of course, and she, an unmarried breastless girl, had known better than to come too close to them. But her mother had told her all about them, and how splendidly they stank. They stank of rancid butter, fermented mares' milk, blood – human and animal – horseshit and sometimes of wine and perfumes looted from the cities beyond the southern mountains. Their loins reeked of the strips of horseflesh they clamped to their horses' flanks in lieu of saddles. Her mother had always said there was a meal in a hug from one of them – from the sweat and sour milk of his beard, and from his richly clotted underbelly. A girl could live off such embraces, said her mother.

ILDICO'S STORY

But this was not living, in this fixed existence, with stores laid by, and constant sufficiency. There was no riotous excess; no hunger followed by surfeit; no uncertainty – except of harvests. Yes, harvests! For now her husband not only kept his herd, like a woman, but had commerce with the soil – the shame of it – growing corn and keeping it in great pots! He would live in a house next!

Oh, yes, the King had built a hall, but only for glory, to receive emissaries bringing tribute and to entertain the generals and princes. Anyway, it was so hung with rich embroideries, silks and furs, inside, that it seemed more like a huge tent. He had been the greatest of those heroes her mother spoke of; the greatest of all men. He was no farmer. He had never touched soil except to shit in it. He owned no mattock or felling-axe, only his weapons: his horned bows, his damascened daggers and swords. They were magnificent, his weapons – but practical, not showy. He had worn gaudy trimmings for the pride and fun of it, but nothing that weighed him down or hindered his movements. His dress was manly, from his good boots to the boar's-tooth cap over which he would strap his great helmet with its horsetail trimmings. There was nothing vainglorious or dandyfied about him. He was a hard man, but he knew how to be generous and magnificent.

It was no wonder that the Roman Caesar's luxurious whore of a granddaughter had sent him her ring. He was a real emperor. His quiet orders did not have to be repeated, and when he raised his voice only slightly, bold men in wolf-mask caps and great horned helmets hurried about his business. He was not tall, but broad-chested and neatly built, striding purposefully and looking sharply left and right. His smell was as it should be: complex, of horses and rancid butter, naturally, but otherwise not as rank as her mother had described. He certainly didn't smell of flocks and cattle, or of any toil except man-slaying.

But his eyes were the thing she remembered most. That keen gaze had rested on her for a moment, had turned elsewhere, then flashed back to her as she lingered at the curtain of her father's tent. In that instant he had seen her, and seen that she was handsome. Her breasts were not quite full-grown then – her brown hands consulted her thorax: she was still well-shaped, but they were softer now. They had been hard like the little pears in the meadows where she had run after goats as a child.

She looked down at her harsh body. Her feet were broad, but strong, and her ankles were still neat. She had been a beauty, and he who saw everything had seen it. He had checked his long stride when he saw her; his eyes, deep-set like a hawk's, darted back to her a second time, and she had stepped back into the tent and let the curtain fall. When she peeped again he was walking away as if she did not exist. But the next day he had come right into her father's tent, and she had shown herself again, and dared to look straight at him before lowering her eyes and going about her business, walking with the proud swaying gait she had learned from the mares.

He had spoken to her father, of course, but it had not been a dynastic affair. He had been – even at his age – in love with her. The Master of the World, Lord of all things, rich in horses, ruler and slayer of men, had lacked something – her. She had agreed. She didn't have much choice, though usually the women of the plains had more say than the poor creatures in Eastern palaces and Roman cities – more, even, than the raw-boned German women with their beer-drinking husbands.

There had followed the wonderful time of preparation. He had sent her presents of things from across the world; from beyond the plains on the far side of the mountains that circled the great camp, from beyond other plains and other mountains, and perhaps from beyond the great water itself. Then he had gone off campaigning, and the preparations had continued. There was the embroidering of cloth, the working of skins, and the accumulation of food. There was talk of a battle, and of a meeting with some great Roman shaman called Popa, or Papa or something like that. At the news of his impending return she had been feasted – the fattening they called it, though she had enough sense to know that he had liked her leanness and would not want to be confronted by one of those

ILDICO'S STORY

fat grinning moons that smirking mothers liked to lead out for mating. Friends came to sit with her. She gave them dried meat, nuts and figs, and giggled with them a little at first. Then she remembered, and was more distant, as befitted a princess.

He came. Dust-caked advance parties brought warning of his approach. A great yellow dust-cloud advanced from the rim of the plain, and under it a dark mass of riders, spread far out on either side, with him riding alone in the hollow of the crescent formation. Deep-voiced horns sounded, shrill trumpets answered; then there were horses everywhere, and in all directions men cavorting and shouting. Dejected prisoners sat in rows with arms bound. Captured princes in torn and draggled finery were put to digging latrine drains and clearing up after the cavalry. Everywhere there were stalking, swaggering men. There was a smell of trampled grass and earth, of horses, of foreign perfumes, of scorched mutton, of spices. At night the din reduced to a murmur of talk and bursts of low laughter round little savoury fires with rings of skewered meat sizzling. Later still, there rose from the tents the moans and cries of women lying in exultation with their men.

Then the day was on her. Her body had been plucked nude of hair, leaving her flat belly smooth; neatly modelled in almond paste between hips that sprang like axeblades on either side. With henna'd wrists and ankles, rouged nipples, and buttered hair gleaming, she was a dish for a king, and she knew it.

The feasting had gone on and on. The sky was lowering with the smoke and reek of burnt mutton. There were horse-races, wrestlings that broke necks, backs, and even friendships that had sustained the shock of battle – so hateful was humiliation here, before the people of the great camp. The young men danced before the swaying lines of girls. She could not be among them this time, but peeped, the unseen cause of it all. The girls looked demure and maiden-soft in their best silk skirts and trousers, but each of them was as tough as saddle-meat, with a knife somewhere under her clothes. Drums swelled and faded, swelled and faded, with occasional sallies of horn-blowing, till in a last great climax of drumming and lowing they brought him to her bride's tent.

He had come into the inner compartment, with its embroidered panels, silks and thick furs; he rinsed his mouth from the jewelled flagon, and came to her in a wave of horseshit, mutton-fat, wine-fumes and civet. He knew his way round a woman, even if he was a little – only a little – fuddled. It was much as she knew it would be – she had lived all her life in a camp. But he did pause a moment, beforehand, to look at her. Then came his sudden convulsion in her arms – much more violent than she had expected, and briefer, with an angry cry and a desperate embrace that drove the breath out of her – followed by terrible panting and another convulsion, then stillness; dreadful stillness. And slowly there came the realization that he was dead.

Her cries had brought men running, and she had thought herself dead as they flung her to one side, gathered him up, then rushed back at her. Perhaps it was her naked helplessness that made them see that a girl could have done no harm to such a man. They pushed her away, and the women hustled her, staring but seeing nothing, hardly able to breathe, let alone speak, back to her mother. In her father's tent, confronted with the familiar chests and hangings and talismans, and the remnants of all the preparations, she had suddenly been seized with a terrible anger. She had been angry ever since.

Meanwhile, the camp that had been quietly rioting towards sleep was roused to a frenzy of wailing. The prisoners screamed as they were slaughtered, and her mother hid her, for fear that her blood might go spattering, along with that of his favourite horses, beside where he lay. But they did not come for her. It was sufficient to kill every man, woman, child, dog, or goat that met them as they carried the corpse eastward.

The funeral, like the wedding-feast, went on and on, with drumming, wailing and horn-blowing, and the sky dark with the smoke of immolations. She had only a vague memory of more killing of horses and slaves, and of her mother getting her away.

ILDICO'S STORY

She was sent to her grandfather. She had not been particularly welcome. As the widow of the King she had a certain cachet, even if it seemed she might be accursed, but till she was remarried she would be at risk. Oh yes, there was talk that she was an evil talisman – may the heart and lungs of those who uttered it be eaten by crows! Who would dare marry such a woman? Only stolid Yurkut, eager like a farmer's pig after a succulent morsel. No doubt he felt that being the son of a shaman gave him protection. Well, he was not a poor man, and he was strong, with the slow strength she had seen in the oxen of the marshes. Shambling, almost to the point of lameness, he came to her with a great wallowing greed that was done with in a few lurching moments. It would never be worthwhile to eat his heart and lungs – no nourishment would come from them.

Her mother had warned her not to let him know she was already with child. Her mouth smiled ruefully. Such a man as the King could sire, even in the moment of death. If she had resented having to conceal her son's parentage then, she resented it more now, though for a different reason. Oh, the shame that he was as he was!

Thinking of it, she sank to her heels and swayed back and forth. She should have been Queen of the World. She would have known how to act the part. The emissaries of the great Khan would have grovelled before where she sat below her husband's cushion. The Byzantines would have entered the great tented hall on all fours, and backed out bottom-first. The Romans would have stammered over their famous sheets of writings; they would have been grimly listened to, then skinned alive. At least, she hoped they would have been skinned alive – or pulled apart by stallions maddened by eager mares with round, cleft croups like the arses of the magnificent women of Pannonia and Samara. She often thought like that, now, and felt excitement rising when the men rode in with stumbling captives, tied by the neck behind the horses.

She had never heard that the King had been cruel. Why should he have been? He had everything a man could have. What would he want with another's pain? He was not interested in screams and cries of mercy, or in watching men writhe, ten feet off the ground with stakes up in their bellies, while he lay on cushions chewing strips of saddle-meat. Only cowards and defeated men and slaves enjoyed those things; men without women, or men who were no good with women, or the women themselves – women like her, without a proper man. She laughed in anticipation, nowadays, when they brought in the captives.

Sometimes she was almost fond of this place, almost felt she liked her grinning slave of a husband. Then she felt contempt for what she had become, and for this soft son of hers, always talking of flocks and herds – herds he had bred, not stolen! Flocks and herds were a man's right, to fight for, to drive off to his women in triumph, to eat up in great slaughters that darkened the sky with smoke, soaked the earth with fat and left whole armies bloated and belching. Her son nursed his flocks like a mother her children. Worse, he had taken to grubbing in the soil like a wild pig or a pink, sweaty-faced settler from the valleys beyond the forests. In this land that his father had burned, he scraped at the soil and grew corn like any farmer! Think of it, when it was his inheritance to ride out in front of the wide horde under its great cloud of dust, leading and slaying men, terrifying the long-nosed city-dwellers and making the Roman Caesar himself send emissaries to beg for mercy.

She had done well not to make herself more ridiculous, by telling people her secret – that this was the last son of Atilla the Hun, of whom men spoke in whispers, calling him the Scourge of God.

THE FARMER'S WIFE
Frank Shon

For a long time Thomas Robertson suffered from pains in the face. Sometimes they lasted ten minutes, sometimes half an hour, but when they happened his whole body was locked in an agonized paralysis. Then one day the condition suddenly and inexplicably worsened. The pains became more intense, like a steel bit drilling into the jawbone; and what was worse, they came more often. Between the attacks he became drowsy and feverish. So in the first week of June, which is a busy time for a fruit farmer, Thomas Robertson went into hospital.

Anna Robertson and their small son Tomas travelled up to Dundee every day to see him. At first they went in the evenings, too. Then Thomas Robertson said it did not make sense to come twice and thereafter they came only once, in the daytime. They sat with him for an hour or two in the warm hospital ward, the sun lying across the foot of his bed and his face in shadow, and then they went out into the fresh air and enjoyed themselves. Now, Anna Robertson did not use the time as you might expect. She went nowhere special, saw no one and did nothing illicit while her husband was out of the way. She simply enjoyed the sensation of being – at long last – alone. Of course the boy was with her, but that was just the same as being by herself. For she still thought of him as part of her, as though the cord connecting them for nine months had never been cut. She performed all the necessary little daily tasks with a new pleasure, and was happy that he should be there.

In the mornings they walked down the length of the raspberry field, past the pickers with their children, past the tractor with the scales on it, all the way down to the yard at the bottom where there was a little office. There were the shipments of fruit out to the factories to be kept track of, occasional phone-calls to make or answer, payment schedules to be kept up, and other matters connected with the crop. But usually they could finish at twelve. Willy the foreman looked after everything else and let her know well in advance when more money would be needed to pay the pickers. In the winter Willy was a drinker, but in the summer he could be relied on absolutely. And always little Tomas was with his mother. When they went into Arbroath to pick up some money he helped her carry the bags.

When they were finished in the office they walked back up the field to the house at the top and had lunch. It was a beautiful June and they nearly always ate outside. From the back of the house you could look out and see all the way down to the coast. There was nothing but fields all the way, greens and yellows, rising and falling. There was no wind and the sun blazed on the flagstones. They lay in it like a hot bath and fell under its spell. And there they would stay until a look at her watch told Anna it was time for them to go up to the hospital. Sometimes the boy pretended to be asleep. Then she would shake his little naked shoulder gently as he lay in the big canvas chair and they would go into the house. They dressed, she combed his hair for him, and they left.

Visiting time lasted two hours in the afternoon. Sometimes she took him a book, but more often a newspaper. Thomas Robertson wanted to keep in touch with the world. Above all, he didn't want to let go of it. So every day he asked his wife how business had been, if the fruit was of good quality, if Willy was doing his job properly without himself there to keep an eye on him; he asked details of the volume of fruit picked the day before and what parts of the field had yielded the most, what were not quite ripe yet. Usually all this took up at least the first half-hour. Thomas Robertson was visibly pleased when she did not have the answer to a question immediately to hand; it reassured him that the business could not really function properly without him. He also took a certain pleasure, now more than ever, from the fact that his wife was younger than himself. She was tanned from the sun, and her hair, which she wore long, had lighter streaks of brown in it. She looked strong and healthy. And sometimes when he pretended to listen to her he cast a furtive little glance around the ward to see if the other men were looking at his wife. Often they were.

Thomas Robertson, from his wife's point of view, looked different. He was a big man, still powerful for his age. Yet there was something in his features that suggested a new delicacy, even fragility, as if the sum of his existence had in some ineffable way diminished. Certainly there were noticeable physical changes. His face seemed a little thinner; some of the colour had gone out of his cheeks. But it was in his eyes that she saw the greatest and most subtle change. For despite his exhibition of acuity, in his eyes there had been a peculiar softening. They sparkled darkly with a lustre she had never seen in them before.

She took in his features with occasional glances while he looked elsewhere. And then it came to her clearly, even as he whispered that he missed her and gave her his suggestive smile, that this figure sitting up in bed issuing his orders and asking questions was nothing other than an old man. For a moment she resisted the idea, then it drew in the man that had been and swallowed him forever. And just as a physical change in someone's appearance takes an initial moment of adjustment before it is accepted, it took Anna only a short time to take in and accept this alteration. The new man was born, the old forgotten. And in bed with half his beard shorn off, proudly wearing the silk pyjamas he bought himself the Christmas before, the new man was suddenly rather absurd.

He leaned over from the bed and said: 'What is it, Tomas?' The boy had been staring at him. But now he said nothing, only looked back to his mother who was sitting on the side of the bed. 'It's the beard,' she said. 'He hasn't seen you without the beard before.' Thomas Robertson said nothing but smiled, and looked at them together, his wife and son. The boy had put his hand on her lap.

Afterwards they went back home. When the business for the day was finished Anna Robertson liked to sit outside in the warm evening with a magazine. There was a big rectangular pool, not deep, which Thomas Robertson had stocked with ornamental fish. About two weeks after he went into hospital it was the brief focus of attention. Anna had drifted into a half-sleep in the canvas chair. Thomas was playing in a little fenced area full of sand. Then all at once there was some splashing and Anna sat up, abruptly. Her dog, a Jack Russell bitch, was in the middle of the pool, jumping and snapping at the water with its sharp little muzzle. The level of the water was low because the pump had broken down and the cycle of drainage and replenishment had stopped. The water had simply drained down to the level of the outlet and stayed there. The dog went after the fish, which had nowhere to go, and because the level of the water was so low it was catching them.

Anna went over to the pool and shouted, but of course the dog ignored her. For the dog knew she did not care about the fish. And there was even something in her voice, a tiny element, that suggested she was only half serious. Then Anna lost interest and at the same moment saw that the boy had come over to the other side of the pool and now stood there, laughing. There was the splashing, gulping sound of the dog killing the fish and behind it the sound of his laughter. And then she found herself laughing along with him. When it was over the dog climbed out of the water and skulked over to a corner. The last of the fish floated on their sides in the dirty green water, their orange and black bodies glistening in the evening sunlight, except where they had been torn.

When she told him about the fish Thomas Robertson didn't shout, as she had expected him to. He didn't even seem angry. He simply nodded and lay back on the upright pillows. His face, from being thin, had become swollen. He said dreamily that the doctors did not understand what was happening to him, but that it was getting worse. The best theory was that the jaw had been fractured some years before and that this fracture had become the seat of the infection. But exactly what it had been infected with they were unable to say. The treatment, likewise, was uncertain. And then he said once, in a quiet, desperate voice, 'I'm scared . . .' and Anna touched the sleeve of his pyjamas. But she could bring herself to do nothing more. And she knew that beneath the pity that glowed momentarily, there was nothing in her heart for this sick creature. She felt awkward, almost embarrassed by him, as if he were a stranger. The quiet human drama of it shocked her, as though it were something extraordinarily vulgar, inappropriate. She looked at him now, stroking the top of his hand with the tip of her finger, and she saw the dull, animal fear in his eyes.

She sat in a chair beside the bed, just as the boy had done all along. Thomas Robertson's interest in the outside world had collapsed. No more exhibitions of acuity. The newspapers she had brought him every day lay unread in the locker by his bed. A shadow lay across his puffed-up face like a blanket. Once he opened his eyes wide and looked at her with a frightened, accusing look, then at the boy, his head starting up off the pillow. Then he sank back down and did not wake again that afternoon. Anna and Tomas hurried silently away half an hour before the end of visiting time, oppressed by the weight of the shadow that was on him, by the unbearable warmth of the place.

It was late in the afternoon but the water at the coast was still warm. She ran into it with the boy and swam for a few minutes. That was long enough, long enough to wash off the uncleanliness that clung to them both from the place. It hung on them like a tangible odour; the shadow of death had settled on her like a colourless film and must be scrubbed off with the salt water and the sharp little breeze that had sprung up at the edge of the water. Tomas wasn't a good swimmer yet and had no natural aptitude for it. He feared the water and when he could no longer feel the bottom with his feet he looked to her for help. She saw his frightened little face above the water and once, when he got into difficulties, stepped forward and took him in her arms and guided him back towards the shore. Yet not before waiting, just for a moment, but for a real interval to pass before she went to him. He saw her wait, saw her watch him struggling there, hung in the water like a helpless, unearthly thing, and for a minute he hated her. Then she took him in her arms and walked with him to the shallower water, stroking his head, talking to him, smiling. It had been washed off. They were clean now, awakened again into the daylight and the world of life. And little Tomas seemed to know what it meant, this moment of loneliness when she held back from him, that it was their bond. When they were home again and standing under the shower he shut his eyes. And as she washed his hair, he unconsciously leaned against her.

They operated on Thomas Robertson's jaw the next day. They scraped off a small amount of bone and took it away for examination, then stitched up the hole and sent him back to the ward. When Anna visited him she was genuinely shocked. He lay back, his arms very still at his sides over the top of the coverlet. His head lay resting on its good side so that the side of the jaw that had been operated on, thoroughly bandaged, was facing upward. His eyes were open, but they were smoky. When she asked him how he was feeling he could not bring himself to speak; he simply raised his open left hand a little in a gesture of resignation.

Now that it was gone, Anna realized that the beard had made him look younger. It had been light brown in colour and slightly pointed, and had given something vaguely elegant to his face. Now that it was gone and the lower half of his face was obscured beneath the bandage, she saw the incipient decay of his features and charted the path they would surely take before long. The outline of the eyesockets announced itself plainly as she sat there looking at him; the wrinkles, usually palliated by the healthy colour of the skin stood out starkly from the pale background tissue; the eyebrows were grey, quite suddenly and completely grey, and the hair above would follow before long. The life seemed to be seeping out of him like a fluid even as she watched, and Anna found herself disgusted by the palpable corruption. For a minute she had been standing over him, looking down into his eyes. And as she leaned over she was aware of a finger on his left hand coiling through her palm. She wanted to withdraw from it but could not. Simply could not. She looked down at the quivering digit that now linked itself to her index finger, so insistently. Anna looked around the ward. Still the finger tugged at her, and there was something suddenly indecent in the gesture which revolted her. It gripped her tightly, a gesture, a symbol of their continuity – he and she. 'If it happens,' he whispered. 'If I go . . .' But she wrenched her hand free before he could finish.

It was raining outside. Anna and Tomas (for he always went with her) came away from the hospital feeling exhausted. They drove back to the house, about twenty minutes away, and immediately went for a walk. They walked down the long field, following the line of the pine wood. The rain hung quietly about the trees and sometimes woodpigeon flew out as they passed by. The ground was full of muddy brown pools. Anna had pulled down the hood on her jacket so that her head would be soaked, and Tomas did the same. He walked beside her, stabbing at the pools with a piece of stick he had picked up. The field was empty and the wide rows of raspberry canes ran down its length like ribs. The smell of the pine wood and the rain soaked through the air and she breathed it deeply, like a tonic.

When they had married, six years before, the difference in their ages had seemed unimportant. In itself it presented no great obstacle to fulfillment. Thomas Robertson was still healthy, he could still father children. And whatever had to be endured in the making, a child was worth it. Indeed Tomas was the reward for that nightly sacrifice she had made of herself on the altar-bed; for the solemn rigour with which she had enacted their conjugal absurdities. Tomas was what it had all been for, and without him it would have all been for nothing. The man had made the boy and now the man must wither.

The next day there was a marked improvement in Thomas Robertson's condition. When Anna and the boy came he was sitting up in bed looking at a newspaper. 'It was the drugs,' he explained. 'They had me pumped full of drugs.' He spoke indistinctly because of the bandages but his voice was firm again. She asked him if he was in much pain. 'Not much,' he said cheerily. 'They gave me something for it.' His features had regained their animation. The future was where it belonged again, no longer written on his face. Like a sacred text, it had been glimpsed once and put away.

'I can only vaguely remember your visit,' he went on. 'You held my hand, didn't you?'

'Yes. I wasn't sure whether to call the doctor, you looked so bad . . .'

'I am glad you were there with me,' he said. He squeezed her hand. As usual Tomas was sitting on the chair by the bed. While his parents were talking he looked around the ward. An old man lay in the next bed and he winked manfully at the boy. Tomas looked around the beds, where clusters of visitors were gathered. The sounds of their voices mingled with the soft music coming from an old-fashioned radio speaker positioned above the doorway of the ward. Slowly he became aware of something, a voice talking to him, saying his name. He turned. 'What about it, Tomas?' His father's eyes were smiling. His mother, looking faintly embarrassed, leaned down and took the boy's hand. 'What about it, Tomas, are you missing me?' Tomas looked at his mother, as if he had not quite understood the question. The expression hurt her, and she felt a sudden surge of shame as though she had failed him. 'Of course he misses you,' she said, not looking at her husband. She had led the boy forward, encouraged him; she could not turn back on him now. The lie must come from her lips. 'He talks of nothing else but when his father will be well . . .'

The father leaned over and ruffled the boy's combed hair with his big hand.

'What have you been doing with me out of the way, eh?'

'Nothing unusual,' said Anna. 'In the office with me. Then we go for walks, don't we?' She looked at Tomas but he didn't answer; he was looking down at the coverlet.

'I dreamt the dog had killed all my fish,' Thomas Robertson said. 'Saw it quite clearly in my head.'

'I told you that a couple of days ago, before your operation.'

'What, all of them?'

Anna nodded. 'We were in the kitchen when we heard the splashes. By the time we got outside it was too late.'

THE FARMER'S WIFE

He was quiet now, and Anna could see the cloud settle over his features. 'Please,' she said. 'Never mind about the fish. Tell me what the doctors say.'

The cloud began to move away. 'They think they're close to cracking it.'

'You mean they haven't yet?'

'Not yet, no. I get injections twice a day, and pills.'

She coughed. 'Do they say how long – before they get it under control?'

'They don't know, but soon now. Definitely soon.'

Anna nodded thoughtfully. Thomas Robertson thought she looked unsettled. 'What is it?'

'Oh, nothing really,' she said. 'I'd just like some idea . . .'

'Don't worry about me,' he said, interrupting her. 'I'm on the mend. Look at me.' She smiled complaisantly, and he thought: perhaps this has not been for nothing, perhaps this illness of mine had brought us a little closer together . . .

Over the next few days Thomas Robertson's improvement continued, so that at the end of the end of his fourth week in hospital the doctors began to discuss his discharge. They did not know exactly what the illness was which had overtaken him, but they had faith in the treatment they were prescribing. Every day when Anna Robertson and Tomas went up to the hospital to visit him they were told that it would not be long before he would be home. And indeed every day he looked a little better. The colour returned to his face and although the bandage remained on his jaw the swelling had all but disappeared. Then at the end of the fifth week a date was set for his discharge, to be the following Friday.

The last few days drained quickly away and, taking on a fugitive quality like the last days before an execution, were spoiled. A shadow had been cast over the woman and her son. On their walks the silence that absorbed them was no longer contented, but filled with frustration. The three little worry-lines were never very far from Anna Robertson's forehead.

Tomas became moody. Their equilibrium had been fractured, disturbed by the impending presence of a third. Two was a harmony, an evenness; three was discordant, an oddity. Not even a question of will, she thought, not even of demands. It would simply be the man's presence, the presence of a third element which would destroy their happiness and their perfection.

The boy didn't hold her hand any more, but lingered behind. Often she had to stop and wait for him, and when she looked at him she saw in his child's face all the sullen resistance of a human being to the inevitable undoing of life. She stepped forward and put a hand on his neck and leaning down, kissed the crown of his head. He, unmoved, stood rigid and unassailable, receiving her offering like a priest or a child-monarch, and despised her. And when he looked up into her face his eyes were cold and full of that accusing male pain she had come to know. And then she knew their lives would return to what they had been. The solitude that bound them together had already begun to dissolve. The dream was nearly over. She could feel the flow of it, carrying her irrevocably towards the future. There would be nothing apocalyptic, of course, only the slow dripping away of her life. If she had had inside her what she saw in those hard little blue eyes it might have been different. But she did not. And she had known all along that she did not. So now she must begin to forget the dream. For grown human beings can forget with remarkable facility. But not a child. A child does not forget, nor forgive.

On a clear day you could see the house from far away, even out to sea. Sometimes the fishermen noticed it on their way back to harbour, a long low structure like a Spanish hacienda, curiously misplaced and white against the dark country that surrounded it. For there was nothing near it, nothing for half a mile down the little tree-lined road. There were only the rows upon rows of raspberry canes, pared back now and tied to their wires and posts for the coming winter. At the bottom of the field was the yard, with its loading-shed where the fruit was sent out in barrels, and the house where Willy the foreman lived, and the little office. After it reached the yard the little road went off towards Arbroath.

There had already been a lot of rain and the earth was black and heavy with it. There had been strong winds too but these had not damaged the canes because of the narrow strip of pine wood that shielded the seaward side of the field for most of its length. Back up at the top of the field, in front of the white house, there was a potato field. It ran down from the house and stopped when it came to a couple of old wooden sheds. Every year the pickers used the sheds to shelter in. It was late September now and Thomas Robertson had begun turning the earth over with a tractor. He ploughed away from the house so that the pickers who followed behind would have the advantage of the slope. The farthest and lower end of the field was damper than the rest and he knew the potatoes there were often rotten. So he always had the pickers start on the high ground, and they went along on their hands and knees in the sodden grooves clawing potatoes into baskets. Many of the pickers, whole families sometimes, had been picking Thomas Robertson's fruit in the summer. Many of them had also come to his field for ten years or more and knew Thomas Robertson quite well by now. They knew he didn't like to work them too hard, as Geddes down the road did, and that he could be trusted to pay them on time, which Geddes could not. Thomas Robertson didn't pay exceptionally well – not even as well as Geddes. But he didn't pay badly either, and because they could trust him and did not have to work too hard with him they remained his pickers and returned to him every year.

Thomas Robertson was glad to be working again, especially to be working like this on his land, as a man should. His jaw was healed and his beard had grown over the small interruption to the line of his face. He could almost forget the sudden phenomenon that had nearly carried him off. Of course it had been a close-run thing. Even the doctors said so, in unguarded moments. Understandably, they took the credit for a successful treatment. But when the question arose – as it did more than once – of what the vanquished illness had actually been called, they smiled at the innocence of the question, like possessors of some profound truth, muttered in their mystic language and moved on, still smiling.

This had annoyed him at the time. He never could bear to be patronized, and besides, he wanted something specific to tell his friends. Yet now, sitting on the tractor with the wind against him and the damp cloying odour of the turned earth in his nostrils, Thomas Robertson was glad that they did not have so much as a name for it. An aberration, a moment of chaos, a mere accidental gust had blown his life off balance. But he had recovered now. The time that had seemed so very extended while he was in hospital had miraculously snapped back into perspective, so that now he could look back on it as a short spell of treatment. Six weeks, that was all. It didn't sound much when you said it. It had been just a short interruption to his continuity, nothing more.

So it was that after only a couple of months he had begun to bury the whole matter. In another few months his memory of the event would start to fall apart, and in a few years he might come to deny that it ever occurred at all. Better by far, he said to himself, to get on with the business of making a living. It was inadvisable, he thought, to 'dwell' on matters, a habit he regarded with deep suspicion. Often he would say that introspection was the enemy of achievement. It was something he had read somewhere and he made the pronouncement with the certain air of authority that farmers and businessmen in general often adopt on the subject of 'getting things done'. Thomas Robertson was a doer, not a thinker, never an intellectual, and he didn't mind saying so. Not that he was verbose: most often when he made any comments on such matters he addressed them to himself.

And yet despite his manful wariness of such things he could not, as he ate his lunch, stop his mind from turning on the night before. Why had she wept like that, he wondered, afterwards? It always made him feel uneasy when it happened and some vague guilt bubbled to the surface of his mind for a while, a few hours perhaps. But guilt for what? That was always when he became confused and secretly rather irritated with her. After all it was supposed to be a pleasurable thing, certainly nothing for a grown woman to cry about. For a moment he considered the question from a technical point of view (it always helped him find his bearings in matters of this sort – that is to say, matters of some awkwardness). Had he done anything wrong, anything clumsy? He remembered as best as he could and could think of nothing . . . no, nothing wrong in that department. Then he thought of how her dog had died, killed on the road outside, and she had cried then, not just at the time but for days and weeks after. There was no doubt about it, she was a cryer. Some people are just like that, he mused. The sort who cry at weddings out of happiness. And the idea triggered something in his mind and he thought, that is it. It was after all the first time since . . . yes, he had moved back into the main bedroom now, and with a vengeance. She had cried from happiness. And he heard again the stifled little moans she had made the night before, and laughed to himself. Women, he thought. Women . . . and carried on eating his lunch.

EXPERIENCE
Alexander McCall Smith

He parked his car at the end of Long Street. It was a dangerous area, at night at least, and he knew that cars could disappear – spirited away to somewhere on the Cape Flats, to be resprayed overnight. And it was really no good going to the police – what could they do? They had riots to contend with, burnings, knifings; all those unsolved murders he read about. They might even ask: 'What were you doing there, sir? Surely you know what that area's like?'

'Taking a walk. I like that part of Cape Town. The old houses, you know.'

That would bring sniggers from some pimply-faced young constable, fresh from some dorp in the Karroo, who would think that three months in the police had taught him everything about human nature.

He turned away from the car and began to walk down the street. It was quiet in that part – one or two antique shops which had been too run-down to move on when the area went to the dogs, one or two private houses of people who were too old to move, or who couldn't move because their affairs were too private for the scrutiny of lawyers.

A man standing in the shadows of his front garden coughed, and spoke to him in Afrikaans.

'Ja, it's a fine evening, isn't it?'

He paused. It was one of the older people, one of the locals.

'We'll get a berg wind one day, though. I can feel it.'

The man in the garden moved slightly out of the shadows. Now, only half obscured by the leaves of an undisciplined bougainvillaea, his face showed, scarred, lined, as if a geological catastrophe had marked a landscape.

'I spent most of my days in the mines,' the man said. 'Up

in Johannesburg. I was a blaster for forty years, you know.'

'A good life.'

The man hawked and spat.

'The mines aren't the same now. They let anybody handle gelignite. Anybody.'

He made a few non-committal comments. Nothing was the same. The whole country was like that. There was no end in sight. Then he continued down the street, watching carefully, his heart thudding within him.

There was a bar coming up on a corner. The door opened out on to the street and he could smell the fumes of beer coming from within, a stale, dank smell. Above the door there was a sign: 'Lion Beer – A man's drink. All Africa thirsts for it.' Below, two men stood in the entrance, engaged in a heated discussion. They glanced at him and then turned back to their argument. As he walked past he heard the words: 'She told me you said she could have the other place. You promised, years back, man. She didn't forget . . .' And then, slurred, 'A man changes his mind.'

A man changes his mind. He didn't have to go on with this. He could turn round and walk back to his car. He could go back and exchange a few words with that man in his yard and then climb into his car and be home within half an hour. It would be easy.

But he went on. The doorways were beginning now, with their unmistakable invitations. He paused in front of the first one, but walked on – too soon. Then, suddenly he was abreast of another and there was a woman standing inside.

'Sir?'

He stopped and looked slowly in her direction.

'You got a light, Sir?' She showed the cigarette between her fingers. It had been half smoked and then stumped out. She watched him.

'Ag, it's only a stompie, I know that. But I don't see why you should waste good tobacco, do you?'

He reached into his pocket and took out a box of matches. Then, striking one, he moved towards her, the flame cupped in his hands.

She put the cigarette in her mouth, and held it there between the index finger and thumb of one hand. With her other hand, she steadied the match.

'You've got those shakes,' she said lightly, exhaling the smoke. 'Your hand.'

He dropped the spent match and raised his eyes to look at her. She was somewhere in her late twenties, he thought; maybe thirty. She was of mixed race, but there was more European in her than African or Malay. She would have an Afrikaans name, he thought, from some Boer farmer generations ago who defied his Church and sought comfort outside the pale. She would be called Coetzee, or de Beer, or something like that.

She returned his gaze, slightly quizzically, and he wondered whether these encounters always went like this. Was he doing the right thing? Was there something to be said, some formula of words which could make it all much simpler, more natural.

'Can I help you, then?'

It was a parody of what a shopgirl might say, but he felt relieved, and answered: 'Yes.'

For a moment she did nothing, but then she flicked the cigarette into the street. He watched it roll into the gutter and lie there, glowing.

'Come upstairs,' she said, stepping back into the hall. 'That's where my place is. Upstairs.'

He had no idea of how such women lived, but had not expected homeliness. Had it been darkened, with a red light glowing, and velvet wallpaper he would not have been surprised. But this room was comfortable, as a bedroom in any home might be. There were photographs on the wall; pictures of a man and a woman and a young boy. In a vase near the window there was a single poinsettia now on the point of wilting.

He looked at the bed but, when he saw her watching him, he turned away sharply and sat down in one of the two easy chairs. It was threadbare, with grease-stains where heads had rested, and he suddenly thought of the dirt that all this involved. Bodies. Dirt. Sweat. Effusions. He closed his eyes.

'I can make some coffee,' she said. 'I don't mind coffee on these hot nights.'

'Yes.' He felt grateful for the ordinariness of the suggestion. 'Yes, I would like that.'

She gave him a mug which was chipped, but seemed reasonably clean. She had a small cup, which she drained quickly.

'Have you got any family then?'

He could think of nothing else to say, although this seemed wildly inappropriate.

The question did not surprise her.

'A son. That's him in that picture.'

'A nice-looking boy.'

'He's just fourteen now.'

There was a silence. She put down her cup and then rose from her chair. She stood beside him and laid a hand on his shoulder.

'Some men just come to talk, you know.' Her voice was low, as if she were imparting a confidence. 'I don't mind that. I can help that way too.'

He said nothing. He had heard that these women performed that role; that some of them were skilful psychotherapists, and cheaper than doctors.

'I'd like to talk to you.'

She smiled. 'We can talk on the bed. You sit there . . . come on . . . There's nothing to be nervous about. We just talk. That's all.'

'You see, I don't really come from Cape Town. I live here now, but I've spent all my time up in Swaziland. I was Chief Magistrate up there for years. Before independence, after independence; I carried on. My father was from Scotland. He went to Kenya and I was born there. Then we came further south. They sent me to school in South Africa because it was close by. I was at a good school in Natal, which was like an English public school. You know what those are like?'

She nodded, but he could see that she had no idea.

'I went to university here – Cape Town – and then went

back to Swaziland. I was magistrate in Siteki, then Manzini. Then they made me Chief Magistrate and I lived in Mbabane. I had an official house, with a driver and a flag in the garden, and I sat in court all day and listened to people lying, lying, lying.'

'People lie,' she said. 'All the time.' She shook her head. 'You tell the truth and nobody believes you because everybody's doing so much lying.'

'And then I couldn't stand it any more and I took early retirement. That was two years ago, when I was just fifty. I had money which my father had left me and it was more than enough to live on, so I came down here. How could I leave Africa?'

He paused, and was silent. She looked at him, an eyebrow raised. She was used to talk of wives who did not understand; of children who were tearing their father's heart apart; of mistresses who had turned cold, who were losing their enthusiasm; but there was none of this.

'So why are you unhappy?' she asked. 'What's wrong?'

He stared at her, wondering whether he could trust her. He had decided that he liked her – there was something matter-of-fact about her which appealed to him, but one could like without trusting. And yet, if he did not confide in her, then he knew that he would never get round to doing anything about it. It was January now; June would be upon them in no time.

She glanced at her watch.

'You don't have to say anything if you don't want to. But this is a working night for me . . .'

He rose to his feet and for a few moments she misunderstood his movements; when he turned around he saw that she had begun to unbutton her blouse.

'No,' he said sharply. 'Don't. I have to be going.'

He reached for his wallet from his back pocket and took out several banknotes. Her eyes followed them as he passed them across to her.

'You don't have to give me that much,' she said. 'Not just for that. You could get much more for that.'

She made a sign with her hands, a crude sign, which he ignored.

'Can I come back and see you again?'

She smiled.

'You can come here any time, listen. Any time!'

In the corridor, she touched him on his stomach and then let her hand slide down his body. He brushed her hand away, said goodnight, and walked down the stairs. At the doorway he hesitated for a moment; somebody was walking past, but the footsteps faded and he was out in Long Street again.

The next day was a Sunday. He had promised to meet Camilla at noon; he would pick her up at the house and they would drive out towards Cape Point. She was ready for him, dressed in lemon slacks and a light silk blouse. She kissed him as she got into the car.

'I want to swim,' she said. 'That's the only thing to do in this heat.'

He nodded. 'The whole of Cape Town thinks the same.'

'Can we go to Hout Bay? There won't be too many people there.'

He agreed. They had the choice of two oceans – the Indian and the Atlantic. The Atlantic would be cooler, more refreshing.

They travelled along the oak-lined road that led over the neck of the mountains. When they reached the bay they parked behind a sand dune and walked down to the beach. Somebody had been riding a horse along the sand and there were hoof-prints tracing down to the edge of the water. She threw her head back, closed her eyes, and let the sea breeze ruffle though her hair.

'Gorgeous. Gorgeous.'

He looked at her, noticing the place where the years of exposure to the sun had dried the skin into tiny lines. She opened her eyes and looked back at him, smiling. He thought: I hardly deserve you. She thought: you can have everything, Jack, everything. I want only you; companionship; to grow older together.

She slipped her hand into his.

'Serious today? Thinking?'

'Nothing in particular.' (Long Street). 'Or maybe just about how happy I am . . . now.' ('People lie. All the time.')

They sat down on the beach. She had a woven mat with her, which she spread out on the fine white sand. They did not touch one another; her leg moved against his, unintentionally; he recoiled.

They swam later; he half-heartedly, she enthusiastically. He watched her plunging into the waves, shrieking as the cold swells lifted her off her feet and tossed her, bundled her downwards. She called out: 'Come on! Come on!' and something else which the waves swallowed.

Drying on the beach, allowing the wind to tease the salt off his skin, he looked out over the waves, over the green of the sea. There was nothing between them and the frozen south; just the ocean, cold, limitless, patrolled by the lonely birds. No home for us, he thought, anywhere.

They lunched in a hotel in Constantia, in a dining room which looked out over vineyards. The floor of the dining room was made of thick oak planks, which squeaked as the waiters walked over them. They drank a chilled white wine, which the toothless wine waiter had recommended to them as the best in the cellar, and then, on the verandah, under domestic vines, they sat and watched the horses grazing in the paddock.

'This is so peaceful,' she said. 'I love peace and quiet.'

He wanted to say: 'It's built on sand,' but there was no point in stating the obvious and equally little point in gratuitous cruelty.

When he dropped her at her house, she kissed him lightly on the cheek. He patted her forearm and smiled.

'Tuesday evening,' she said. 'Bridge – as usual?'

He said: 'I wouldn't miss it for the world.'

Then he watched her walk up the driveway, past the beds of roses and the orchid house, to the icing-white housefront with its tall wooden shutters and its air of wealth and stability. They had decided to live there, after the wedding, after June.

*

'You came back?' She smiled at him. 'I knew you would.'

He did not want to stand in the doorway and so he jerked his head in the direction of the floor above. Once in the room, he took off his jacket and flung it over the back of the chair. He felt less awkward now and he felt no embarrassment in taking off his shoes and sitting on the bed, leaning against the headboard.

'You got a wife?' she asked.

'No. But I'm going to get married.'

His answer surprised her.

'Soon?'

'A few months.'

She looked at him with curiosity.

'I can tell what you're wondering,' he said. 'You're wondering why I'm here if I'm going to get married soon.'

She nodded her head. 'I was.'

The levity he had felt on entering the room now seemed to desert him. He felt his heart thudding again, just as it had done when he had first walked down Long Street. It was not going to be easy.

'I told you about myself last time,' he began. 'You remember what I said?'

'About Swaziland? About your being a magistrate?'

'Yes. About that.'

She nodded. 'I remember.'

He reached for a cigarette, lit it, and handed it to her.

'I lived by myself there, you know. I had no woman.'

She stared at him uncomprehendingly. Then a glimmer of a smile appeared around her lips.

'I mean never,' he said quietly. 'I never had women.'

There. He had said it. The whole pretence of masculine worldliness had been destroyed by those few, honest words. From the smutty conversation in the dormitory of the boarding school in Natal to the double-edged jokes of the Manzini club bar; all that was shown to be based on a lie, like everything else.

She tugged at the cigarette and then blew the acrid smoke into the air above the bed.

'I have lots of men like that,' she said quietly. 'They come here all the time. All their lives they talk, talk, talk, but they've never known a woman. You're not alone.'

He raised his eyes to hers.

'I don't care about it,' he said. 'But now . . . now I'm getting married, and she had a husband before, and I . . .'

She leant across and laid her hand on his wrist.

'You don't have to worry. Really, you don't. There's nothing to worry about.'

At bridge they played as partners, as usual. They played slowly, interspersing the game with conversation, as she called it, or gossip, as he called it. After the years of widowhood, his presence imbued her with a feeling of completeness and security. Often he would look up from his cards to see her smiling at him, as if sharing a private joke. He felt embarrassed lest the others notice; he did not relish the thought of the remarks that he knew would be being made by others, remarks about late-flowering love. Yet secretly, he basked in her affection. After years of being peripheral to the emotional lives of others, here was something in which he was central. A line of poetry, half-remembered, haunted him: 'Bless you, darling, I have found myself in you.' It doesn't matter that this all falls down about our ears, or that nobody wants us – I have found myself.

The next day, they went to an auction and bid for a writing bureau. It had belonged to a successful Jewish lawyer who had left for Australia. They paid more than the valuation, but that did not matter; it was perfect for the room they planned to turn into a study, a room where he could keep his papers, all those records of his cases which he intended one day to write up – medicine murders, internecine feuds amongst Swazi chiefs, long-forgotten passions. She signed the cheque, refusing to allow him to contribute.

'A present, Jack. A present.'

He kissed her, closing his eyes, breathing the expensive perfume. In his mind he was in the room in Long Street, in the heat of the night, with the long, honey-coloured body beside him and every touch and gesture remembered.

She said: 'You seem distracted by something.'
'Of course not.'
She took his tie between her fingers and straightened it.
'We could go for coffee in the square. We could look around some of the stalls.'

He nodded, and they walked out of the auction room into the light of the street; then past the Anglican Cathedral, where a man stood at the doorway, holding up a placard: 'Pray for them. Pray for the imprisoned, the suffering. Pray for our land.'

He read the message, and then he looked away. What was the use? What was the use of prayers against whips and guns? And where would the whips and the guns be in the new order?

That night he saw her again. She knew his name now, or rather she knew his first name. She talked about her son and his plans – he was bright, and she was paying for his education. She was encouraging him in his ambition to be a dental technician because whatever happened, whatever went wrong, there would always be false teeth to fit.

He only half listened. It struck him as bizarre that somebody could aspire to be a dental technician, or get vicarious satisfaction through a son's aspiration along those lines. He could think only of her body; of the feel of her in embrace with him; of the daring, abandoned gestures; of the refutation, in each and every moment they were together, of the whole distorted, crippling edifice imposed on their sad, neurotic country.

He saw her every week after that, always on the same evening. She showed him a book she had, but he became angry with her and said:

'Put that filthy thing away!'

She was chastened.

'It's just what people do. I thought you wanted to learn.'

He stared at her, began to say something, but checked himself. As he left that night, he slipped an envelope into her hands.

'I won't be back. I'm sorry.'

She smiled.
'I'm used to saying goodbye. I say goodbye every day.'

In June, after the wedding, they went to a hotel up in the mountains. It was cool, and the trees were bare. He took a walk before breakfast each morning, and again in the evening while she had her bath before dinner.

'You seem so distant,' she said over a pre-dinner drink. 'Not that I'm complaining! I like you just as you are.'

He averted his gaze and picked up his glass.
'I like to think.'
'About what? About Swaziland days?'
'Yes.'

About Long Street; about how she had appeared so suddenly, completely naked; and the memory made him ache, for he had been shown a secret, and lost it, and he feared he would never again find what had been vouchsafed him.

Then, in November, when it was getting hot again, they walked through the gardens in the city centre and stopped for coffee under the giant palm trees.

'Look at that ridiculous gull!' she said.

He glanced across at the gull which had perched on the head of the statue of Cecil John Rhodes, and then his heart leapt. She was there, walking slowly up the path, smartly dressed, carrying a small shopping bag.

'Rhodes had no sense of humour. He wouldn't have liked that.'

But he wasn't listening.

'I'm going to stretch my legs,' he said. 'I've got a cramp coming on.'

He rose from the table and walked away. She couldn't see him yet, but would soon; once they were screened by a hedge, and he could speak.

'Hello.'

She gave a start, and then a smile.

'I've been shopping,' she said. 'It's my boy's birthday tomorrow. Fifteen! Would you believe it?'

He smiled weakly. He did not want to discuss the boy.

'I've thought about you every day,' he said. 'There hasn't been a day gone past – not a day – when I haven't thought of you.'

She looked at him curiously. 'You're only telling me that.'

'No, I'm not. Every day. Every night. I remember everything we did. Everything.'

So she said: 'You're the one who used to . . .' She faltered.

He looked at her aghast.

'I'm sorry,' she said. 'I know so many people. Of course I know who you are. Ag . . .' She smacked at her head. 'My stupid brain always letting me down. I should get a doctor to fix it one day.'

He made his way back to the table, and sat down.

She said: 'You've had a shock? Are you all right?'

He replied: 'It's nothing. Only . . .'

The palm fronds moved above them. There was a warm wind from the ocean and it would soon blow the mountain clear of cloud.

'I was thinking,' she said. 'I was thinking while you were away – shall we play bridge again tonight?'

'Of course. There's nothing I'd like better.'

'Do you mean that?'

He wanted to answer: 'No. I don't. I want to go to a room I know in Long Street.' But he knew that he couldn't say that, because we have to lie, and lie.

LETTERS FROM ANOTHER PLACE
Esther Woolfson

July 1982

How the hell should I begin this? Sir? Dear Sir? OK. Dear Sir . . . *Dear Sir, I feel I can no longer.* But I have always felt that I can no longer. This time, though, I can't. I can no longer . . . *serve with an army, the actions of which.* They are actions, oh yes, they're actions all right. Of this fact, there's no possible doubt. Unfortunately, I cannot find the words to describe these actions and I wonder if such words exist in any language because they don't appear to exist in mine or in any other I know anything about. Perhaps it's just as well that they don't. The actions of which . . . *I abhor.* At this point, I should really say that I do realize that there must be more appropriate words than abhor but I can't bring one to mind at the moment so it will have to do. Abhor sounds so thin and insubstantial but what other word could cover so much ground? What other word could contain in a few letters the heat of the anger I feel which seems to have the power to strip my bones of flesh so that I walk about a skeleton? Flesh is what makes me human, that and certain activity of the brain over which I am denied control and since I am rendered no longer human and without flesh, I must be a skeleton and since that's all I am, I'm not much use to you, am I? Nor, do I have to say, do I wish to be of any use to you. Actions I abhor . . . *carried out for reasons I consider immoral.* There, now you can feel free to laugh. The word 'moral' or even 'immoral' always makes people here laugh. There you are. I present myself to you in full, skeletal naivety.

LETTERS FROM ANOTHER PLACE
February to August 1982

Camp Zafon

My dear Irit

How strange it seems to be writing to you again. One gets out of the habit and even a few days' leave seems to break the chain. It's something to do with coming to a new place I expect. It feels a bit like starting the whole, horrible business all over again, except that this time, it's winter.

The move was completed with the usual mixture of tedium and panic and I felt, again, the old familiar (and utterly loathsome) feeling of having to keep awake at any price.

In spite of my general reluctance to adapt myself to change, I have to say that it all looked magnificent at dawn this morning. The sun was bright, bright red and the mist rising from the hollows and valleys turned pink and then gold as it rose and dissipated. We have glimpses of snow and sea and mountains and while we settle in to get ready to do the various things which I assume we're here for, I have a deep sense of unease when I consider our proximity to places I'd rather be a lot further from.

I'll write again soon
Gavriel

* * *

Camp Zafon

Dear Irit

I've felt torn since my last leave having regretted, of course, my decision to go back with Ya'ariv the very moment it was made. I bitterly regretted that I wasn't coming back to Jerusalem to spend the time with you, and Ma and Pa. It's not that I didn't enjoy being at

Ya'ariv's, I did and since he's the one person here I can really talk to, I wanted to do something to please him.

It was lovely going to Safed, if a trifle disorientating. It made me reflect a bit on the nature of geography and how things are only north if one is south and vice versa. The bland assurance that Safed is a town in the far north will not appear with such complacency on my Grade 4 geography exam paper next time round, I can assure you. It made me think about the way countries see themselves – China calling itself the 'Middle Kingdom' while we all know very well that it's the Far East and us calling ourselves 'The Land' as if it's the only land and everything else is purely incidental and not really land at all (until we put our godly feet on it, anyway).

Do you remember the school trip to Safed? It still seems a place of mystery and medievalism. That feeling was increased somehow by the fact that Ya'ariv's father is a rabbi. Did I tell you that before? Anyway, that meant synagogue on Saturday, an unusual event in my life, as you know. Pa will mutter about 'the grip of the clerics' if I tell him. Ya'ariv's father didn't display any untoward tendency to grip, though, he's very thoughtful and liberal and concerned.

In the afternoon, Ya'ariv and I went for a long walk, up to the ruins of an Arab village, high, high up. It was very clear and we stood and looked in the direction we had come from, back over the grid squares of fields and fishponds, over borders and mountains and snow and sky. It was as if we were so high up that we had no identity at all, nothing which related to what happened in the distant world below, as if that world had no claim on us. I felt all my knowledge of who I was draining away from me, there, in what felt so much like someone else's place. Ya'ariv felt it too. We talked about the people from the village and what might have happened to them and where they might have gone.

Our talk make me feel more like a shadowy figure than I do usually – you know that feeling, that the process of following in others' footsteps and treading on layer upon layer of the past is stealing something of your own reality, turning you into a shadow. It's what we do here all the time, sheltering behind an army of shadows from the past so that I wonder what we'd be without the shadows. I don't know that I like thinking about that.

I was glad that if I couldn't be with you, I was with Ya'ariv. He's got this very dry, spare way of talking which gave me a chance to think – one thing that's difficult here. 'No 4988752, you have a dreamy look coming into your eyes, the kind of look that usually precedes cerebral activity. Cut it out now I say, we have no use for that sort of thing here.'

Ya'ariv has theories about the progress of events in the next few months. I suspect that his predictions are dreadful enough to be accurate. We shall no doubt see, in time, if he's right.

I'll have leave in three weeks, I think. Will you be at home that weekend? Write and let me know,
     Yours
     Gavriel

* * *

        Camp Zafon

Dear Irit
First of all, a big hello to the censor. That said, hello to you too. Thank you for writing so soon. You can't imagine how cheering it is when you do.

You're right, it is only a matter of time. I feel reconciled to it in a day to day sort of way but if I think about it enough, I'm deeply uneasy about the whole thing. I find I've got to call on all the reserves of energy and strength I've got and it's made me realize how much I owe to my parents for giving me some independence of mind. It really is only now that I see how visionary they are and how easy it must be just to bring your children up the same as everyone else. We're both lucky. When I was younger, I resented it and felt hard done by – a bit of a pariah in fact. Having parents who were different was a burden most people didn't seem to have. What a disgusting little conformist I must have been. Now, I see how valuable their world view is and how much broader a view they've given me than most people here seem to have. Its easy to appreciate how fantastic they are when most of the people you meet are so monumentally small.

Some mornings, Irit, I wake up and wish that I was Superman like just about everyone else around here. I wish I could go around like they do saying 'Why are we so clever?' and grinning and beating my chest, while all the time I'd be as content and as fucking brainless as they are. Amazing.

To be fair, there are some OK people here, people who take care not to be noticed. I work so hard at it that I expect to wake up some morning and find someone else climbing into my uniform not having noticed that I'm here.

Sometimes, I'd like to run amok with grass in my hair and nothing on. They'd think I was nuts and throw me out. Hang on, no, they wouldn't. They're all nuts themselves. They'd love me suddenly. Do you love me?

Gavriel

* * *

Camp Zafon

Dearest Irit

I went for a walk today and the cyclamen were out, tiny pink cyclamen in the grass. What am I doing here?

There are times when I wonder if I've woken up in the middle of some awful dream. There are times too when I do wake up in the middle of some awful dream but on the whole, it's better not to scream aloud. I let my mind come gradually back to the thought of you, one sane, fixed point in my life, and then it's better.

Someone asked me about Pa the other day, a fellow who was a student of his. He's a reservist, quite nice, very sombre. The way he spoke made me conscious of the fact that he knows Pa's non-conformist views. Mind you, who doesn't? I felt quite disconcerted. It doesn't do to be different here and this thought makes me ashamed. That I should care!

I'm very fed up, having dropped my watch on the shower floor the other day. The glass smashed and it stopped working in protest and so I can't even see how slowly the time passes.

I'll see you soon, though not soon enough,
Gavriel

* * *

Camp Zafon

Dearest Irit
This is the morning of what promises to be a long and boring Saturday. I don't know which is preferable to be honest, activity or inactivity. God what am I saying? The latter, definitely.

It always takes me days to reconcile myself to being back again after being on leave. Bits of me seem to stay behind snivelling in corners of Jerusalem and even now, I feel as if I might, in some other form, be found lurking under your father's hibiscus in its spring guise.

I enjoyed my last leave tremendously. There was a special quality about it, I don't know exactly what but there was. It was lovely to have some time with you and I think you know how much I appreciated that.

I really enjoyed the time I spent talking to Pa. It was very nice being on our own before Ma came back from her conference. You know what kind of organizer Pa is, so it was all very relaxing, very laid back. I didn't say much to you about my conversations with him because for a start, we had other things to talk about and also because I wanted a chance to think them out a bit before writing. It's all given me a lot to ponder.

I realize that I adhere to an infinitely childish belief that my parents should be now, and should always have been perfect and to have Pa tell me of what he sees as his failures has been quite hard. I found myself thinking that his failures are very elevated ones, so it appears that I can't relinquish the idea easily. I don't know why I should think it because they're always so open and willing to talk and not hide things, especially about themselves. In a way, he didn't say anything I didn't know objectively before, it's probably because I didn't know the right questions to ask before and I do now.

When I got back on Tuesday evening, I discovered that Pa had raided his little cellar in anticipation and had put some wine in the fridge. I was touched by that because usually, he finds it a bit much to put the kettle on. To be honest, I was surprised he knew where the fridge is. We sat in the garden and drank wine in the darkness and talked. It's so comfortable to be at home after the hell-hole.

We talked about its being the eve of my twentieth birthday. I hadn't realized till then that Pa spent his twentieth birthday in Auschwitz. I knew he'd been there, and about the family of course – it's just that being the same age now has made me look at him in a different way. I asked him what he remembered about that day but he couldn't remember much. He did remember wondering if it would be his last birthday – lots of people he knew hadn't even made it that far. He talked a lot about why he was there, because of his politics and not just because he was a Jew; he said it was the same for a lot of his friends, some of them Jews, some not. That all seemed very important to him and when I asked him, he said, 'Yes, it is, and it was at the time because it made a world of difference to be dying for your ideas.' I can see, I think, what he means by that.

Inevitably I suppose, we got on to talking about freedom and choice and compulsion and he began asking me about the way I feel about it all, the army and what's happening now and everything. I felt tearful suddenly at the way he knew how I felt and the way he seemed to extend a vast gentle sympathy all around me. (Not that I feel I'm so deserving of sympathy.) Pa's so angry about the way things have turned out here. He says that we've misused our past and that we remember history for all the wrong reasons and force everyone else to remember what happened while forgetting it ourselves. He said that he and his friends fought in the streets against the kind of things that are becoming commonplace here.

He says he's seen enough of societies going wrong to know that he's justified in feeling frightened of the future. He says that he's not cynical – for Pa cynicism is a kind of disease – but that he's worn down. I can't quite believe that, he has too much fire left inside him for that, surely. He even said he has moments of despair. When he said that, I had an awful feeling of everything coming to bits in my hands. I know that I'm wasting these years and that there are some pretty dreadful things about this place that seem to be overtaking the ones which made it bearable to live in, but writing to you and moaning is altogether a different thing from hearing Pa saying it. It endorses it all for me in a way which scares me.

The crux of it all is that he feels that his life and his work have been a compromise and that he's given them both to something which has turned out to be deeply flawed. He says that he's afraid I'll be the price he pays for it.

I recognize that as being irrational and though he would never admit it, it's superstition, the idea of paying for mistakes by suffering and sacrifice, but as you can imagine, it's not an idea which appeals on any level. I asked him if Ma feels the same about it and he said that she does but that women (please don't rush round and take the matter up with him!) have the unique ability to work so hard that they can sublimate the rumblings of their consciences – so there.

Anyway, I look at him with new eyes. I don't like leaving him. After all these years when he's been so protective towards me, I find myself worrying about him. He's working on some gigantic project which he tried to explain but which I could scarcely grasp at all. He potters away doing God knows what in his lab all day so that should stop him from getting too fed up.

Look after yourself,
Gavriel

Your birthday present ticks loudly in my ear all night. Thank you.

* * *

Camp Zafon

Dearest Irit

Even very early this morning the sun was warm and I heard doves cooing on the roof tops. For lo, the winter is past and the voice of the turtle might be heard if it wasn't for the noise of things going crash and bang.

I can sympathize with your parents, Irit. I know you want to avoid a fight and I'm sure you're right to want to go but I can't help seeing it their way a bit. (The new, mature me, you see.) They've always tried very hard not to over-protect you which must have been difficult in the circumstances, considering your father's first family and what happened. The fact is, it's still your responsibility, our responsibility, to deal with the effects of the past even if they were someone else's deeds. They're only asking you to plan a bit more. It doesn't seem unreasonable and I'd be happier that way too. Anyway, it isn't for quite a while yet, is it?

It sounds like a good idea to go to Beersheba to see Nurit. I doubt if I'll be back that weekend anyway. Send her my love. I send you mine,
Gavriel

*　　*　　*

Jerusalem

Irit, dear Irit

I can't seem to find the words to tell you how much I wish you were here, now, and how much I wish we could go out and walk, perhaps in the Old City and I could tell you about my week, my bloody, awful week and I could tap some of your fund of sense and goodness and decency to try to restore the balance of my world which at the moment is all madness and badness and evil. But you're not here, this one damnable weekend when I have a bit of unexpected leave and a need to talk to you so great that I feel weak and hopeless.

This week, I watched one man kill another in cold blood. It's a funny expression that, cold blood. Blood appears to be many things in such circumstances, but cold isn't one of them. I don't want to distress you but I have to tell you and I have to write it down.

The circumstances were so ordinary and day-to-day that my vision of the day-to-day has been ruined. I keep on thinking about how I knew it would happen, or rather that it does happen and that I've never done anything to alter the fact that it does and did.

A patrol brought in two men, fedayeen or villagers, I don't know which. I saw them when they first came in and then they took them away to be questioned. I didn't expect to see them again – they're usually transferred elsewhere pretty quickly here. They had both had some close attention from someone's boot before they came in and looked grim. One was young, our age I suppose, nice looking and ordinary. The other one was older and kept spitting out smashed teeth.

I was away elsewhere most of that day and about five, just when we got back, I had to take some things over to deliver to someone. It had been a beautiful warm day, a day when spring seemed to be winning and I kept thinking about the lizards coming to under their stones. It was a very still afternoon and I was just drinking in that moment of peace when I saw them bringing the two of them out. They were just standing there, waiting for transport, I assumed. It was suddenly preternaturally quiet, as if someone had switched the sound off. There was no shouting, no talking. A man came out of the doorway, a man I have seen often and whose name I cannot write. He was carrying a pistol, very casually. He seemed so relaxed, so easy, not smiling, but almost. I thought it must have gone OK with them, the atmosphere seemed almost friendly. He motioned the younger one aside and then I saw what was going to happen. I couldn't say anything, the silence was so vast and so unbreakable. It was as if the noise was what shattered his head apart. I couldn't see the moment his face changed from absolute fear and disbelief. The impact blasted away his skull and the whole of the top half of his face. The other one began shrieking and I have been pursued unceasingly since by his wails of grief and horror though I didn't see him again after that.

I went off then and was sick and later when I had a shower, I combed fragments of bone from my hair and stood in a pool of the dilute substance of another man.

I think I'll go for a walk anyway and drop this into your house on the way. I feel bad sharing it with you like this but I know how well you will understand.

The knowledge that you will be travelling back to

Jerusalem while I am travelling away from it fills me with dread.

I've just heard Ma coming in – I'll go and see if she'll come for a walk with me. I crave company at the moment, especially yours,

Love,
Gavriel

* * *

Camp Zafon

My dear Irit

Two letters and a parcel of books – you are kind and thoughtful and more patient than I deserve. Yes I'm fine, honestly.

Ya'ariv asked me there for the weekend but I gave him a resounding (but polite) 'No!' I did suggest that he might come back with me some weekend which he's promised to do sometime. He's going home this weekend because it's his sister's birthday and she's coming back from Haifa. He's done a small landscape in watercolour for her – it's very good. I asked him if he's applied to Bezalel but he refuses the discuss these things and says he will when the moment comes to do so, some fifteen months hence I suppose, stubborn bastard.

Anyway sweetheart, I count the minutes, the seconds even. Till Friday,

Gavriel

* * *

Camp Zafon

Irit, was that the way to tell me? Why in hell didn't you say something when we were together? I knew something was wrong when you didn't sleep. You were so tense and I didn't want to ask why so maybe it's my fault.

I suppose in a way I understand. You said you didn't want to spoil my weekend and how dreadful it would be for me to have to travel back to camp in the early morning knowing you were leaving. As it was, I travelled back feeling so desperately miserable and worried that in a way, I'd rather have known. It's easy to say that though, isn't it?

I do understand and accept your need to go and to go now. I realize it's very hard for you to feel that you're leaving me a virtual prisoner but don't allow yourself to feel too bad about it. One does change and I know quite well that you've been planning it for a while and have a perfect right to decide as you have done.

You know I can't pretend not to be sad, more than sad, but I don't want my feelings to be like a stone for you to have to carry round in your rucksack. I either have, or will have, enough distractions to keep me going. I've been meaning to do a lot more reading so that I'll have covered a lot of ground by the time I get to university, and there are people I've been meaning to see more often.

It seems an odd way to leave a relationship – hanging in mid-air. You say it's not like that but I can't see what will happen now. I'll change too and anyway, God knows what will transpire in the next few months in this madhouse. All this is something which works so much on my mind that I can feel myself changing and becoming distant from the world. I used to retreat into the knowledge of you and now I can no longer do that I'm not sure where I'll go, if you know what I mean. Anyway, there isn't a lot of point in continuing this.

Take care of yourself. I may write, I'll see how it goes. Irit, you'll leave such a large gap in my life.

Gavriel

* * *

LETTERS FROM ANOTHER PLACE

Camp Zafon

My dear Irit
You're right and I know you're right and I am ashamed of myself. I admit that my response was childish and sullen and petulant but that's because I am childish and sullen and petulant. I do acknowledge your right to go away and your need to go away and never, never, whatever I may have sounded like, would I ever want to prevent you from doing anything you chose. I know you understand what it's like for me but I won't let it be an excuse for my bad behaviour.

Your plans sound so exciting. You'll love the big, wide world, especially after this little hot-house of a place. I admire your ability to make friends and be at home anywhere. I wish I could learn the skill but I can only stand and stare in awe at your tremendous warmth and the way I see ice-people melt before you. You're lovely and the thought of you sustains me through the everyday dreadfulness of all this, about which I'm not going to write for fear of letting you know the small, petty things which assume weight in my life. Write soon and look at everything for me, think of me, admire things for me,
Gavriel

* * *

Jerusalem

My dear Irit
My first weekend home since you left and I was dreading it more than a little but since I had had more letters than any of the rest of them, my ego was in a fit state to meet the challenge.

Ma was still at work when I got back yesterday afternoon so I went right round to your house. Your mother was in the garden marking the ubiquitous jotters and your father was home, watering something in the jungle which is fast taking on its summer lushness. The twins were there and old Mrs Gluckstein from next door, ranged round a large cake. The twins went indoors to watch television and I took over their place at the cake. There was a large and unexplained gap in your house and a huge space in the garden and I wanted to jump into the enormous hole which had appeared in the sitting room in case it was the beginning of a tunnel which led to you. But I didn't. Instead, I went home in time to greet Ma and we danced in the kitchen together. Pa came back and we had an elegant Friday night dinner and equally elegant conversation.

Most important was that Pa has been offered a job in the States. I don't need to tell you the issues it raises, there are so many. He did ask me what I thought but I don't really feel able at the moment to say anything disinterested. All very unsettling.

That's not all that's unsettling. The atmosphere here is terrible with everyone waiting and wondering exactly what's about to happen. I suppose you'll be reading the papers and will know just what's going on. I'm feeling pretty anxious about it. I've never invaded anywhere before. I can write flippantly because I'm at my desk, in my room at home. But tomorrow . . .

I'll let you know what's happening while I can still write reasonably freely. You don't know how lucky you are to be out of it,
    With my love,
    Gavriel

   *   *   *

           Jerusalem
Dearest Irit
Today is the day, right on target, just like Ya'ariv predicted. If we survive, maybe I'll get him declared a prophet.

It's 6.00 a.m. and I'm just off back to the unit. I hate everything that's happening and I'm very scared too. I can see nothing that can make what we're about to do right.

I'll take care of myself and I'll write when I can. I just wanted to write before I go to say, without the censor sharing my most intimate thoughts, that I love you,

Gavriel

* * *

Address unspecified

Dearest Irit,
Just to let you know that I'm OK. Uninjured, not OK.

My usual degree of mental preparedness for everything has let me down on this one. I've never even imagined anything this bad. I'm glad I haven't.

I hope I'll see you again,
G.

* * *

Address unspecified

My dear Irit,
This is hard to write because it's so hot here and because I don't have the words to tell you about it. I'm dry and empty and I don't have the words. I've come to where my imagination ends and where words can no longer describe things. This is experience beyond words.

It's weird to think all the time about how you'll be seeing some of this on TV. Not all of it, they won't show all of it. I'm so glad you're abroad and not tainted by all this. I don't know what it must be like though, having to face the world with all this going on. I'll never be able to face the world.

When we made love for the first time, suddenly,

suddenly I understood everything I'd ever read about it, a new universe of insight opened and spread before me; I felt as though I'd stepped over into a realm of knowing and inclusion and now I've stepped into another, a different kind of inclusion. I don't know if I can do this, Irit, even my small, lousy, insignificant little bit.

I'm perpetually awake. Dry and empty and awake. It's so bloody hot. All the time, I'm living other people's lives and dying their death and wondering if death'll be the same for me. I can't see any good reason why it shouldn't and lots of reasons why it might and worse, many reasons why I might deserve it more than they do.

I keep going on pure reason. Finer things exist. I say this to myself but I don't really believe that they do. Not now.

G.

*   *   *

Jerusalem

My dear Irit

I've done it. I kept feeling that I would and now I have and if it didn't seem so much like dancing on corpses (lots of them) I would perform a tarantella in Ben Yehuda Street and an old fashioned minuet (by myself) in the lobby of the King David Hotel and a courtly pavanne in front of the Knesset. One half of me is elated and the other, larger half (if I may be so mathematically bold) is manacled to a pillar of solid horror and dread and sheer, sheer guilt.

I wrote the letter and wait for a reply. I expect it will be of the mind-concentrating variety, but I feel light within myself. I have answered that persistent, nagging voice which whined in my ear like a mosquito. I threw my shoe at it and squashed it against the wall in the night and the voice went quiet.

It goes on, in spite of me. It goes on.

I'm not sure what happens now. Nothing nice I expect. I'm prepared for all possibilities, please don't worry. There wasn't really much choice, you know. If you don't hear, write to Ma and Pa. One day, Irit, we'll see the galleries of Europe together,

Love,
Gavriel

* * *

Jerusalem

Dearest Irit,

I'm still waiting and have nothing to do but think. The trouble is that thinking is a mistake. It leads me into pools of dreadful, neurological mud. I've tried everything to prevent it. I've tried reading trash. (A copy of a cartoon mag. Mr Nussbacher in the paper-shop said, 'Gabi my boy, what does a clever fellow like you want with that?' I said, 'My brain's gone on holiday, Mr Nussbacher.') I've also tried more challenging stuff designed to keep the neurons fully occupied. Pa's study is stuffed with suitable material but alas, I find stray thoughts escaping from the grasp of dialectical materialism and I'm too debilitated to lift down some of the more improving works on physics.

I have come reluctantly to the conclusion that I'll never feel better. Part of me is destroyed. Pa's been a great help and I wonder how far it's all influencing his decision about the future. We haven't discussed it. It's his future and I have my own, though at the moment I have no real sense of having one at all.

Could we really meet up sometime? I'm scared to let myself think about the possibility,

Love,
Gavriel

* * *

  Jerusalem

My sweet Irit,
For days now, I've been in Pa's study pretending to read. I'm not really together enough yet. I see things I would rather not see obtruding between the lines. Most distracting when one is making a serious attempt at the Russian authors. I also find the distracting presence of you between the lines in ways not to be detailed in letters and between bad angel and good angel, I cannot give the best of what remains of my mind to *Crime and Punishment* and *The Brothers Karamazov*. I'll pretend to read Pushkin for a day or two.

Pa has decided on the job in America. It's a bit much to take in. I'll let you know the logistics as soon as we've planned some.

By the way, the letter came and with it a summons. I expected a court-martial at least, it's happened to other people. The oddest thing, though, they think I'm mad. They sat there with their slimy, yellow teeth and incipient mania and said that I'm mad. I'm also free. Oh Irit, what do I do now?
                              Gavriel

                         *   *   *

                                                            Jerusalem

Dearest Irit
What a question. Would Paris do? Yes, Paris would do,
                              G.

BIOGRAPHICAL NOTES

ELIZABETH BURNS was born in 1957 and lives in Edinburgh. Primarily a poet, 'A Roomful of Birds' is her first published story.

WILLIAM BOYD was born in Accra, Ghana, in 1952. He was educated at the universities of Nice, Glasgow and Oxford. He has published four novels (*A Good Man in Africa, An Ice-Cream War, Stars and Bars* and *The New Confessions*) and a collection of short stories (*On the Yankee Station*). His fifth novel – *Brazzaville Beach* – is published in the autumn of 1990.

MICHAEL CANNON was born in 1958, left school at sixteen to work and later to travel. After many desultory occupations, he worked at an oil terminal in the Shetlands before attending a college of further education and then Glasgow University. He graduated in 1986 and is currently employed by Strathclyde University. 'The Trader' is his second story to be published in this annual collection.

FELICITY CARVER was born in Edinburgh in 1945 and has lived mostly in Scotland. Educated at Edinburgh University, she is married with two teenage children. This is her second story to be published in this annual collection. Others have appeared in the *New Edinburgh Review* and *Punch*.

DOUGLAS DUNN's first collection of stories was *Secret Villages* (1985), and he is preparing another. His most recent collection of poetry is *Northlight* (1988). Other recent books are *Poll Tax: The Fiscal Fake* (Chatto & Windus, CounterBlast series), and *Andromache* (Faber & Faber).

MARGARET ELPHINSTONE has worked as a writer and gardener in various parts of Scotland. She has published poetry, short stories, and two novels, and is also the author of two books on organic gardening. She now lives in Edinburgh, and as well as writing, she teaches Scottish Literature at Strathclyde University.

RONALD FRAME was born in 1953 in Glasgow, and educated there and at Oxford. His plays for radio and television have received several prizes and many literary plaudits. His eighth book, a novel called *Bluette*, is published in 1990.

DOROTHY JOHNSTON was born in Ayrshire in 1959. After graduating from Edinburgh School of Art with a degree in painting she worked

BIOGRAPHICAL NOTES

abroad for two years, mainly in Italy. She now lives in Glasgow with her husband and baby daughter. 'Incubus' is her first published story.

FRANK KUPPNER was born in Glasgow in 1951. Poet, critic, lover of beauty, and general all-round Renaissance failure, he has published four books of various sorts. A fifth, *A Concussed History of Scotland*, is published by Polygon in mid-1990.

CANDIA McWILLIAM is the author of two novels, *A Case of Knives* (1988) and *A Little Stranger* (1989). She was born and brought up in Edinburgh, read English at Girton College, Cambridge, and now lives with her husband in Oxford. She has three children.

JAMES MEEK was born in London in December 1962. He went to school in Dundee and university in Edinburgh and London. He has worked as a newspaper reporter since 1985. He lives in Edinburgh. In 1989 his novel *McFarlane Boils The Sea* was published.

WILLIE ORR was born in Northern Ireland in 1940. He has worked in Harland & Woolf's shipyard in Belfast and in the Gate Theatre, Dublin. He left Ireland in 1959 to work with the Iona Community and remained in Scotland, working as a hill shepherd in the Western Highlands for thirteen years. He attended Stirling and Strathclyde Universities as a mature student, and is now a research worker at Strathclyde University. In 1988 he was awarded a Writer's Bursary by the Scottish Arts Council.

PETER REGENT has lived in Fife since 1965. His collection *Laughing Pig and other stories* was published by Robin Clark in 1984. 'Ildico's Story' is his fourth story to appear in this annual collection.

FRANK SHON was born in Arbroath in 1963 and educated at the High School, Arbroath, then in Sussex. He has worked ever since as a labourer in factories, on building sites and in horticultural nurseries; for a while he was a kitchen porter in a hospital. He now lives in Oxford where he is training to be a teacher.

ALEXANDER McCALL SMITH was born in Zimbabwe and educated there and in Scotland. He is the author of over twenty books, many of them books for children. His collection of African stories, *Children of Wax* (Canongate) appeared in 1989. 'Experience' is his fourth story to be published in this annual collection. He lives in Edinburgh.

ESTHER WOOLFSON was born and brought up in Glasgow. She studied Chinese at the Hebrew University of Jerusalem and Edinburgh University. She has worked as a translator and as a journalist and has had short stories published in *New Writing Scotland*. After years of moving around, she now lives in Aberdeen.